PRAISE FO

"Don't miss the Laurel McKay books. Like me, you'll be 'dying' to read the next one."
—*Brenda Novak, USA Today Bestselling Author*

"*Dying for a Deal*, Book Seven of the Laurel McKay Mysteries, is another worthy addition to this crackerjack whodunit series. Known for their humorous dialog, fast pacing, and intriguing plots, this go-round author Cindy Sample offers the reader even more, highlighting Laurel's growth as a woman and sleuth. It is a total and complete delight."
—*Heather Haven, IPPY Award-Winning Author*

"Sample's sleuth is an endearing character readers will adore."
—*RT Book Reviews*

"*Dying for a Deal* showcases author Cindy Sample's talent at dealing readers a mystery from a trick deck of cards complete with Jokers. Laughs, surprises, and danger mingle when Laurel McKay Hunter joins the PI agency formed by her detective husband and stepfather. Laurel's first cases prove to be real killers as she takes on a shady Lake Tahoe timeshare resale company preying on old folks and attempts to shadow the fiancé of her former boss to determine if he's cheating. The heroine's whole lovable but wacky cast of friends and relatives add to the fun."
—*Linda Lovely, Author of the Brie Hooker Mystery series*

"Cindy Sample's writing is positively fun, imaginative and all around tantalizing."
—*Romance Junkies*

"Cindy Sample knows how to weave a story that satisfies and excites. Time literally flew by as I turned the pages... simultaneously harrowing, exciting, tender, and uplifting, a true who-done-it combined with a romance that will warm the heart and sheets."
—*Long and Short Reviews*

"Cindy Sample has mastered the art of REAL dialogue. The characters are wacky and believable. Any woman who constantly finds herself in awkward situations will love this book. This is a story that will make you wonder "who did it" and make you laugh out loud. Of course, the romance simply is divine!"
—*BookReviewsRus*

"All of the elements of an excellent cozy mystery. Interesting characters, plot and setting. Fast paced writing. I struggled to figure out what it was that stood out that made me really enjoy the book and I decided it was the tone. *Dying for a Dance* is a feel-good book, it makes you smile."
—*Examiner.com*

"*Dying for a Date* is packed with zany characters, humorous situations, and laugh-out-loud narrative. Consider reading this book in one sitting, because once you start, you will be reluctant to put it aside."
—*Long and Short Reviews*

The Laurel McKay series

DYING FOR A DEAL

A LAUREL MCKAY MYSTERY

Cindy Sample (signature)

CINDY SAMPLE

DYING FOR A DEAL

By Cindy Sample

Copyright 2018 by Cindy Sample

Cover Art by Karen Phillips

ISBN: 171887880X
ISBN: 978-1718878808

Visit us at www.cindysamplebooks.com

DEDICATION

This book is dedicated to my wonderfully supportive children,
Dawn and Jeff. How lucky and proud I am of both of you.
And to my mother, Harriet Bergstrand, who came up with the title.
We miss you, Mom.

Also to those readers from around the world whose emails
make this journey so much fun. Your words bring a smile
to my face and magic to my fingertips.

CHAPTER ONE

Day fourteen on the job, and I already knew the real reason fictional private eyes kept a bottle in their lower desk drawers. As I tapped my pen against the barren surface of my desk, my gaze roamed around the freshly painted walls of our brand new detective agency. The silence was deafening. Almost enough to drive a person to drink.

I glanced at my watch. 10:00 a.m.

A tad early for a cocktail. Not that I had any whiskey stored in the bottom drawer of my desk. My secret stash consisted of a jumbo bag of M&Ms if needed. Which, at the rate business was coming in, could be sooner rather than later.

I picked up my nameplate from the desk and blew a speck of dust off the shiny gold letters: *Laurel McKay Hunter, Investigator*.

If only a new client would walk in the door.

Or a dead body. Even a zombie.

At this point, I wasn't too picky.

When my new husband, Tom Hunter, suggested I join Gold Country Investigations, the agency he and his former partner, Robert Bradford, had started, I was ecstatic. Bradford, as we affectionately referred to him, also happened to be my stepfather.

But so far this job was not the glamorous profession I'd envisioned when I agreed to quit my previous job at a local Placerville bank.

My caseload, at best, could be defined as light. Or—to be precise—nonexistent.

In the short time I'd been with the agency, my duties had encompassed such important tasks as selecting our coffeemaker and choosing the font for our signage. My most significant accomplishment to date was scoring forty-eight rolls of toilet paper for $9.99.

Since both men were retired homicide detectives, and I was merely a person who stumbled through life occasionally tripping over corpses, I shouldn't complain. Plus, I needed to put in six thousand hours of casework before I could become officially licensed as a detective.

At the rate my casework was progressing, my first social security check would arrive before my P.I. license.

The tiny bells over the front door tinkled as someone entered our Main Street office. A new client? If this were a scene from one of my favorite hard-boiled detective novels, the visitor would be a tall blonde dressed in a designer suit, with a mysterious past and an intriguing case for me to solve.

I swiveled my chair in anticipation. My shoulders drooped as I contemplated the new arrival—a five-foot-tall octogenarian in a Shirley Temple wig, a vision in pink from her polyester jogging suit to her sequined tennis shoes.

Virginia T. Sprinkle. My eighty-nine-year-old grandmother.

Not quite as enticing as a mysterious blonde or a dead body, but definitely better than spending the morning talking to myself and devouring my candy stash.

I walked around the desk and bent over to air-kiss her soft, wrinkled cheek. She handed me a cardboard carrier containing two heavenly smelling cups of coffee. I sniffed again. One of the cups exuded two of my favorite scents: chocolate and cinnamon.

They didn't call me a detective for nothing!

Gran settled into the visitor chair across from my desk. She straightened her wig, which tilted to the left, then reached for her coffee while I sipped on the hot Mexican-style mocha. She glanced around the agency nodding approvingly at the almond walls, taupe carpet, and mahogany furniture.

"Nice digs," she said. "Where's the menfolk?"

"Tom and Bradford are in San Francisco working on a big insurance case. Did you want to talk to them about something?"

"Nope." Gran pointed at me. "I want to hire you."

CHAPTER TWO

I choked on the hot liquid but managed to swallow without leaving any mocha splatters on my white blouse.

"You want to hire me?" I repeated. "For a case?"

"Of course, isn't that what you do?"

I narrowed my eyes at my grandmother. "What kind of trouble did you get into now?"

She put her palms up and met my gaze with sincere pale blue eyes. "Not me. A friend of mine needs help."

"Okay, I'll bite. What's the problem?"

"Well, it's kinda complicated, and I'm not sure I've got all the facts down. I was hoping you could meet with her tomorrow."

I looked at my old-fashioned desk calendar. The blank pages stared impertinently back at me.

"What time tomorrow?"

Gran shifted in her seat. "Well, here's the thing. Iris is a tad embarrassed about her situation and isn't comfortable seeking professional help. Plus, she doesn't have a lot of money. She's a widow and barely getting by on her social security checks. So I came up with a plan to get the two of you together. I think she'll really warm up to you. And you're darn good at worming stuff out of folks."

What a recommendation. Maybe I should add it my business cards—*I can worm my way into anyone's confidence*.

"So where are we going to hold this semi-clandestine meeting with my prospective client?"

"I thought of the perfect setting," Gran said, her smile so wide it displayed every one of her gold fillings. "The all-day senior bus trip from Placerville to the South Lake Tahoe casinos. It will be perfect." Perfect for whom?

"But I don't qualify. I'm forty, not sixty." For a visual effect, I fluffed my coppery curls. Nary a silver thread, but only because I'd yanked out two of them this morning.

She flipped a liver-spotted hand at me. "Pish, tosh. They don't care. If you want to go incognito, you can borrow my Queen Elizabeth wig. You'll fit right in."

Unfortunately, that's what I was afraid of. But it wouldn't kill me to spend a day with Gran. And meet her friend, a potential first case for me.

I might even win a jackpot and come home with a pile of money.

Although, with my luck, I was more likely to come across a crackpot than a jackpot.

I left the office a little after five, stopped at the store and picked up a roasted chicken with a couple of sides, a salad mix and dessert. In our house, this was considered a home-cooked meal. Somebody cooked it, right?

I was pleasantly surprised to see Tom's car in the driveway. Then I realized he'd been forced to park there because my ex-husband's truck blocked entry into our garage. Since my marriage to Tom four months ago, the two men in my life had stopped circling each other like combative lions and formed a somewhat amicable relationship. Hank had finally realized I was no longer in the picture as far as he was concerned, and Tom had concluded my kids' father would remain in our blended family picture frame for the rest of our lives.

I'd even gone so far as to create an online dating profile for Hank, thinking it would be one way to keep him from being underfoot. But the man was way too fussy. I'd like to think it's because I'm irreplaceable.

I chuckled to myself before attempting to walk through the front door juggling three shopping bags.

"I could use some help here," I called out to anyone within listening distance. Our cat, Pumpkin, appeared instantly, the scent of roasted chicken wafting through the entry. Seconds later a set of strong arms grabbed two bags while another set snatched the third.

4

A duet of "Hi, hon" greeted me.

Tom glared at Hank before placing a soft but sensuous kiss on my waiting lips. I would have gone for round two if Hank hadn't cleared his throat and interrupted my welcome.

I pointed toward the kitchen. "Thanks for the help. Goodbye." Hank headed down the hallway. I turned to Tom and frowned. "What's he doing here?"

Tom shrugged. "Who knows? He's here so often, I regard him as part of the furnishings." He plopped another kiss on my lips, hefted a bag in each arm, and then led the way into the kitchen, leaving me with one of my favorite scenic viewpoints.

Tom's jeans-clad posterior.

It took less than ten minutes to assemble dinner for our combined families. My marriage to Tom meant adding another member to our household—my eight-year-old son Ben's best friend, Kristy, who happened to be Tom's daughter.

Since my house had been my children's home for most of their lives, Tom and Kristy had moved in after we returned from our honeymoon. The sale of Tom's house provided the funds needed to open up the agency plus pay salaries, albeit small salaries, to all three partners.

The only negative with the move was that my house contained only three bedrooms, so my eighteen-year-old daughter, Jenna, was forced to share her room with an inquisitive stepsister. Since Jenna would be leaving for college in the fall, it wasn't too much of an inconvenience. For me.

I'm not sure my daughter would agree with that comment.

Thinking of Jenna's upcoming move made my eyes grow misty. I swiped at my right eyelid as I set the salad bowl on the table.

"You okay?" asked a soft voice in my ear.

I glanced up at Hank. "Sure." I rubbed my eye once more before adding, "Just thinking about Jenna going off to college."

Hank placed a calloused palm on my shoulder. "It's hard to believe she's heading out on her own."

"Not quite on her own," I replied, thinking of the impending tuition and dormitory bills. "*We* have some big bills coming up."

"I know. I'm prepared to pay my share," he said. "I'm bidding on a new job this week."

As a contractor, Hank's bottom line was more of a hilly slope than a flat line of profit. But I was grateful for whatever contribution he could make to our college fund. Speaking of which, the fund's beneficiary, our star pupil, popped into the dining room. Jenna grabbed a plate and began loading it with her dinner. "Hey, what's going on?" I asked her. "We're ready to sit down and eat."

She shook her head so fiercely her long auburn ponytail smacked against her freckled cheek. "I'm taking it to my room. I need to study. Finals begin next week. And then I'm done." My five-foot-eight daughter punched a fist into the air, narrowly missing the brass light fixture over the table.

Jenna had inherited my klutziness along with my chocolate addiction. Not to mention my love of crime investigation.

"I'm so over high school," she announced with a dramatic sigh. "College can't begin soon enough."

My checking account somewhat disagreed with her. But I remembered the excitement of my freshman year attending the University of California at Davis, which ended up being Jenna's university of choice.

"Did you line up a summer job yet?" Hank asked with a worried look.

"Yep." Jenna looked at me with quizzical cornflower blue eyes that mirrored mine. "Didn't Mom tell you about my new job?"

I was completely confused by this conversation, and I hadn't even had a glass of chardonnay yet. "What are you talking about?"

"I'm going to work at the agency with you."

6

CHAPTER THREE

The bodies were multiplying. The bodies working in our agency, that is. How could Tom hire my daughter without asking me first? The detective in question joined us, an open bottle of chardonnay in hand. I reached for the nearest wineglass. "Pour," I ordered. He looked taken aback but obligingly filled my glass. I took a much-needed sip before grabbing hold of his arm and dragging him into the kitchen, where I could begin my interrogation in private.

"Jenna just informed me she'll be working at *our* agency this summer." I elevated my voice as I glared at Tom. "Don't you think I should have been consulted?"

"Jenna was supposed to ask your permission," he said. He marched back into the dining room and I followed.

Tom addressed my daughter. "You were supposed to run that idea by your mother first, Jenna. She's the office manager and will make the final decision."

"I didn't think you were serious. Of course, Mom wants me to help out, right?"

Three pairs of eyes zoomed in on me. I chugged half the wine in my glass while I contemplated my reply. I loved my daughter but working together day in and day out for three solid months might be more mother/daughter bonding than either of us wanted.

I chose my words with caution. "I'd love to have you work with us, honey, but there isn't that big of a caseload right now. I'm not sure we can keep you busy enough."

Tom rebutted my comment. "Between research and some clerical tasks, Bradford and I can keep Jenna occupied. It should prove a useful experience before she starts her criminal justice classes in the fall."

Far be it from me to fire my daughter before her first day on the job. I finished my wine, set the glass on the table, and opened my arms to my daughter.

"Welcome to the agency."

I convinced Jenna to join us and after we all filled our plates and commenced eating, the conversation shifted to school events. Ben and Kristy couldn't wait to update us on some of their end-of-year third-grade activities.

"We're gonna go through the Gold Bug Mine up in Placerville," Kristy said. "I've never been."

"Sounds like a fun way to finish the school year," I said. "The mine is rated a five-star tour, one of the highlights of El Dorado County as far as I'm concerned."

"They got a blacksmith shop, too," Ben announced, then asked, "What do blacksmiths do?"

"They put shoes on horses," I explained.

He sent me a puzzled look. "Horses wear shoes?"

Jenna nudged him with her elbow. "Horseshoes, dummy."

I started to reprimand Jenna when Ben interrupted. "They need parents to help chap...chap...um, go with us," he said. "Can you come, Mom?"

"As long as it's not tomorrow, I can do it," I told him. "I have my first case to investigate. Finally."

"A walk-in?" asked Tom and I nodded.

"Your marketing is finally paying off," he said. "What kind of case?"

"Um, I'm not sure yet."

"Who's the client?"

"Not sure of that either."

Tom looked perplexed.

"It's a Gran referral. I'll know more tomorrow." I speared a piece of lettuce and turned the conversation in his direction. "So how was your meeting at the insurance company today?"

"It went well. I think Fidelity Insurance will continue to utilize our agency."

"What kind of case?" Hank asked Tom.

"Insurance fraud," Tom replied. "Guy claimed he couldn't walk because of a car accident. He was suing the other driver's insurance agency for several million dollars."

"Was he lying?" Ben asked midchew.

"Looks like it, Ben. Last week his wife drove him to the Galleria, helped him into his wheelchair and then entered the mall, apparently to do some shopping. But instead of hitting the stores, she rolled him to the north side of the mall where he was met by an SUV. I didn't have time to get back into my car to follow him, but Bradford was standing by. I texted him the make of the car and license plate number, and he followed them."

"Where did they go?" Jenna asked, clearly engrossed with their surveillance operation.

"To a golf course," Tom replied with a smile. "And Bradford has the photos to prove not only is the guy perfectly capable of walking, he's an excellent golfer."

Ben turned to Kristy. "That sounds cool. We should join the agency when we're older. Do we get to wear disguises?"

"Sometimes," I replied. "Tomorrow I'm going up to Tahoe disguised as a senior."

"Try not to get into any trouble, Laurel," Tom said, his deep brown eyes twinkling with humor.

"How could I possibly get into trouble when I'm hanging out with a busload of seniors?"

Silly me.

CHAPTER FOUR

I followed my grandmother up the steps of the large tour bus. In order to forestall any possible questions regarding my age, Gran introduced me as her caregiver.

The bus driver chuckled. "You got your hands full, miss," he said.

Didn't I know it. Hanging out with my grandmother could prove dangerous to a person's health. Most likely mine.

She claimed her middle initial "T" stood for Theodora, but our family designated it T for TROUBLE.

Groups of seniors clambered on board. The women, and some of the men, wore comfortable leisurewear in every shade of the rainbow. Between the canes, walkers, and mandatory hugs among friends, it took fifteen minutes to load everyone up.

Gran seemed to know most of the passengers, which came as no surprise since she'd lived in Placerville all her life and remained active in a number of local organizations. But I wasn't prepared to hear one white-haired jug-eared man address her as "hot stuff." Maybe those Wednesday night bingo games were rowdier than I realized.

Gran introduced me to Iris, a petite woman with wispy white hair and kind hazel eyes who sat across the aisle from us. I grabbed the window seat and looked forward to enjoying the beautiful scenery the bus passed on its route to the Stateline casinos straddling the Nevada-California border.

Late spring snow frosted the mountaintops, providing breathtaking views. As the bus wound its way up the serpentine two-lane highway, I could see the American River roaring through the canyons with the pent-up energy of a third-grade class released for summer break.

The rolling motion of the bus as it maneuvered its way up, down, and around Highway 50 lulled me into a brief nap. The screech of aged brakes woke me with a start.

"Wake up, kiddo. We're here," Gran's voice blared in my ear. "No sleeping on the job now."

I glanced out the window at the eighteen-story hotel and casino. Even on a weekday, people bustled in and out of the revolving doors. The seniors, sensing riches ahead, exited the bus far quicker than they'd climbed on board. The bus driver assisted each of them as they stepped down onto the sidewalk. When I reached the bottom of the bus steps he handed me a blue coupon. Everyone else seemed to be holding onto a similar item.

"What's this?" I asked Gran and Iris, who joined us.

"That coupon entitles you to ten dollars' worth of chips and one dollar off the buffet," she said. "Heck of a deal."

It certainly was, and a heck of an incentive for the seniors to spend more than they should. But who was I to disparage whatever form of entertainment kept Gran and her friends excited. If you're going to lose a pile full of money, you might as well enjoy a great view of beautiful Lake Tahoe while you're at it.

As we entered the casino, I whispered to Gran, "When am I going to interview Iris? That's the reason I came on this trip, you know."

"All in good time. You youngsters are so impatient." She stopped and stared across the enormous casino, the lights from dozens of crystal chandeliers gleaming above the blackjack and craps tables in the middle of the room. Line after line of colorful slot machines beckoned us. Gran's nose twitched, as if she were on the scent of a winning machine. "C'mon," she said, pulling me along with her. Iris followed behind, evidently more than willing to let Gran determine which slots would pay off the best.

Not being much of a gambler, I was happy to discover the bank of machines Gran led us to were nickel slots.

An hour later, I rolled my shoulders, stiff from sitting on the stool, punching buttons nonstop. Years ago, when you hit a jackpot, the slot machine would light up and clamor while a pile of coins fell into your bucket. These days, an electronic tinkle heralded your winnings and the money remained in the machine until you wisely stopped playing and left with a piece of paper in your hands.

I chose not to do that and my twenty-dollar bill now belonged to the casino. Gran and Iris were each playing three machines, way too much work for me. I stood, stretched, and then joined Gran.

"How are you doing?" I asked her.

She squinted. "Not sure. I can't tell how many nickels I got left. But I haven't run out of money yet."

"How about you cash in and we grab something to eat?"

Gran looked over at her friend. "Iris can probably use a break, too. You're on."

Twenty minutes later we were finally seated at a booth in the buffet. The joint was hopping. I guess when you're a senior on a fixed income, you can't beat "all you can eat" for $3.99, especially when you have a buck-off coupon.

After platefuls of overcooked vegetables and batter-fried strips of something or other, we finally got down to business. Detective business.

With a few nudges and encouraging words from Gran, Iris hesitantly shared her story with me.

"Ten years ago, my husband, Jim, and I were on vacation up here," Iris said. "At one of the casinos, there was a guy offering discounts on activities like rides on the Tahoe Queen or free dinners. All you had to do was sit through a timeshare presentation."

"Sounds like a good deal to me," said my grandmother, who loved nothing better than a freebie.

"It would have been except we got talked into purchasing 'points' equivalent to two weeks of vacation time anywhere in the world," Iris said wryly. "I didn't think we could afford it, but Jim got all caught up in the presentation. He thought it was a great idea, especially since he planned on retiring in a few years."

"Did you get to use them much?" I asked.

She shook her head. "We were supposed to be able to use the points at resorts all over the world, places like Australia and the Caribbean. But every time we tried to use our points someplace, the resorts we were interested in were already booked." She looked down at her hands. "Then Jim got cancer and it was all chemo and radiation and recovery after that. Until the day he didn't recover."

Gran patted her friend's hand and we both made sympathetic noises. No matter how long it's been since a spouse has died, it's never easy for the one left behind. Gran and my mother had both suffered when their husbands passed many years ago.

The three of us remained silent for a minute, which was probably thirty seconds too long for my chatty grandmother because she jumped in. "So Iris here got stuck with this timeshare ownership. Every year she pays these huge fees that just keep going up and up."

"Can you sell it?" I asked her, having seen numerous advertisements online and in magazines from companies that specialized in timeshare sales. That seemed like a viable option to me.

"I tried," Iris explained. "One company called me multiple times and said for a set fee of three thousand dollars they could sell my timeshare for me. They explained the cost was much lower than paying a commission. That made sense so I signed up with them. But after a year, there was nary a sale. Then a different company contacted me called Timeshare Cancellation. They assured me they could get the money back that I paid for the timeshare points because the original company made promises they couldn't keep. They charged me forty-five hundred dollars."

"Still nothing, I presume," I said.

"Nope. In the meantime, the fees, which weren't so bad to begin with, were now up to two thousand dollars a year. I've been living on my social security and a wee bit of interest from our savings, which rapidly declined after I paid off Jim's medical bills. The fees are getting too expensive for me to pay every year."

"It's tough for us old folks," Gran chimed in.

"We also financed part of the cost of the timeshare." Iris grimaced. "At eighteen percent interest. Thought we could pay it off once Jim got his bonus. But then he got sick. One day six months ago, I got a call from another company that promised to take over the loan and absolve me of everything. They sent me testimonials to prove how great they were."

"Hah!" I said in detective-speak. "Never trust a timeshare testimonial."

13

"This company, Timeshare Help, promised to assume the loan and the ownership for a small fee."

"Define small."

"Six thousand dollars. For each week."

"Not so small," I mused.

"No, but the loan payments and the increasing fees were killing me on my limited income." The lines surrounding her thin lips deepened as she frowned. "I was relieved to finally find a way to get rid of it."

"That sounds like a good solution, although an expensive one."

"It would have been," said Iris, "except my loan was never paid off, and I'm still getting billed for the annual fees and loan payments. When I called Timeshare Help, they claimed they knew nothing about the transaction and never heard of the person I'd spoken with. I keep trying to talk to a manager, but I just get the runaround going from one automated extension to another before eventually I get cut off."

I pondered her situation for a few minutes. "Have you discussed this with a lawyer?" I asked her.

She nodded. "I met with a Placerville firm, but they wanted a retainer of five thousand dollars. They indicated their fees would probably run much higher, and they couldn't even guarantee they could recover any of my money."

Iris grabbed my hand in hers and squeezed it tight. "Can you help me?"

CHAPTER FIVE

I slid my palm out of Iris's surprisingly strong grasp and patted her hand. "Of course, I can help," I reassured her. "My specialty is investigating financial fraud."

And I now had my first case to prove it.

"When we return home, can you get me copies of your initial purchase agreements and any paperwork you have from Timeshare Help?"

"I sure can. I found the address in the yellow pages for their local office in South Lake Tahoe. I thought maybe Ginny"—she pointed to my grandmother—"and I could visit them today. I don't drive anymore, so this bus trip was the only way to get up here to talk to them in person." She hesitated before going on. "But since you're a fraud expert, it might help if you came along." She grabbed my left hand again and squeezed so hard my diamond ring probably left an imprint on her palm. "Would you go over there with us?"

Since the alternative to visiting Timeshare Help would be spending the next three hours losing more nickels than I could afford, my answer was an easy affirmative.

Gran completed one last trek to the dessert buffet before we left. The woman had the metabolism of a professional cheerleader. One genetic trait I did not inherit. I settled for two bites of her apple cobbler and half of a chocolate chip cookie. Enough of an energy boost to get me through an afternoon of detecting.

I needed to be sharp for an encounter with a team of timeshare experts. Those folks are slicker than an Exxon oil spill. Hank and

I had almost succumbed to their sales chicanery when Jenna was little. Fortunately for us, my young daughter tipped her cup of hot chocolate onto the salesman's lap. His yelps of pain combined with her shrieks provided us a quick and painless exit.

Painless for us.

Our trio stepped out of the casino. We grabbed one of the cabs lined up at the entrance and gave the driver the address. He frowned at us and I wondered if he was having a bad day. Then we discovered the Tahoe office of Timeshare Help turned out to be located in an L-shaped strip mall less than a mile from the casinos.

I gave the cab driver a large tip, which must have made up for the brief ride because he offered a nicotine-tinged smile as well as his business card for our return trip. I shoved the card in the side pocket of my purse and joined the two women. Timeshare Help's office was wedged between an art gallery and Palomino's Pizza. Despite eating a short while earlier, the scent of garlic floating from the restaurant made my stomach growl.

I turned to the women. "Are you ready?" I asked in a hearty voice, wondering why I sounded like I was about to lead a platoon into warfare.

Gran squared her shoulders, fearless as ever. Iris's hands shook. Did she suffer from Parkinson's or was the thought of confronting the timeshare scoundrels enough to make her quiver?

I latched an arm through each of theirs as we approached the office. The Three Musketeers, ready for action. One for all, and all for one. Our grand entry was halted for a few seconds when an older couple burst through the doorway. The man's pudgy face glowed magenta under a shock of white hair. The scowl creasing his face was not the expression of a happy timeshare owner. His wife patted his arm, murmuring what sounded like calming words. She sent us an apologetic look as they barreled past our threesome.

Interesting. But none of our business. I held the door open and we entered an office decorated in standard Lake Tahoe décor—beige walls, forest green carpet, a couple of tweed visitor chairs in the foyer. Large framed photos of popular vacation destinations hung on the walls.

A row of empty glass-walled cubicles greeted us.

"Halloo," I called out to the empty room.

"Hello yourself," shouted a male voice in the back of the office. "I'll be right out."

Thirty seconds later, a six-foot-tall salesman greeted us with a smile so white it practically lit up the neutral office. His slick-backed hair gleamed as if he'd covered it with a coating of black lacquer.

"Please sit down," he said, pointing to two green tweed chairs in front of his desk. A cloud of musky aftershave caused me to cough. I chugged from my water bottle while he grabbed a third chair from the empty cubicle behind him.

Once we were all seated, he introduced himself as Gregg "with two g's" Morton. I glanced at his nameplate and contemplated whether I should inform him he was actually Gregg with three g's, but decided it wasn't relevant to our conversation.

"So what can I do for you lovely ladies today?" His voice oozed enough charm to woo a cobra out of a basket.

"We got a problem and you're it," Gran announced.

"Well, we certainly can't have that, can we?" he replied. "How can I help you?"

Iris introduced our trio, explaining her situation to Gregg. He made sympathetic noises, jotting down notes on a small legal pad. While we were chatting, a short, stout man with reddish hair and a tall, slender blonde dressed in a tight-fitting sheath dress entered the office suite. They both glanced in as they walked down the corridor past Gregg's office. The man entered a cubicle two stations behind the one we were seated in while the woman walked down the hallway to a larger office in the back.

Iris finally wrapped up her story, and we all waited for Gregg's response. Iris looked optimistic, while Gran sat with her skinny arms folded and a surly expression on her face. Gregg typed Iris's name into his computer and scrolled through a variety of screens. After a couple of minutes he turned to face our trio, leaning forward and making individual eye contact with each of us. I had to commend the man on his body language. His posture and sympathetic expression gave us the impression he could solve Iris's problem in a matter of minutes.

"I can't locate your name in our database. While I certainly sympathize with your situation," he said, focusing his attention on Iris, "I'm positive no one in our company would charge a resale fee and then not follow through on the sale." He pointed to a one-foot-tall brass trophy on his desk. "Our office received this award from the local chamber of commerce, confirming our dedication to our customers. Are you certain you didn't confuse us with another timeshare sales company? There are a significant number of them out there and not all are as consumer-oriented as we are."

Iris looked flustered. "I didn't bring the papers with me, but I'm positive it was this company. Although I suppose I might have mixed it up with one of the other places I dealt with." Her shoulders slumped at this setback. Even her white curls seemed to wilt in response.

Gran narrowed her eyes at the man. "Don't think just because we're old that you can get away with this scheme. Cheating widows out of thousands of dollars." She grabbed the chamber of commerce trophy from his desk and waved it around. "This is *unacceptable* and we won't stand for it."

Gregg stood and carefully eased the brass trophy from Gran's grasp. "I assure you Timeshare Help would not tolerate such a practice. But we would be happy to sell your timeshare points for you. That is our specialty and we have a very successful track record."

The blonde stepped out of her office, gliding down the corridor in four-inch heels.

"Is there a problem, Gregg?" she asked, managing to sound both gracious and intimidating at the same time.

"No, Kimberly, I have it covered," Gregg said in a stiff tone.

"No you don't," replied Gran before addressing Kimberly. "My friend, Iris, here got conned by one of your employees, and this guy claims that's not possible."

Kimberly frowned at Gran. "That is quite unlikely. I'm sure your friend is merely confused."

I opened my mouth to protest, but Iris spoke up first.

"C'mon, Ginny," she said. "Let's go." Iris fumbled with her handbag, which fell onto the floor. I bent over and returned it to her.

"We'll go," Gran said, waving her finger in Gregg's face, "but mark my words. We will be back."

CHAPTER SIX

We walked out of the office with as much dignity as an octogenarian version of the Terminator, her flustered best friend, and a granddaughter could muster.

"Well," Gran said, "I sure told them."

"You certainly did," I replied. "But I'm not sure that accomplished anything."

"Are you kidding? Didn't you see how nervous I made the two of them?"

Uh, no. But I didn't have the heart to share my opinion. Iris chewed on her lower lip while we pondered our next move.

"I'm sorry I dragged you all the way over here for nothing," Iris apologized. "This stuff is so confusing. I guess I must have the wrong company like he said."

"It was worth visiting their office while we were in town," I reassured her. "And I didn't appreciate Gregg's attitude. After we return to Placerville, I'll stop by your house and pick up all of your paperwork. Then I can start reviewing it tomorrow."

"You're so kind," Iris replied. "You make your grandmother proud."

Gran and I beamed at each other.

"We have a plan," I said. "So let's enjoy the rest of our day."

We stopped at the pizza parlor for sodas to go. Even in midafternoon the place bustled with activity and plenty of to-go orders like ours. I wondered if it was the quality of the pizzas or the handsome owner who drew in the mostly female clientele. One sip

19

of my flat-tasting soda offered the answer. The dark-haired owner with the soulful eyes offered the only fizz.

We decided to walk back to the casino. The sun shone and, due to the high altitude of six-thousand-plus feet, the high-sixties temp felt closer to eighty degrees. The walk back to the casinos was flat all the way so we took our time, stopping at a store here and there. The fresh mountain air with its piney scent invigorated me and was far more appealing than the stale smoke-filled casinos.

We arrived back at Harrah's with thirty minutes to kill before the bus was scheduled to leave. It allowed us enough time for a pit stop and a few minutes at the roulette wheel. The attractive female croupier reminded me of my daughter with her freckled face and long auburn curls trailing down her back. She flashed me a winsome smile so I went all out and placed twenty dollars on red. I doubled my bet and ended up with forty dollars, a huge win for a lightweight gambler like me. I gave Cherie, the croupier, a five-dollar tip, then went to cash in my winnings before I lost them on the slots.

Gran and Iris also managed to add a few nickels to their wallets, so everyone wore smiles on the bus ride home. Herb, the white-haired, large-eared friend of Gran's, insisted on occupying the seat next to her on the bus. I might have to do some detecting into Gran's extracurricular activities one of these days.

The bus returned to Placerville a few minutes after five. I dropped Gran off and drove Iris to her cute Craftsman-style cottage in downtown Placerville.

I followed her up the crooked brick-lined path to her front porch and waited while she searched for the key. The smell of lemon oil tickled my nostrils as I entered her tidy foyer. Even though she was a half-century older than me, the woman was obviously a better housekeeper. Maybe I could add housecleaning to my daughter's job description at the agency. I smiled imagining her expression when I informed her of her additional job duties.

Iris told me to wait in her small parlor while she shuffled off to her office to retrieve the paperwork. I sank into a cushy flowered sofa far more comfortable than the hard bus seats.

Just as I was pondering what to prepare for dinner my cell pinged. I pulled it from my purse to see a text from my mother. She wondered what I thought of her bringing over lasagna for dinner for Bradford and her and the rest of my family.

DYING FOR A DEAL

I quickly typed "Thanks," followed by an emoji with the largest smile I could find, then stood to gather the pile of papers Iris held in her hands.

"I'm afraid they're not too tidy," she said, "but everything should be there."

Given the fact I now held a five-inch-tall stack of documents, I certainly hoped it was the case. I felt bad leaving the widow alone, but I had a family to feed. Well, technically, I had a family I wanted to dine with. I promised Iris I'd get back to her sometime the next day.

The pungent scent of garlic greeted me as I walked into my house. I love garlic bread, but it smelled like my mother's version contained enough to take out an army of vampires. Tom, Bradford, and Ben sat at the oak table while my mother bustled around my kitchen. Her beige linen dress not only complemented her short platinum hair style, but it remained immaculate. How did she do that? If I were cooking lasagna, a trail of tomato sauce would already be decorating my ample chest.

I kissed my husband and thanked my mother once again for bringing dinner.

"I thought you might be delayed," Mother said. "Whatever possessed you to go on a casino trip with your grandmother?"

"She wanted to introduce me to her friend Iris," I replied with a smile, "who is officially my first client." I pointed to the stack of documents. "I'll be working my way through the papers tomorrow."

"Tomorrow?" cried Ben. "You can't go to work tomorrow. You're chap... chap...you know, going with us on the field trip to Gold Bug Mine tomorrow. You didn't forget, did you?" he asked, his hazel eyes concerned under an overgrown thatch of messy chestnut hair.

"A chaperone." I mentally added "haircut for Ben" to my growing to-do list before responding. "Of course, I'll be chaperoning your trip. Iris has waited this long to resolve her problem. Another day or two won't matter."

"They got special hats and everything," Ben informed me.

"Hats?" I sent a puzzled glance to my husband.

"Hard hats," Tom explained. "And given your klutzy..." His voice tapered off at my glare. "Gotta wear protective gear in those mines. We can't have our children getting hurt."

Bradford snorted. "Or your wife."

21

The sound of the oven timer going off muffled my uncomplimentary reply to my stepfather. Within minutes we were all enjoying an excellent meal. Between forkfuls of extra-cheesy lasagna, I updated the family on my new case.

"An agent in my office has a client who's been trying to clear up their credit report," said my mother. "One of the disputed items was a delinquent timeshare loan."

"The guy we spoke with today emphasized their company would never swindle a client," I replied.

"Did you expect him to admit it?" asked Bradford, the most senior detective in the room.

"Well, no. And we did catch him off guard by just showing up in the office. After I review Iris's documents, I'll have a better idea where she stands. So how was your day? Any new cases while I was sleuthing with the seniors?"

Bradford nodded. "Yeah, we got a call from a woman who wants to meet with us. I set it up for Friday. She wouldn't disclose her problem over the phone, but she works at Hangtown Bank. You might remember her."

"Who is it?" I knew almost everyone at Hangtown Bank from the time I'd worked there.

"Adriana Menzinger," Bradford replied. "The name sounded familiar to me. Does it ring a bell?"

I almost choked on my half-chewed piece of garlic bread. Adriana's name didn't just ring a bell. It chimed louder than Big Ben at midnight.

Now why would my former boss need help from our agency?

CHAPTER SEVEN

I was dying to know why Adriana had contacted our firm, but I'd have to wait until her Friday appointment. Depending on her needs, I could end up with my second client.

Although I'd prefer a client who wasn't such a witch.

There was a witch or two among the mommies accompanying their children on the field trip the next day. One woman suffered a meltdown worthy of *The Real Housewives of Beverly Hills* when she learned that hard hats were optional for kids but mandatory for anyone over five-feet-two-inches tall. Heaven forbid her perfect coiffure get squashed under the protective helmet.

Another mother declared the mine too scary for her daughter. My rugged kids, and I included Kristy in that description, couldn't wait to check it out. As far as they were concerned, the darker, dirtier, and scarier the better.

My cell rang as we were about to enter the mine. The docent frowned so I silenced it and shoved it into the side pocket of my purse without looking. Probably another one of those darn telemarketers who called my cell intermittently all day long. Despite being on the Do Not Call list. Someone ought to do something about them.

And maybe I would, but first things first. We had a cave to explore.

My phone vibrated once and then a second time. Geesh. I would have thought there would be no reception inside the dark mine. I slipped the phone out of my purse and looked at the recent calls. All from my grandmother's cell instead of her home phone. That couldn't be good. And why wasn't she at home today?

I turned the ringer back on and dialed her cell. She picked up on the third ring, gasping out my name.

"Gran, what is it?" I tried to keep my voice low so the docent wouldn't chastise me. But between my hard hat and the noisy third-graders voices echoing throughout the small cavern, it was impossible to understand what my grandmother was saying.

I punched the speaker button and Gran's voice boomed out over the speaker, caroming around the limestone walls.

"Help," she yelled. "We got a murder."

CHAPTER EIGHT

Two dozen wide-eyed children stared at me while their parents looked aghast. One little girl began to cry. The docent strode up to me and glared, his bulbous nose almost touching mine.

"Ms. McKay, please take your detective business outside. I'm attempting to conduct a tour here."

"Sorry," I said to him, "it's my grandmother on the phone."

He stepped back, a concerned look on his ruddy face. "Oh, is Ginny okay?" Evidently my grandmother's charitable work in the community, as well as her role as El Dorado Rose a few years back, gave her more credibility than I had.

"That's what I need to find out. Can I go back outside the entrance and complete my call while you finish the tour?"

He nodded and I picked my way down the gravel and dirt path, still trying to hear my grandmother's garbled words.

Once I passed through the timbered exit of the mine, I removed my hard hat. "Gran, what's going on? Did you say someone was murdered? Where the heck are you?"

"I'm in Tahoe and the answer is yes."

I couldn't stop the questions from coming. "Where? Why? What are you doing there?" I screeched.

"You were tied up with Ben's field trip, so Iris and I decided to take a field trip of our own back up here. Remember my friend Herb?"

"Herb? The guy with the jug ears? What does he have to do with any of this?"

"I asked him to drive us to that timeshare place. Herb's real accommodating if you know how to wet his whistle." She cackled, making me cringe. The last thing I wanted to know was how one wet a senior's whistle. The first thing I wanted to know was who was dead.

"Is Iris okay?"

"Well, she kind of fainted when we discovered the dead guy. The police aren't too happy with us. Said she messed up the crime scene when she landed on top of him."

"Gran, who is him?" I asked between clenched teeth.

"Oh, sorry. Remember the timeshare guy we spoke with yesterday? Gregg with two g's?"

"Technically, it's three g's," I felt compelled to say. "Is he there now?"

"More or less. And I don't think it matters how many g's you put in his name. He's the dead guy."

CHAPTER NINE

"Gran, this is terrible news," I said, my heart sinking almost as low as the mine shaft. "Are you on your way home?"

"I'm not sure the police will let us go. They kinda suspect we might have bashed the guy's head in."

"Why would they think that?" I couldn't imagine why the police would think Gran or Iris capable of a physical assault on the much younger man.

"That nasty female manager told them I threatened Gregg yesterday when I grabbed that trophy and waved it around."

"That's plain stupid."

"Sure is, except my fingerprints are on it along with a lot of his blood, and no one else's, so far as they've told me."

"Do you want me to come up there? They haven't arrested you or anything?"

"No, although they keep giving us the evil eye. So far, they just want us to sit tight in case they have more questions." She sighed. "Herb's got cataracts and he don't see well at night so I hope this doesn't take too much longer."

I shuddered at the thought of Gran's elderly friend weaving his way down Highway 50 in the daylight, much less driving at night.

"I'm stuck on this field trip with the kids and don't even have a car. Did you call Mom yet?"

"Are you kidding? Your mother would bawl me out if she knew we'd driven up here by ourselves."

"You are right about that. Expect to hear from her soon."

27

I ended the call and dialed my mother's cell. She picked up immediately.

"What's wrong?" she asked, her maternal intuition kicking in. "Are you okay?"

"I'm fine," I said. "Enjoying the tour of the mine with the kids."

"And you chose the middle of the mine tour to call me?"

Geesh. The woman was so suspicious. You'd think she was a detective instead of a Realtor.

"Gran called. She and a couple of friends decided to go back to Tahoe and talk to that timeshare guy again."

"Oh, dear. Are they okay?"

"Other than Iris fainting and landing on a dead guy, who coincidentally happens to be the timeshare salesman we met yesterday, they seem to be fine."

Mother's response included a few censorable words, but I finally calmed her down. "Gran's worried they won't get released until late. And she's not too keen on Herb chauffeuring them down the hill once it turns dark."

"Oh, dear. I have an appointment at one thirty, but I can have someone else handle it for me. I swear, we need to put one of those pet microchips in your grandmother so we can keep tabs on her."

She hung up and left me chuckling over her Orwellian suggestion. Gran had so far successfully fought my mother's efforts to relocate her into a retirement community. Mother only relented when Hank moved into Gran's house and became her roommate a year ago. The partnership seemed to work for the two of them, although it didn't give my ex much privacy on the romantic front.

And I truly wanted Hank to find the happiness I had with Tom, who would be far happier when Hank was occupied elsewhere.

A gaggle of grade-school children exploded from the mine, indicating the end of the official tour. Ben and Kristy loped over to me. My stepdaughter, who'd inherited her father's genes, towered over my son, a late bloomer.

"Who called when you were in the mine, Mom?" asked Ben. "It sounded kind of like Great Grandma."

"It also sounded like someone was murdered," added Kristy.

I looped their sweaty hands in mine, one kid on each side, before answering. "There was an unfortunate incident up in Tahoe, and Gran coincidentally happened to be there. Nothing for any of us to worry about right now."

At least I hoped not. My phone chimed and I yanked it out of my purse. A text from Mother: *Heading up to Tahoe with Robert. Will keep you posted.*

I breathed a sigh of relief that my mother and her detective husband had taken over. With luck, everything would be sorted out by this evening. And I could enjoy the second half of the kids' field trip—an authentic Forty-Niner BBQ.

Later that night, my mother called to update me. "Your grandmother is home safe and sound," she said, "although knowing how she loves to play detective, she'll probably want to get involved in this dreadful situation up in Tahoe."

"Were you able to get any information out of the local authorities?" I asked.

"Robert knew one of the detectives from his time at the sheriff's department, and the officer was willing to share some information, what little they had, with us. By the time we arrived, they'd transported the victim to the morgue."

"How are Gran and Iris doing?"

"Iris seemed overwhelmed by the events, but your grandmother said the murder proved this Gregg person was up to no good."

"Hmm." I mulled over her remark. "His death could be due to a myriad of reasons, and none of them might have anything to do with Timeshare Help."

"That's what the office manager insisted to the lead detective. She made an offhand remark about the guy having a drug problem."

"Maybe he owed money to a drug dealer. Or was involved with one of the Mexican cartels."

"Laurel, there aren't any cartels up in Tahoe," she said.

"And you know that for a fact?"

"Well, no. The only thing I know for a fact is that I do not want my daughter and my elderly mother investigating the murder of some lowlife."

"Don't worry, I'm only concentrating on Iris's timeshare case."

It was just a coincidence my very first agency case involved a timeshare salesman who was recently murdered.

CHAPTER TEN

The next morning I dropped Ben and Kristy off at school, then headed for Placerville. I cruised down Main Street past the nineteenth-century brick and pastel-painted clapboard buildings. An enormous banner stretched across the historic bell tower welcoming everyone to the annual Wagon Train Parade event in early June. Less than a month away.

Last year's Wagon Train Parade ended in a chase scene involving a runaway carriage and a stagecoach driven by an unwitting volunteer—me. There was also a shoot-out involving real guns, not the pretend scenes performed by the Hangtown Posse every summer.

This year I planned to stay on the sidelines. No participating in the parade in any capacity—not even as one of the Sassy Saloon Gals, a group formed by my best friend, Liz Daley, to entertain at various local events.

With Liz eight months pregnant and feeling more surly than sassy these days, I doubted she would be up to entertaining anyone other than her newborn arrival. I should give her a call once I got to the office.

I parked the car in my leased spot, then meandered down the sidewalk, stopping to admire my former employer's window displays. Last year, my friend and co-worker Stan Winters and I had been assigned the task of decorating Hangtown Bank in a style befitting the California gold rush.

We ended up enjoying the project far more than expected. And solving a murder. Which, given my history, is always to be expected.

I glanced at my watch. Not even nine yet. I could grab a mocha from my favorite coffee shop. I pulled open the door and smiled in delight. The customer standing in front of the register beamed back. He shoved a few bills into his wallet and hurtled toward me.

Speak of the devil. Stan placed his hands on my shoulders as he scrutinized me from the tips of my bangs down to my battered sandals.

"Laurel, you're looking..." His voice trailed off as he searched for an appropriate adjective. "Comfortable," he managed, my fashionista friend's tactful way of saying I looked like I'd thrown my clothes on this morning.

Totally not true. I'd spent at least twenty seconds on my wardrobe selection.

"So what's new?" I asked. "It's been ages since I've seen you."

"There is so much going on at the bank. You wouldn't believe it. We have to squeeze in a gabfest."

I mentally perused today's calendar. Blank as usual. Which reminded me of tomorrow's meeting with my former boss.

"Hey, is anything weird going on with Adriana? She called the agency and..." My voice dropped when I realized client confidentiality meant I couldn't actually tell Stan that Adriana was a potential client. Okay, that totally sucked.

Stan's gray eyes widened behind his nerd-chic wire-rims. "OMG. So much to dish." He peeked at his watch. "I'm late. I know your schedule must be crazy busy with your cases, but are you doing anything for lunch today?"

I hesitated to tell Stan today's lunch hour was a designated Costco run. I didn't want to burst his bubble about the glamourous nature of my new job.

"I'll reschedule. Let's meet at Cascada."

"You're on." He gave me a quick hug before racing out the door. I walked to the counter but found myself concentrating more on Stan's purported gossip than the pastries lined up in front of me. I finally decided to get a half dozen assorted donuts since both guys were expected to pop into the office today and they were former cops.

Enough said.

I arrived at our office and was attempting to juggle the donuts, my mocha and my keys when the front door opened with a whoosh. Bradford's craggy face lit up as he caught sight of the pink box.

"Let me help you." He grabbed the box with one of his ham-hock-sized hands.

Robert Bradford and I first met during a murder investigation when he was determined to pin the murders on me. The crotchety detective, whom I'd dubbed Tall, Bald and Homely, had interviewed my mother, who informed him her daughter was far too disorganized to commit a murder.

Once I was proven innocent, to everyone's surprise, including his, Robert Bradford fell in love with Mother. Even more surprising, she fell in love with him. Although I grudgingly accepted their engagement at the time, it wasn't until he risked his own life to save mine that I learned not only to respect him, but love him.

I set my mocha and my purse on my desk, following Bradford into our tiny breakroom, barely larger than my kitchen pantry.

"Thanks for helping with Gran's situation," I said. "How did it go?"

He reached into the box, grabbed a chocolate-covered cream-filled donut, and took a hefty bite before replying.

"Well, you know your grandmother. She can be a tad —"

"Cantankerous," I suggested.

He nodded. "Yeah, that works. They'd originally asked your grandmother, Iris, and Herb to wait at one of the sidewalk tables in front of that pizza place. But Ginny kept popping back into the office and getting in the crime techs' way, giving them pointers on how to do their job. They finally stuffed all three of them in the back of a squad car. That woman watches way too many crime shows."

I giggled. I could totally visualize my petite grandmother bossing the CSI team around.

"So what's your take on the murder? Was the detective willing to share anything with you?" I tore off half a glazed donut and bit into it. Yum.

Bradford polished off his own donut before answering. "Someone clobbered the vic on the back of his head. The techs found a trophy covered with blood, but they'll have to check to see if there's a second blood type or DNA left behind."

"The cops don't seriously suspect Gran or Iris, do they?"

"I wouldn't think so, given their size and age. Although your grandmother told me they'll probably find her prints on the trophy from the day before. That won't help. Especially since the murder seems to have occurred not too long before she and her friends walked in. Must have just missed the killer."

"No one else was in the office when they arrived?"

"Your grandmother said the door was ajar so she walked right in. She waited a bit, then decided to cruise through the office. She discovered him on the floor. The office manager and some other fellow supposedly wandered in right after your Gran found him. Your grandmother had already dialed 911 and an ambulance and cops were on their way."

"Did they seem shocked?" I asked.

"Who? Your grandmother or the guy's co-workers?"

"His co-workers. Nothing fazes Gran."

Bradford rocked back on the heels of his sturdy size-thirteen Rockports. "I couldn't honestly tell. The office manager kept asking Henry, the lead on the case, when they would be done. Claimed she had work to do and the crime scene tape was a customer deterrent."

My jaw dropped. That Kimberly had some nerve. "Did she look guilty?" I asked.

"Mostly pissed off. Like the victim had ruined the décor or something."

"Crabby."

He shrugged. "She's a piece of work all right. The sales guy with her looked scared enough to pee himself."

"I'd be freaked out, too. Maybe he's worried about a serial killer offing all the timeshare salespeople. I'm sure Iris isn't the only person who's been screwed by their company."

"Which means there could be a very long suspect list," Bradford said.

"And it could make my investigation into Iris's situation far more complex. I should check in with her today, see if she wants me to continue or not, given the situation."

Bradford snorted. "Are you kidding? Your grandmother is even more fired up than before. I'm kind of surprised she didn't beat us into the office today."

The office phone rang and I hotfooted it out of the breakroom, hoping the caller on the other end would be another new client.

Nope. Just the same old bossy one.

"Good morning, Gran. Have you recovered from your frightful experience yesterday?"

"Are you referring to your mother's driving us back to Placerville?" she replied. "I think Iris and I would have been safer with Herb, even if he can barely see over the steering wheel. Or at night. Barbara drives slower than the Wagon Train when it rolls down the hill."

Gran must have woken up on the wrong side of her sleigh bed this morning.

"How come Robert didn't drive?"

"Your mother says she gets carsick if someone else is driving that winding road."

My mother is also a control freak with a capital C.

"Does Iris still want me to follow up on her timeshare problem?"

"Sure. Why wouldn't she?" Gran asked.

"Okay, let me do some more research and I'll get back to you. Try to stay out of trouble today."

She hung up without assenting to my request. Hopefully her busy schedule involved something tamer than a murder investigation. Like her weekly bridge group. Although I'd seen her group in action. When it came to cards, those ladies were out for blood.

CHAPTER ELEVEN

Stan was already seated at Cascada when I arrived. A large turquoise Kate Spade purse perched on the chair next to him. I'd invited Liz to join us for lunch, and it looked like she'd been able to escape from the spa she owned in El Dorado Hills. With a baby due in a month, today's lunch could be one of the last times we dined together without the background accompaniment of a squalling infant.

Not that Liz would allow her child to cry or behave less than perfect in public. My demanding friend would find that totally unacceptable.

Liz duck-walked toward us, her ankles swollen and her belly so huge she looked as if she would be giving birth to both a basketball player and a basketball. But dressed in designer maternity togs, she remained the classy Brit I'd known since we'd met twenty years earlier at a fraternity party. After our dates decided to drink themselves into a stupor, we bonded over the three-mile hike back to campus.

We'd been best friends ever since, through thick and thin, marriage, divorce, pregnancy—and the occasional murder investigation.

Liz lifted her hefty purse from the chair and dropped it on the floor before plopping into the wooden seat. The chair and Liz both groaned in protest.

"I've decided I'm too old to bear a child," she announced, as she squirmed on the hard surface.

"Perhaps you should have come to that conclusion eight months ago," suggested Stan.

"Only four more weeks to go until D-day," I said. "And once you deliver your little bundle of joy, you'll be filled with joy." Not to mention her life would be filled with dirty diapers. But now was not the time to share how much my friend's life would change. Or to warn her the early years were the easiest. With my eldest going off to college, there would be a host of new things for me to worry about.

"So why are we all here today?" asked Liz with a grimace.

"Just wanted to see your smiling face," I replied with a grin of my own.

"Not really," Stan corrected me. "I mean, of course, we want to spend time with you before you pop your little Cinnabun out of the oven. But I have dirt to share—on Adriana Menzinger."

Just the mention of my former boss and nemesis gave me heartburn. But since it looked like Adriana might become a new client, the more dirt, I mean, information I could gather in advance, the better.

Stan lowered his voice so Liz and I leaned forward to catch every word of his scoop. Or rather, I leaned in and Liz hunched herself forward to better hear him.

"Adriana met this hot guy through some online dating site a few months ago. Had to tell the entire office about how great he was, blah, blah, blah. So annoying for some of us," voiced Stan, whose partner, Zac, a stage director, was traveling across the United States on a three-month tour.

"That's your idea of dirt?" Liz curled her lip at him. Stan's news wasn't exactly on the scale of TMZ celebrity reports.

"Let me finish, ladies. Two weeks ago she came into the office flashing a huge diamond. She met with the president of Hangtown Bank and gave him three weeks' notice."

"She quit?" I practically shouted at him. "After stealing that job away from me?" Despite my gratitude toward my husband and stepfather for inviting me to join the detective agency, I was still ticked off at Adriana for snatching the marketing director position after my boss retired last fall.

"Supposedly. That's what the bank rumor mill was churning out all week. Then yesterday we heard Adriana changed her mind and she's staying after all. She's still wearing that mega diamond, but there hasn't been any talk of her fiancé for a few days. Sounds suspicious to me. What do you think?"

What did I think?

I smiled, thinking how wonderful it was my friends were such excellent gossips. It certainly made my job easier.

CHAPTER TWELVE

The next morning was even more chaotic than usual. With a client meeting scheduled with my former boss, I needed to present the appearance of a successful private detective, even if I hadn't quite succeeded in that capacity yet. I pawed through my closet and finally settled on what I refer to as "vintage" and what most fashionistas would describe as "old." But the black gabardine suit fulfilled all my criteria: It was clean and it still fit.

Since Tom was providing chauffeur service today, I hugged all three kids goodbye, stepped into the Subaru, and backed out of the garage. I was running late so I gunned all four cylinders. I zipped up Highway 50 in record time, my tires squealing as I slid into my parking space at 8:27. Which gave me three minutes to trot down the sidewalk and greet our new client. If I was lucky, she'd be running late.

No such luck. With a frown on her cherry-red lips, and her arms firmly crossed, Adriana stood outside our office, one four-inch heel tapping the sidewalk in frustration. I quickly opened the door to the agency and ushered her inside.

Her frown morphed into a quizzical expression as I hit the light switches and opened the blinds. "What are you doing here?" she asked.

"I work here. Remember, that's why I left the bank?" Actually I left the bank for multiple reasons. An enormous dislike of my former boss—the one standing in front of me, her arms still crossed. And a huge like for my current partners and family members.

Her gaze roamed around the empty office. "Where are the investigators? I spoke with a Robert Bradford on the phone when I made the appointment."

"Robert was unavailable so you'll be meeting with me." I tried to put a positive spin on it. "Since we know one another so well, I'm more suited to help you with your problem."

Her pert nose crinkled as if smelling my bullsh** and not liking what she'd encountered.

"Why don't you have a seat in Tom's, I mean, my office," I said hurriedly. "Can I get you some coffee? We have an assortment of flavors."

She sighed, mumbled "French roast," and stomped on her stilt-like heels into Tom's office. I hoped he wouldn't mind me confiscating his digs for the interview. Once our firm grew, we'd be able to expand to larger quarters, including an office of my own.

The Keurig coffeemaker took four minutes—yes, I counted every second—to deliver Adriana's dark roasted brew. I brought her mug of coffee and an assortment of creams, sugar and sweeteners, wishing there were a way to sweeten her up as well.

I fixed a smile on my face, settled into Tom's comfortable chair, grabbed a pen and one of his legal pads and began the interview.

"So what type of situation can our agency help you with?" I asked, trying to maintain a professional demeanor instead of sounding like one of the Gossip Girls.

Adriana picked at a manicured fingernail, the vermillion-red color matching the color of her artificially plump lips.

"What I'm about to tell you is confidential, of course."

"Of course," I parroted back. "Everything you share with me is confidential. Just like it would be with an attorney." I couldn't resist adding, "Or a therapist."

She frowned at my remark, took a deep breath, crossed her legs and began her story.

"I got engaged two weeks ago." She thrust her jawbreaker-sized diamond ring at me, apparently thinking visual aids would assist her storytelling.

"Congratulations."

She smirked at me, but surprisingly the smirk morphed into an expression that could best be described as—sad.

"Gino Romano, my fiancé, swooped into my life several months ago and swept me off my brand new Louboutins." She threw me a half smile. "I'd never met anyone so bold, so exciting, and I have to admit, sexy. Obviously, I'm a great catch," she added, throwing back her mane of dark curls.

"Obviously," I said with an internal eye roll. "May I ask how you met?"

"On the *Hello Cupid* site," she said, her color rising to match her lipstick. "It's the most progressive and analytical online dating service these days."

In my opinion, there was nothing wrong with using a dating site or agency. As long as you didn't use the one I'd signed up with two years earlier. Talk about drop-dead dates. Although, if I hadn't joined the Love Club, I'd never have met Tom.

"Many people have found the perfect match online," I continued. "However, there are scam artists out there, as I'm sure you're aware. Looking to take advantage of women, and men as well."

"I'm not an idiot, Laurel," she replied. "I can take care of myself."

I remained silent, since there must be something she couldn't take care of herself. Otherwise, why was she ruining my morning and depriving me of my daily donut fix?

"Even though we recently became engaged, we don't live together. Gino lives in Granite Bay and I live in El Dorado Hills. His firm is in Roseville, and I have the drive to Placerville every day."

I nodded and jotted down the geographical aspects of the case, wondering if they were truly relevant.

"Last week I dined with a girlfriend in Roseville, at a restaurant near the Galleria, and as we were driving by R. C. Steakhouse, I noticed Gino standing by the entrance, his arm around a blonde." Her dark eyes flashed with anger as she added, "A very young and very shapely blonde."

"You shouldn't jump to conclusions. Perhaps he was meeting with a client."

"He's a financial advisor, specializing in seniors and their investment portfolios." Her voice dripped with sarcasm. "This girl was barely legal, much less one of his baby boomer clients."

"A relative, granddaughter of a client, masseuse?" I couldn't stop throwing out possibilities, none of them likely.

"Seriously? Plus, the only reason I chose to meet with Beth that particular evening was because Gino told me he had a dinner meeting in San Francisco and wouldn't be home until close to midnight." I tapped my black Bic against the desk. "Is that the only time he's misled you?"

She shifted in her chair, crossing her left leg over her right and then switching once again. "I don't want to seem like one of those paranoid girlfriends always worried their boyfriend is going out on them."

"You're cautious. There's nothing wrong with that."

"Earlier this week, he informed me he had another meeting in San Francisco. After work, I drove to his house." She paused, looking reflective. "I'm not really sure why. Intuition, I suppose. A red convertible was parked in his driveway. The house was lit up, so he was obviously home and entertaining someone."

"Did you see who he was with?"

She shook her head. "His nosy next-door neighbor waved at me as I drove past. The guy is always outside pruning and planting. I waved back and took off, terrified Gino would learn I was there. Spying on him."

"You haven't said anything to Gino?" I asked, knowing I would have been hard-pressed to keep quiet if I'd been in her situation.

Her eyes downcast, Adriana mumbled, "I don't want to rock the boat. I love him, Laurel."

"I understand," I said and meant it. Love can do strange things to people. Like turn an assertive female bank executive into a lovesick teenager. "But how can the agency help?"

"I'd like you to, um, I guess, tail him. Like they do in the movies. Take photos of him and whatever woman he's with. He's already told me he has to spend a couple of nights in Tahoe next week on business. I want to find out if it's legitimate business or monkey business."

I attempted to maintain a professional demeanor, but internally I was jumping up and down. My first surveillance job. So cool.

I quoted our rates, which given the newness of our agency, were very reasonable. Adriana reviewed our client agreement, skimming past the fine print, including our requirement of a fifteen-hundred-dollar retainer. She pulled a checkbook out of her purse, wrote the check without batting an eyelash and handed it to me.

"You'll ensure Gino will have no idea someone is following him, correct?"

"Of course," I replied, wondering how hard this tailing thing could be. It was a good thing I'd given my periwinkle Prius to my daughter. Not the best car for blending into the scenery. But my almost new silver Subaru Forester would be ideal for this type of operation.

Adriana gave me all the information I requested: Gino's home and business addresses, the dates of his Tahoe trip, as well as all of her contact information. I ushered her to the front door, closing it behind her.

I walked back to Tom's office and relaxed in his comfortable leather chair, a wide smile on my face as I stared at my first retainer check, as pleased as if I'd won the California lottery. Then the front door flew open, and my husband burst into the office, his tie askew and his eyes frantic as he searched for me.

I rose from the chair, puzzled, as he raced to my side.

"What's wrong?" I questioned him.

"Have you talked to Jenna?" he asked. "Is she okay?"

Only three little words, but they were enough to make this mother's heart drop to the floor.

CHAPTER THIRTEEN

I grabbed Tom by his firm bicep. "What do you mean?"

"You haven't heard?" he asked.

"Heard what? I just finished a client meeting."

"There's been a single-car accident on Green Valley Road. A Prius was run off the road. I was afraid it might be Jenna."

I staggered to a chair and fell into it. "Do they know what model or color the Prius is?" I asked. "There are a ton of them on the road these days."

"I'm not sure. I heard it on my police scanner just a few minutes ago. I thought I'd check with you first to see if you heard from her. After I dropped the kids off this morning, I stopped at Home Depot to pick up some irrigation supplies. I caught the tail end of the announcement so I didn't catch the license plate number."

I glanced at my watch. Jenna would still be in class, assuming she wasn't the accident victim. I didn't want to turn into one of those overwrought mothers who race to the school every time they hear a siren in the distance. But still, I'd feel better if she confirmed she was okay. I grabbed my cell out of my purse to see if there were any messages. None.

That was a good thing. Unless she was injured and couldn't contact me. My stomach clenched at the realization. I texted her in all caps.

CALL ME ASAP.

I stared at my phone, willing it to beep or ring. While we waited, Tom called one of his buddies at the El Dorado County Sheriff's

Office to see if they had the name of the victim or the specific year and color of the car. The only response was it was a young female driver, no passenger, and an ambulance was on the way.

I didn't think my stomach could get any more nauseous, but I was wrong. I dashed off to the bathroom, locked the door and stood over the sink gasping for air. I kept telling myself to settle down, but my maternal instinct had kicked into high alert. Tom pounded on the door to see if I was okay. I decided I wouldn't be okay until I knew my daughter was safe at the high school, so we locked up the office, jumped into Tom's car and headed for Green Valley Road.

It was a good thing Tom handled the driving. Despite the gravity of the situation, he maintained a speed barely above the speed limit, a wise move because the two-lane country road contained more twists and turns than the current mystery I was reading. Although I mentally urged him to speed it up, I tried to relax and concentrate on something pleasant.

If only I could think of something.

We zipped down the road on the lookout for signs of an accident. Just as we passed North Shingle Road we caught up to a canary-yellow tow truck from a Placerville body shop. Tom followed the truck while I checked my phone once again.

Nada. And Jenna's calculus test should have been over by now. Although she would have switched off her phone before class began and might not have turned it on again.

The tow truck rounded a bend, with us trailing a few feet behind. The right indicator light on the truck blinked red and Tom slowed, but not before I caught a glimpse of a black-and-white CHP patrol car, a dirty white county sheriff's car and a very smashed Prius.

A periwinkle Prius.

CHAPTER FOURTEEN

It was a good thing I hadn't snacked on any donuts this morning, because there is no way I'd have been able to keep my breakfast down once I saw Jenna's totaled vehicle. Despite my desire to view the damage and find out any pertinent facts, like where my daughter was, the spot where we'd parked wasn't exactly safe for any pedestrian activity.

Tom clicked on the emergency signals before opening his door and checking for traffic in either direction. After walking behind the car, he carefully helped me out so I didn't slip on the gravel-lined sloping path that paralleled the ditch alongside the road. We traipsed through dried leaves and twigs that crackled underfoot until we reached the squad cars.

Tom hailed the deputy who was deep in discussion with the tow truck driver. "Hey, Bill," Tom said to the officer. "This is my stepdaughter's vehicle. Can you tell me what happened and where we can find her?"

"Do you know if she's okay?" I asked as a waterfall of tears cascaded down my cheeks.

"The ambulance took her to Marshall Hospital. The airbag hit her pretty hard and she might have a sprain or two." He looked at the Prius—the passenger side completely smashed into the hill alongside the road. "Your girl was mighty lucky."

"What happened?" Tom asked.

"She was still pretty freaked out when I questioned her, but from what she said, I guess a car whipped around that curve," Bill said, pointing twenty feet ahead of us, "halfway in her lane. She veered to the right, but he hit her front bumper and sent her crashing into this hill."

I shivered. Bill was right. Jenna was mighty lucky.

"I can't believe the other car just kept on going," I said, indignant that someone could leave the scene of an accident they created.

Bill shrugged. "Probably some young kid afraid he'd get in trouble or lose his license."

"I presume Bodyworks will tow her car to the shop," Tom asked the driver of the tow truck, who nodded in response.

I elbowed Tom. "Can we go to the hospital? I need to see my daughter. Now."

Tom handed his business card to the deputy in case they uncovered any evidence regarding the car that caused the crash. Jenna had given the Bodyworks driver her contact and insurance information, so he was good to go.

I took one last look at the car. I didn't know much about auto repair, but it looked like my ancient Prius might have taken its last ride.

As we were driving to Marshall Hospital, my cell pinged with a message from Jenna. It was brief, basically saying she was okay but to come to the hospital right away. Please. Followed by a very sad-faced emoji. I kept my reply short, informing her we were on our way. Tom dropped me off at the emergency room entrance and went off to park. I almost crashed through the automatic doors into the hospital, which were not moving as quickly as my feet were.

The front desk directed me to Jenna's room, where I broke into tears again. At the rate I was blubbering, I could lose three pounds in water weight today.

"It's okay, Mom. I'm not hurt bad." Jenna's lower lip quivered and it looked like she might start bawling as well. "But I missed my calculus final," she wailed.

You had to admire a daughter who prioritized academia over accidents.

I bent over and gently kissed her forehead, smoothing out her matted hair. "Don't worry about your exam. I'll stop at the school and speak with your teacher. I'm sure he'll let you do a makeup test."

"I still can't believe those boys didn't stop. They must have seen me crash. I could have been *killed*," she said with the eloquence of an Oscar-winning actor.

"There were two people in the car? Did you recognize either of them?"

"No, but I had a very close visual of the driver who tried to sideswipe me. I won't forget him or his car," she emphasized. "And once I'm out of here, I'm going to track him down."

"You let me handle it. The most important thing is that you're okay." I stroked Jenna's arm and wondered if she'd seen herself in a mirror yet. The large bruise on her forehead would soon turn the same color as her indigo jeans.

A nurse entered the room and greeted us. "How are you doing?" she asked Jenna.

"Much better, thanks. The ibuprofen helped."

The nurse turned to me. "And how is Mom doing?"

"I've been better, and I could definitely use something stronger than ibuprofen." When the nurse frowned at me, I elaborated. "I was thinking of chocolate."

"It calms her down," Jenna said to the nurse. "Even better than Xanax. So can I go home now?"

"The doctor wants an X-ray of your ankle as well as your ribs to make sure nothing is broken. But after that, you should be good to go. Although we highly recommend resting all weekend."

Jenna frowned. "But it's Katie's senior party this Saturday night. I can't miss it. How long do you think it will take to fix my car, Mom?"

My phone beeped, saving me from giving a reply that could lead to more angst for my daughter. Then I chastised myself for having such a negative outlook. The body shop might be able to repair her car.

And I might lose ten pounds by tomorrow.

As the nurse loaded Jenna into a wheelchair for her X-rays, I glanced at my phone. Multiple messages from multiple family members who had heard about an accident involving a periwinkle Prius. Probably the only one in the county.

I called my mother first and assured her Jenna would be fine, although her car was most likely fatally injured.

Gran had also left a message since her phone network occasionally outpaced Twitter.

"Is my great-granddaughter gonna be alright?" she asked when I called her back.

"Yes, she was very lucky." I gave her a CliffsNotes version of Jenna's accident.

"Do you need me to come down there?"

"Nope." My bossy grandmother was more likely to alienate the medical staff than assist in any way. After her last hospital visit, she'd annoyed the nurses so much they'd recommended she switch to another medical group, one that didn't include Marshall Hospital as a designated facility.

"I'm sure they'd be thrilled to have you help out," I said, then switched to a diversionary tactic, "but how about we work on Iris's issue instead?"

"Good point. We can't let the fact that scumbag was murdered interfere with our case."

Technically, it was *my* case, but since Gran referred Iris to me, it wasn't worth arguing over.

"Correct. Let me do some more research, then I'll visit their office and try to get Iris her money back."

"That's my girl detective. I wouldn't mind hitting the craps table again neither. We can multitask while we're up there."

"I'm not sure you should visit the timeshare office again. Especially since Gregg was murdered. We don't want you to get into trouble with the police in Tahoe."

"Don't be silly, Laurel. There's no reason anyone would suspect me of killing that twit."

No reason other than her fingerprints were all over the murder weapon. I hoped the Tahoe police department had come up with some suspects other than my grandmother by now. She might love going up to Tahoe, but I didn't think she'd be too keen on taking advantage of the South Lake Tahoe jail's overnight accommodations.

CHAPTER FIFTEEN

May weekends are normally filled with a variety of school or local events. In Mother's free time, between her real estate career and helping her daughter with her grandchildren, she actively participated in several local philanthropic organizations.

This weekend was the annual Sierra Foothills Assistance Club garden tour. Mother had roped me into helping out at one of the houses on the tour. I could hardly object since my job entailed standing next to an amazing infinity pool situated in a lush garden. All I had to do was chat with the folks on the tour.

Flapping my lips was definitely a skillset I'd perfected. And today I'd have the opportunity to do just that with hundreds of visitors. One of the other volunteers, a brown-haired woman with a sweet smile, stopped to talk to me.

"You're Barbara Bradford's daughter, aren't you?" she asked me. When I nodded she introduced herself as Jeanne Lehmann, a member of the club, "How is your daughter doing? Barbara told me about her terrible accident. She was quite beside herself with worry."

"Jenna should be fine. Teens are resilient. She has a cracked rib, a sprained ankle, and a few bruises."

"She's lucky," Jeanne said. "By the way, your mother mentioned a few days ago that you were investigating a resale timeshare scam up in Tahoe."

"I am. Have you encountered a scam yourself?"

"Not me, but one of my friends got involved with one of those scammer companies. A few months back she and her husband paid a significant amount of money to a company to take over the ownership of a two-week timeshare in Florida. The deal also included absorbing the timeshare loan. And now the phone number for the company has been disconnected. They don't know what to do."

"Interesting," I said. "Was the company Timeshare Help?"

Jeanne shrugged. "All of these timeshare resale companies sound the same to me. Can I have them contact you?"

Another possible client? Yes, indeedy. I pulled out my business card and handed it to her. Jeanne said goodbye, then hustled down the path to her assigned station by a wisteria-framed gazebo in the corner of the owner's two-acre lot.

It might be time to order some T-shirts with our agency name plastered across the back. With an intriguing design on the front that would get people's attention. Like a chalk body outline.

Maybe not. The heat must have been impacting my creativity. The climate in late May could range from the fifties to well over one hundred. I wiped perspiration off my brow. Today was fast approaching the high end of the spectrum.

I glanced at the stairs leading to the patio above the pool area where I stood, wondering if there was time for me to grab a bottle of water before the next onslaught of visitors. A couple descended the steps holding hands. Her dark hair shone in the midday sun as it cascaded down the back of the short sleeveless red sundress she wore. I envied her long bronzed legs. My semi-long legs had yet to make contact with the sun this year, which explained why they were ensconced in dull black pants. Although she wore Jackie O-style sunglasses, I recognized Adriana immediately. No doubt the man standing next to her was her fiancé. My future tailee.

Tailee? I needed a lexicon for sleuthing terminology.

But what a timely encounter. As they drew closer, I waved at my client, who seemed intent on her conversation with him. She finally noticed me throwing my arms around like an out-of-control school crossing guard.

She shot me a wary look as they approached, but I knew better than to spill my guts.

"Hello, Adriana," I greeted her. "Are you enjoying the tour?"

"Yes, it's been great."

Gino smiled at me, waiting for an introduction that never occurred. I jumped in and said, "I'm Laurel. Adriana and I used to work together at Hangtown Bank."

Gino shook my hand. "You're no longer in the banking business?" he asked. Adriana's worried eyes grew as large as the planters surrounding the pool.

"I'm doing freelance work now," I replied. "But I miss working with you, Adriana." She smiled in surprise, either at my complimentary statement or my skillful fibbing.

"Are you in banking too?" I asked Gino, pretending I didn't know.

He shook his head, his spicy cologne overpowering the delicate fragrance of the roses on the walkway. "I'm in wealth management. Are you looking for someone to manage your portfolio?"

My toilet paper portfolio far exceeded my stock portfolio at this point, but since my job included investigating him, I might as well discuss investing with him. "Yes, I'd love to talk to you sometime."

Gino handed me his card and they walked away. The couple was a few steps away from the gazebo when Adriana pivoted and headed back in my direction.

"Whew," she said. "I was worried you'd tell him I'd hired you."

"I told you, discretion is my middle name."

"Thanks. Listen, Gino just told me he has a client meeting tomorrow night. Any chance you can stake out his place or tail him without him recognizing you?"

"Of course. Not to worry."

She left with a smile on her face while my smile scrunched into a frown. I now knew what Gino looked like but the same went for him. I'd have to wear some type of disguise when I was tailing him. My closet contained a multitude of disguises if I wanted to dress up as a clown, a witch, or a vampire.

It looked like I might need to check out Gran's spare bedroom, which Mother and I kiddingly referred to as Wigs R Us.

The next hour was spent chatting with locals from all over El Dorado County as well as Sacramento. It was getting near the end of my shift when another familiar couple walked down the pool steps.

To be more specific, Stan strolled while his companion waddled. Good grief. What was Liz doing here in her condition?

As they drew closer, I noticed Liz's stomach protruding even more than during our lunch two days earlier.

"I hate to mention this," I said, "but you look like you're about to pop."

She sighed. "Yes, that's the plan. I'm officially done with being pregnant. Brian's getting ready to go to trial on that big kidnapping case, so Stan volunteered to escort me today. We thought all of this activity might encourage this baby to make his entrance into the world." She uncapped a bottle of water, took two sips then dumped the rest on her head.

I gasped and Stan stepped back, almost landing in the pool. The always elegant Elizabeth Daley, proprietor of Golden Hills Spa, had reached a new low.

"What?" she said in a very non-regal tone.

"Oh, nothing. You look cooler," Stan said encouragingly, although with streams of water pouring down her face, she looked more like a beached whale.

"Was that Adriana you were talking to a few minutes ago?" Liz asked.

"Did she hire you for a case?" Stan chimed in.

I shrugged. "You know I can't say. Client confidentiality."

"Oh, balls," said Liz. "C'mon, grant a pregnant woman her last wish."

"That's what they give condemned prisoners," I informed her.

"Not much difference," she said with a sigh.

"Give it up, girl," Stan said to me. "You know you want to dish."

Stan was right. I really, really, really wanted to dish. But I was determined to be professional.

I mimed a zipper and said, "My lips are sealed."

Stan looked off in the distance where Adriana and her beau were chatting. "I bet she hired you to keep an eye on her fellow. Right?"

"It's not for me to say."

"She probably wants you to tail him or do a stakeout," Stan said. "I could help with that."

I shook my head. "No can do."

"Laurel, you know you can't go more than an hour without peeing," Liz said. "You're worse than a pregnant woman. How on earth are you going to do a stakeout?"

Uh oh. Tom forgot to include tips on that in my lesson plan. How was I going to manage stakeout activity without help?

"I'm not saying I need to tail anyone, but if I did, Jenna could go with me. She's going to be our intern." Then I snapped my fingers in dismay. "Shoot. She'll be hobbling around for a week or two, and she has finals to study for next week."

Stan waved a hand in my frustrated face. "Does the agency have room for one more intern? One who owns a car that would be perfect for stakeouts? It comes equipped with a supply of Godiva chocolate."

I wasn't certain what Tom would say to this arrangement, but I threw out my hand to Stan and said, "You're hired."

CHAPTER SIXTEEN

Monday morning I agreed to drive Jenna to school and Tom said he'd take the little kids. Tom and I shared a quick kiss before driving off in our respective vehicles. I pondered how nice it was to have someone in my life to share all of my chauffeuring responsibilities.

It was even nicer to have someone share my bed. Thinking about the previous night's amorous activities made me blush. I peered over at my daughter to see if she'd noticed, but she was nose deep in her math book.

Jenna finally slammed her book shut and looked up when we were a few blocks from the high school. She stuffed the textbook in her backpack and shifted in her seat. "I can't wait for school to end and my new job to start. What kind of cases do you think I'll be working on?" she asked eagerly.

How best to answer her question. The other day the UPS guy dropped off two cases of copy paper that needed to be stored. That would be one less "case" for this detective/office manager/mom to deal with. But I didn't think that was the kind of case my daughter alluded to.

This internship would be quite an eye-opener for her.

"My caseload is fairly light, right now," I replied. "But I'm sure the guys will keep you busy doing…detective, um, stuff."

"I'm willing to start at the bottom and work my way up," she said.

Ah, to be young, enthusiastic, and not responsible for a household budget. I pulled up behind a row of mom-driving SUVs, shifted into park, then raced around the car to help my daughter. But she'd already maneuvered herself out of her seat, backpack and all. I kissed her on the cheek and wished her good luck on her makeup final. She thanked me, then limped off to class, instantly surrounded by solicitous girls anxious to check on their injured friend.

I was proud of my plucky daughter. The females in my family don't let little things like multiple injuries stop them from getting things done.

Traffic into Placerville was light, and I arrived at the office around eight thirty. I brewed some coffee, then hit the internet in search of data on timeshare resale companies. I'd barely typed in the word "timeshare" when Google spewed a myriad of links and timeshare resale advertisements at me.

Talk about a booming business. Timeshare resale companies proliferated from one coast to the other. Every site possessed smiling staff offering to whisk away your financial problems for a minimal fee.

Guaranteed.

Two hours and four cups of coffee later, I'd gleaned more information than I'd ever thought possible on the topic. I'd also perused multiple Better Business Bureau sites and discovered complaints exceeded compliments by a lot.

Almost one hundred to one.

The majority of the companies pitched their one-time fee as far lower than paying a commission tied to the sale of the timeshare. The problem with that theory is that commissions are tied to an actual sale. If the timeshare isn't sold, then there's no charge. Whereas the one-time fees seem to have produced few, if any, sales from almost all of the companies I'd queried.

Instead of Timeshare Help they should be named Timeshare Rip-off.

The front door opened and Tom and Bradford walked in, one behind the other.

"Hey, fellows," I said. "How did your meeting with the District Attorney's Office go?"

Tom bussed my cheek, then both men settled in the chairs in front of my desk.

"Good meeting," Tom said and Bradford nodded back. "The D.A.'s office is out one investigator for a significant sick leave so they want us to interview some of their witnesses for multiple cases."

"We need to send them a contract agreeing to our terms," Bradford chimed in, pointing his finger at me.

"Hey," I protested, "I'm not your secretary. I have my own casework, you know." Geesh. Men! "Surely senior investigators such as yourself are competent enough to fill in the blanks on our standard contract."

Bradford grunted.

"But you're so much faster than we are," Tom said, his dark eyes locking on mine.

I sighed since I'm a pushover for my husband's Godiva-brown eyes. "Fine, but you can add this to the job description for our new intern. By the way, I'd like to add another intern to the agency."

Now both men frowned. "Honey, we'll barely have enough work to keep Jenna busy. And we can't afford a paid intern. How did you come across this person?"

"It's Stan," I said, barely maintaining a straight face. "He wants to help me on my stakeout tonight." Before Tom or Bradford could object, I added, "It would be safer to have a partner, just in case something happens."

"Nothing better happen," Tom growled. "Or we'll pull you off stakeout duty without a moment's hesitation. The goal is to sit in your car, possibly follow the person, take notes, and then return home safe and sound. You can do that, right?"

"Of course, but having an extra set of eyes can't hurt. Especially when I need to make a pit stop."

Bradford rolled his eyes but wisely kept his mouth shut.

Tom heaved a sigh. "Just make sure Stan realizes anything he learns is confidential. Not to be disclosed to anyone." Tom's voice rose and he did as well. "I better not see him tweeting *#amdetecting* or *#bigclue* tonight."

Hmmm. I was beginning to regret taking on my new intern. I certainly hoped before the evening was over I wasn't tweeting *#help*.

CHAPTER SEVENTEEN

I should have known. When Stan picked me up for our surveillance detail, he was dressed to detect in a long beige trench coat with a soft gray fedora cocked over his sweaty brow.

"You realize it's ninety degrees outside," I said.

"I thought the outfit would get me in the zone. You know, enhance my Spidey sense."

I stared at Placerville's version of Columbo.

"It will cool down later on," he said. "This could be an all-nighter, right?"

"Gosh, I hope not." But since this was my first surveillance job, who knew? Although Adriana had given me an idea of Gino's normal daily routine, she also forewarned me it wasn't uncommon for him to leave the office early, stop at his gym for an hour and then work from home. He could drive straight from the office to his alleged business meeting or stop at the house first to change his clothes for said client meeting.

Or romantic assignation. The reason we'd been hired.

Stan had taken the afternoon off work, and we were prepared to give it our all. Assuming our all would be representative of a classy team like—who?

I pondered for a minute, and thought of a detective show from the eighties I'd recently discovered on the Hallmark channel— *Hart to Hart*. Sure, Jennifer Hart, portrayed by Stefanie Powers, was taller, slimmer, and more glamorous than me, but we both had coppery brown curly hair.

I glanced at Stan as he backed his silver Beemer down the driveway. With his receding hairline, Elton John specs and insignificant jawline, he wasn't quite a doppelganger for Robert Wagner.

Stan glanced over at me and winked. But he was my partner. At least for tonight.

Four hours later found us sitting in Stan's car, bored, hungry and crabby. Real-life stakeouts were way more tedious than portrayed on television. Although, if the man sitting next to me had been my husband instead of my gay friend, it might have been a different story.

We'd initially begun our surveillance at Gino's Roseville office, waiting in the parking lot for a dull two hours before following him to his contemporary-style house in Granite Bay. An additional two hours passed while we caught up on all the gossip either of us could think of, discussed our favorite TV shows, and burned through the Godiva goodies Stan brought along. Although we'd stuck to water instead of soda, my bladder was practically shouting at me.

"I think he's in for the night," Stan said as I shifted uncomfortably in my seat. "Should we take off?"

"I don't know how much longer I can hold it. Having a partner is great, but not having access to a bathroom is problematic. I thought Gino would have left for his meeting by now, but maybe it was cancelled. I guess we'll have to try again another night."

"Okay," Stan said. He inserted his key in the ignition, shifted into drive, and we rolled forward. Suddenly, I whacked him on his right arm.

"Hey, what's the matter with you?" he asked, slamming his foot on the brake.

I pointed down the street. "It's Gino."

We'd discreetly parked half a block away from Gino's house, but it was close enough for me to see Gino backing his navy Mercedes coupe out of his garage and down his driveway. When he reached the street, he braked for a second, gunned the engine, then barreled down the narrow road.

Stan proved an intern has his merits. Especially one who owned a sleek BMW with an engine zippy enough to follow the speediest suspect. And who drove skillfully enough not to lose him once we reached a four-lane road.

"You're not half bad at this tailing thing," I remarked, keeping an eye on Gino's vehicle, three cars ahead of our own as he drove south down Hazel Boulevard.

"I used to practice tailing cars just for fun," he acknowledged. "In case I switched careers and ended up with the cops."

"You never told me that," I said.

He shrugged. "Eventually I realized I probably wouldn't fit in. I think I'm more comfortable hanging out on a stage than in a squad room."

The conversation died as Stan concentrated on his mission. It was dark now and more difficult to follow Gino's vehicle. Fortunately, he drove a newer model fitted with a bright display of rear taillights that practically screamed luxury car.

Gino also assisted us with our tailing maneuvers by utilizing his blinkers to indicate whenever he planned to turn left or right. Something most drivers seemed to disregard these days.

When Gino hit Highway 50, he headed west toward Sacramento. Ten miles later, he exited the freeway. Instead of going straight, which would lead to Sacramento State University, he turned left on Howe Avenue, heading south for a brief distance before going right onto Folsom Boulevard. Shortly after, Gino drove into a strip mall. Garish fluorescent lights in eye-opening shades of hot pink, lime green and banana yellow advertised a smoke shop, nail salon, laundromat, a few vacant stores, and at the end of the mall, a larger venue, with one of the more tasteful signs, simply titled The Gray Goose.

"Interesting spot for a business meeting," Stan said.

"It looks like Adriana has good instincts."

"Yes, although Gino wouldn't be the first male to conduct business in a bar."

"It's a long way from his home, though. Lots of bars closer to his house to choose from."

"True," Stan replied. "And this isn't the classiest part of town either."

I chewed on my lower lip. "I guess I should go in and see who he's meeting."

"I'll go with you."

"Not dressed like that you won't. Lose the raincoat and hat."
Stan clutched his fedora. "Not the hat. It's part of my image."
"Whatever. Look, I'll go in there first. See if he's meeting with a woman. If I'm not out in fifteen minutes, come in after me. But be cool."

"*Moi?* I am the epitome of cool," Stan replied before giving me the once-over. "But you are totally not dressed for the occasion. You need to look hot, and right now you look more like a soccer mom than a gal out for an evening."

I glanced down at my white button-down shirt and jeans skirt. Perfect for a stakeout—not so ideal for nightclubbing. Stan leaned over and unbuttoned my top button. I swatted his hand away.

"What do you think you're doing?"

"Attempting to turn you into a sexpot. Two more buttons will help."

I reluctantly unfastened the next button. Then I reached into my surveillance tote bag and pulled out one of Gran's auburn pageboy wigs. I found a dangling pair of earrings stuffed in the bottom of my purse I'd worn a few weeks ago when Tom and I enjoyed an infrequent date night and added them to my ensemble. I slipped out of the car and rolled the elastic waistband of my jeans skirt up twice, revealing shapely, albeit pale, legs.

"Go get 'em," Stan said, leaning out of the car window, "and try to look sexy. Don't stomp around like you usually do."

"I don't stomp," I said with clenched teeth. "I merely have a brisk stride."

"Yeah, well, slow down and put some swivel into those hips." He punched the power button on his window and waved me forward.

I clumped away from the car, realized Stan was right about my heavy tread, and switched to a slower, more seductive pace. It took me awhile to find my rhythm and at first I probably looked more like an arthritic redhead than a hot-hipped hussy. By the time I pushed open the heavy door to The Gray Goose, I'd fully embraced my new role.

It took a few minutes for my eyes to adjust to the dimly lit interior. Booths lined two of the walls with a few scratched wooden tables in the middle of the room, half of them occupied. The clack of colliding billiard balls echoed from the back of the L-shaped room. To the left of the entrance, a long bar welcomed couples and singles.

I guessed their primary goal was to end up as one half of a couple by the end of evening.

The Gray Goose epitomized your standard neighborhood bar. The question remained—why was Gino in this particular neighborhood?

I glanced around the room, my senses assaulted by the smell of booze, cologne and hot grease. A few patrons shot lewd grins in my direction, making my skin crawl. I took care of my most imperative mission first—the ladies' room located way in the back of the building. I fluffed up my curly wig, added two more coats of lipstick, took several deep breaths, then headed back out. My first objective: an empty seat at the bar. Maybe I could learn something about Gino from the bartender.

The tall burly bartender sidled over to me. "What can I get for you, hon?"

"What kind of chardonnays do you serve by the glass?" I asked. He hooted, and a woman a few seats over snickered at my request.

My face heated in embarrassment. "Just give me a glass of your house white," I mumbled, reaching into my purse for my wallet. A large hand stopped the movement and a figure slid onto the bar stool next to mine. In a deep baritone, he said, "Put it on my tab."

CHAPTER EIGHTEEN

I turned to thank the man for my drink and almost fell off my stool. Seated next to me was my quarry—Gino.

Some detective I was.

"First time here?" he asked me, his thick dark lashes framing curious eyes.

Wasn't it obvious? But I simply nodded and took a sip of the white wine the bartender placed in front of me.

Blech. Their house chardonnay tasted more like house vinegar. I reluctantly swallowed since I didn't see any spit jars nearby, then asked my own question.

"What about you? Come here often?" I fluttered my lashes at him, feeling like a bimbo straight out of a B-movie.

Gino gazed into my eyes. Briefly, before his gaze dropped to my chest, which is not nearly as talkative as my lips. I placed my index finger under his chin and helped him locate the correct visual coordinates for our conversation.

"Sure." Gino smiled seductively. "You never know who you'll meet."

I could see how Adriana fell for him. The guy simply oozed charm. And wealth. His silk shirt, slacks and lizard shoes screamed designer duds. He'd paid for my drink from a huge wad of cash in a silver money clip.

So if he was that well off, why was Gino hanging out in this dive?

"You live around here?" I tried to sound sultry and mysterious, like a husky-voiced Lauren Bacall or Kathleen Turner, but I was so nervous it came out more like Betty Boop. I needed to drown out my soccer mom persona. And keep him from recognizing me from our brief exchange during the garden tour.

"Not far. And you?" He leaned closer as if anxious to hear my reply.

"Not far." I gave my best attempt at a Mona Lisa smile. I picked up my glass, hoping to find some investigative inspiration and sipped again. Double blech. This wine did not improve with age. "So what do you do for a living?" I asked, back in fluttering female mode, curious how truthful he would be.

"I dabble in a variety of things," he replied. "My goal is to make sure my clients are"—he leaned in, his chin practically resting on my bosom—"completely satisfied with the service I provide."

Hmm. I'd been out of the dating scene for a few years now, but that sure sounded like a pickup line to me. Or maybe that's how he reeled in his clients.

"And your line of work?" he asked.

"Oh, this and that," I said. "I get bored easily."

"Well, maybe you haven't discovered the right position?" His dark eyes held a hint of laughter at his innuendo-laden comment.

Me. I just wanted to barf.

The door to The Gray Goose burst open. A giant of a man, clad in a leather vest, jeans, ginormous metal-studded belt and a multitude of colorful tattoos on both arms, strode into the bar. A bushy black beard and moustache covered most of his face, but his beady black eyes looked annoyed as they scanned the room. His gaze finally settled on the bar, and he sauntered in my direction.

The bearded giant claimed the seat next to me as he growled at the bartender. "Pete didn't show?"

Great. I was sandwiched between a Hell's Angels lookalike on my left and Mr. Suave on my right. It might be time to head for home. As I started to rise, the bruiser placed a firm hand on my shoulder and pushed me back down.

"Don't leave on my account, babe," he said before telling the bartender, "Shoot me a Bud." Then he turned his attention back to me. "I'm Jake. What's your name, sweet thing?"

Uh oh. I hadn't prepared a new identity and my own name was somewhat uncommon.

"I'm Tiffany," I squeaked out.

"Tiffany, huh. Does that mean you cost a bundle?" He roared with laughter, almost knocking over the beer the bartender set in front of him.

What?

Gino leaned in and covered my hand with his warm palm. "I'd say she's a real gem of a gal."

Jake also leaned forward, a cloud of beer breath permeating the air as he wrapped his arm around me, squeezing me tight enough to make another of my buttons burst open.

Okay, it was past time for this detective to disappear. I attempted to escape from Jake's iron-fisted grip, but the guy had superhuman strength.

Now if only a Superman would appear and rescue me.

CHAPTER NINETEEN

The door to The Gray Goose opened once again. Although not quite the superhero I'd envisioned, a rescuer stood in the open doorway, the neon lights from the sign highlighting him in shades of blue, pink and green.

My fedora-wearing friend didn't exactly fit the mold of The Gray Goose's clientele, but at least he'd dumped the raincoat. Stan's gaze finally landed on me, and he sidled over. Beneath his wire-rims his gray eyes looked concerned.

"Hi..." Stan stopped as I shot a warning glance at him. "Um, hon. I've been waiting for you," he said in a whiny voice. A perfect imitation of a petulant spouse.

Jake's arm dropped and so did his jaw as I responded to Stan's plea. "Sweetie," I said, "you're here."

I jumped off my barstool and gave Stan a big hug. "Nice meeting you boys," I said to the two men before grabbing Stan's hand and racing out of the lounge.

The cool night air felt fantastic after the stifling heat and sweat-scented aroma in the bar. I peered over my shoulder as Stan beeped his clicker. I fretted that one of the men might follow us out of The Gray Goose, but both remained inside.

"Thanks for rescuing me," I said to Stan as I slid into the passenger seat.

"I wasn't certain what to do, but you were in there so long I got concerned. What did you learn?"

"Not a heck of a lot."

"That big dude in leather looked like he wanted you for his dinner." Stan chuckled as he reversed out of his parking space.

"You might be right. Say, do you think we should find a more discreet place to park and see if Gino ends up going home with someone other than Adriana?" I asked.

Stan looked at the clock on his dashboard. "It's not quite ten yet. I could manage another hour here. How about you? Do you have a curfew?"

"Nope. I'm being paid to hang out with you. Let's see if we can learn something other than Gino's poor taste in bars."

I woke with a start when Stan jerked his elbow into my shoulder. "Wake up, sleepyhead."

I wiped drool off my chin and straightened in my seat. "I can't believe I fell asleep. Next time I'll bring a thermos of coffee."

"If you drink coffee, you'll have to make more bathroom stops," Stan reminded me.

"Yeah. I might not be cut out for this surveillance stuff, after all. Wait a minute." I scooted forward in my seat so I could get a better look through the windshield. "That's Gino walking out with Jake and another guy in leather."

We watched as the three men conversed. Gino was the more animated of the threesome, using his hands to emphasize his point. The other two, both dressed in all leather, listened, sometimes nodding at Gino's remarks. Other times shaking their heads in disagreement. Whatever they were discussing, the big dudes seemed far more in agreement with one another than with Gino.

What an odd trio. Jake eventually walked over to his bike, reached into a saddlebag and removed a small parcel. He handed it to Gino. Then Jake and his friend yanked helmets over their heads, climbed on their motorcycles and roared out of the parking lot, turning right on Folsom Boulevard. Gino got in his car and drove off behind them, although he made a left turn, most likely returning to his home in Granite Bay.

"Now what?" asked Stan.

"I wish we had X-ray vision and could see what was inside that bag."

"It could be anything," Stan said. "Drugs, money…you're not going to make me follow those guys, are you?" He groaned before turning onto Folsom Boulevard, a few cars behind Gino.

I yawned. "Nope, that's enough detecting for tonight. I'll report in to Adriana and tell her what we found. She might not care if Gino is up to something suspicious, as long as he's not with another woman."

"Adriana can be a bit of a bulldog. I have a feeling you'll be following Gino again."

"Fine with me. It's a fairly easy detail."

Sometimes I'm too naïve for my own good.

CHAPTER TWENTY

It was after midnight by the time I returned home. I'd intended to shower off the remnants of my time in The Gray Goose, but I hated to wake up Tom, who snored softly into his pillow.

I slipped into our king-size bed, pulled the sheet up to my chin and rolled over on my side, ready to sink into a welcome oblivion. Seconds later, my body tingled as fingers lightly caressed my neck and fluttered across my back.

I flipped over on my other side, where my husband's mischievous eyes met mine.

"I've been waiting for you," he said. "Your last text said you'd be home several hours ago."

"Sorry. We were determined to get a lead tonight."

Tom moved closer and wrapped his arms around me. Then he pulled back looking repulsed. "I'm not sure how to say this delicately, but you stink."

"The perils of being a P.I.," I countered. "We ended up in a dive bar in Sacramento."

"I'm not sure I like the idea of you hanging out in seedy bars."

"Don't you trust me?" I asked, somewhat annoyed at his comment.

"Of course. I just don't like the idea of you being around a bunch of sleazeballs."

"It's all part of the job, isn't it?"

"I suppose," he said reluctantly. "I never envisioned you doing surveillance work. It could be dangerous."

"Did you expect me to remain in the office all the time? That's somewhat chauvinistic."

"I'm only concerned about your safety, hon." Despite my aromatic scent, he nestled closer to me, tickling my neck with his hot breath, trying to distract me from our conversation.

A conversation that needed to be continued another time. Right now, I was ready to be distracted.

Tom left early the next morning, so our late-night discussion was postponed for the time being. With Jenna's car out of commission, I dropped the kids off at their respective schools and drove to the office. My first item of business was to type up a report detailing the events of the previous evening's stakeout. Despite four cups of coffee, two at home and two more at the office, I could feel my energy level ebbing to the point that I wistfully eyed the cushy client sofa in our tiny lobby area.

If I locked the front door and flipped the open sign to closed, maybe I could squeeze in a short catnap. Although whoever originated that term had obviously never lived with a cat, because our pet's naps lasted for hours on end.

My cell rang as I stifled yet another yawn. I bent over to check the display.

Gran. Probably calling to bug me about Iris. I was tempted to ignore the call, but I clicked the green button and greeted her as cheerily as I could.

"Hi, Gran. I'm working on Iris's case as we speak."

"Good girl. But you may need to switch your attention to my case."

"You have a case for me? I hope it's not another missing coupon investigation." My grandmother lost coupons as quickly as she scooped them up. But nothing made her smile faster than a discounted purchase.

"Nope. There's some police officers here want to drag me to their station."

"What?" I shrieked so loud the front blinds rattled in protest.

"Ouch," complained Gran. "You just about busted my hearing aid. It's no biggie. At least I hope not," she muttered under her breath.

"Start at the beginning. What's going on?"

"Two detectives stopped by my house this morning. They want to take me up to Tahoe and grill me."

The sound of other voices in the background echoed over the phone line.

"Good grief. About the murder?" I asked. "Do you need an attorney?"

"Not sure. The only lawyer I know is the guy who did my will for me." She let out a gasp. "And since I can feel a heart attack coming from all this scrutiny, you might be meetin' with him sooner rather than later."

CHAPTER TWENTY-ONE

I managed the drive to Gran's house in nine minutes flat. And I only broke the speed limit for eight of the nine minutes. An SUV with a South Lake Tahoe police medallion emblazoned on the side of the vehicle was parked in her driveway.

I scooted around the official vehicle and trotted up her sidewalk. Hank's truck was gone so he was probably at his current job site. I pounded on the door hard enough to bruise my knuckles. My grandmother finally opened it and I skidded into the entry.

"Take it easy, kiddo," Gran said as we hugged. "You're looking kind of flushed. Wouldn't want you to have a heart attack, too." She emphasized the last word of her greeting then cocked her head to the right, indicating I should follow her into her parlor.

Normally, Gran's blue and pink flower-sprigged wallpaper, white wainscoting and comfortable wing chairs with homey needlepoint pillows provided a welcome refuge for me. I'd spent much of my childhood playing in this room while she babysat me and my older brother when Mother had to work at the real estate office.

But today, the two officers in their pressed navy uniforms tarnished the room's ambiance. Even more irritating was the identity of one of the officers.

"Detective Reynolds, what are you doing here?" I asked the attractive dark-haired woman who previously partnered with my husband in both the El Dorado County Sheriff's Office and the San Francisco Police Department years earlier. Last fall they'd worked together in an undercover operation. Ali Reynolds played the role of Tom's girlfriend during that particular investigation. She didn't bother to hide her desire to continue in her role long after the case had been solved.

Her appearance in my grandmother's house did not improve my agitated state.

"Didn't Tom tell you?" she asked. "I switched to the Tahoe P.D."

"No," I replied. "He probably didn't think it was important enough to mention."

Her face darkened and I instantly regretted my snarky remark. The last thing I needed to do was annoy one of the detectives interrogating my grandmother. I quickly switched gears.

"Congratulations on your new position. It's beautiful up there."

She narrowed her eyes at me but merely nodded.

"So what brings you down the hill to Placerville?" I asked cheerily.

"As I'm sure you know, your grandmother is a person of interest in the murder of Gregg Morton. We need to conduct an in-depth interview with her. If she wishes to arrange for an attorney to be present, it's within her rights."

"I think I'll plead the fifth," Gran said. "Of gin." She chuckled but the rest of us remained silent. The detectives had driven a long way. This was no laughing matter for them.

"Gran, why don't you make some coffee for these nice officers," I suggested, figuring Gran was less likely to get in trouble if she were out of the room. Ali and her partner, whom she introduced as Sergeant Gomez seemed to welcome the suggestion. Gran bustled out of the parlor, and we got down to business.

"So you have questions for Gran," I stated.

"Obviously," Ali said sarcastically. "We're not here to sightsee. Now, do you want to arrange for legal counsel for your grandmother?"

"I work in the detective agency with Tom, so Gran is technically my client. Does that count as representation for now?"

Ali snorted. "I can't believe that after stumbling into a few murder situations, you think you're equipped to work for an actual detective agency."

Some things never change. Once a bitch, always a bitch. I kept my cool and simply reiterated that I'd like to sit in on their interview.

"You don't need to take my grandmother back to Tahoe, do you?" I asked as Gran brought out mugs of coffee for everyone.

"Tahoe?" Gran asked, her eyes gleaming bright. "Can you drop me off at the casino when we're done chatting?"

"Gran, this is serious. Please sit down and answer the detectives' questions."

Gran settled into her bentwood rocking chair and, for a brief moment, the only sound in the room was the creaking of the decades-old rocker.

Ali pulled out an iPad and thumbed through a few screens. Gomez broke the silence by complimenting Gran on her coffee.

"Only the best for the fuzz," she said, her eyes twinkling.

Ali rolled her eyes and began questioning Gran. "We understand you threatened bodily harm to the victim the day before he was found murdered. Why did you threaten him?"

"He was trying to pull a fast one on my friend. I wanted to incent him"—Gran made air quotes—"to come clean and fess up."

Ali looked puzzled. She turned her attention to me. "Can you interpret what your grandmother just said?"

I gave the detectives a brief summary of why the three of us were in the timeshare office the day before the murder. I added that it was the first time Gran had met Gregg Morton. "So obviously she had no reason to kill him."

"She had no real reason to threaten him either," Ali replied. "Based on what you just told me."

Gran hung her head and gave them an abject look. "Sometimes I get a little carried away. No harm, no foul, you know."

"Except someone did get harmed, and so far you're the only person with a grudge against our victim," Ali said to Gran.

"Surely you have other suspects, other unhappy clients," I said. "It's been five days since he was killed. What have you guys been doing all this time?"

Ali glared at me. "Our job. Which is why we'll be taking your grandmother up to our office. Now."

CHAPTER TWENTY-TWO

"You can't do that," I shouted and placed a hand on her forearm.

"Try and stop us," Ali replied with an insincere smile, brushing my hand away. "Yes, why don't you try and stop us. Then we can bring you in on an obstruction of justice charge."

I watched, mouth agape, while the other officer read Gran her rights as he led her out of her house.

"Don't worry, Laurel." Gran winked at me as they escorted her into the backseat of their squad car. I supposed I should be grateful they didn't handcuff her, but the idea of my petite grandmother committing a murder was so ridiculous, I felt like whacking both detectives on their hard and stupid heads.

What to do now? Since I was today's designated family chauffeur, I couldn't drop everything and follow the officials back to Tahoe. I texted Tom, Bradford and Mother about what had occurred and waited for their replies.

Mother was the first to respond. "How could you let them take your grandmother away?" she asked.

"I didn't have a choice, Mom. They threatened to arrest me for interfering. Remember Ali Reynolds, the female detective Tom used to work with?"

"I do," she replied in a puzzled voice.

"She's the lead detective. I think she's still mad Tom ended up marrying me."

"That's ridiculous. Although it's equally ludicrous they arrested your grandmother."

"I'm not sure Gran was officially arrested, even if they insisted on driving her up to their office in Tahoe. But they claim there are no other suspects at this point."

"Well, then, you better just go find some for them."

"I'm on it."

Tom called twenty minutes later. He and Bradford were tied up with witness interviews on behalf of the District Attorney, but he promised to give Ali a call and get the real story.

"Now don't get your hopes up, Laurel. Just because Ali and I worked together previously doesn't mean she'll tell me anything. I'm a private investigator now, and she doesn't need to share diddly-squat with me."

"Well, you have my permission to use your famous Hunter charm on her," I said with a reluctant sigh.

He laughed. "Okay, I'll see what I can do. But don't count on it." He lowered his voice. "Are you okay?"

"Not really. But don't worry about me. You need to work your magic on Ali."

Tom promised to call Ali's cell right away and also to get the name of some good criminal defense attorneys in Tahoe. Just in case.

I decided to find another chauffeur to pick up the kids from school. Just in case.

An hour later I was back on Highway 50 heading east toward Lake Tahoe, but I was not alone and not in my SUV. An extremely pregnant woman sat in the passenger seat next to me, the seat belt of her Jaguar convertible barely making it over her baby belly.

"Thanks for letting me tag along," said Liz. "When I'm at the spa, I drive all the staff crazy, and when I'm home alone I make myself crazy."

"Are you sure it's okay for you to be going to Tahoe?" Even though I'd birthed two babies, I felt zero desire to play a role in Liz's delivery.

"Of course. And the change in altitude might encourage this little bugger to come out. This will be the last time I can enjoy the sun on my face and the wind in my hair. Next week we trade in this car for something more practical." She turned to gaze out the window. "I haven't been up here in a while. The river is roaring."

I peeked at the river on my right before returning my vigilant gaze to the road. Normally this time of year, a few intrepid kayakers would be barreling down the American River, but with the currents fast and freezing cold, there didn't appear to be any daredevils willing to risk their lives.

We spent the next hour chatting about babies. It had only been eight years since Ben was born, but the number of items invented to assist new moms boggled my mind. In no time at all we arrived at the South Lake Tahoe Police Department.

We entered the rock-walled lobby and through an automatic door into the reception area. I told the clerk seated behind a thick glass window that we were there to pick up my grandmother, Virginia Sprinkle. The clerk made a call, then told us Gran was still being interviewed by the two detectives.

"Should we sit here and wait until she's done?" I asked Liz, whose stomach gurgled in response.

"I'm starving. Why don't we lunch on the lake? This could be one of the last times I can enjoy a peaceful meal for the next few months."

I smiled, fully aware it could be the last time Liz enjoyed a relaxing lunch for the next eighteen years.

We settled on Riva Grille, a mutual favorite, perched next to the lake. The overhead umbrellas protected us from the sun and the breeze off the lake helped cool down my overheated friend.

Shortly after we'd ordered, our server seated nearby a middle-aged man wearing a red polo shirt. He was accompanied by a young woman, possibly his daughter as there was a slight resemblance. He glanced in our direction but didn't seem to recognize me, although I remembered him.

I leaned in to whisper to Liz. "That's one of the guys who works at Timeshare Help."

She whispered back, "Do you think he's the killer?"

I sat back in my chair. I hadn't bothered to contemplate who the killer might be. I only knew it couldn't be my grandmother. "I don't know. I can't just go and ask him now, can I?"

"That might have been your M.O. in the past, but now that you're a real detective, you should probably be more subtle." Liz broke into a wide smile as our server approached with a Cobb salad for me and a plate piled high with pasta and chicken marinara for Liz.

"It might be a while before they let Gran go," I said, optimistically believing she would be released eventually. "Maybe after lunch we should stop at the timeshare office. You look like someone who could be in the market to purchase one of those resale units. They're perfect for a growing family."

Liz pointed her breadstick at me. "You sound like a salesperson yourself. Do I really look like a believable prospect?"

I eyed her bulging belly and nodded. "Yep, and if nothing else, it should be a speedy presentation."

CHAPTER TWENTY-THREE

After the timeshare salesman settled his bill and walked out with his companion, we waited ten minutes, hoping that was sufficient time for him to return to his office. In the interim, I checked in with the SLTPD. Gran was still stuck in the interview room. I wondered whose fault that was. As a young child, my grandmother's ability to detect the smallest white lie was annoying. Knowing her curious nature, Gran could be grilling the detectives even more than they were grilling her.

Liz and I drove the one short block to the timeshare office. I parked the car, then ran around the vehicle to open the passenger door. Although her convertible was beautiful, when it came to the interior, it wasn't too accommodating for pregnant women. Especially women the size of my friend.

"How much weight have you gained?" I asked when she tripped and almost knocked me over. I'm not exactly on the light side, but Liz seemed to have doubled her pre-pregnancy weight.

"Too much," she said in a dejected tone. "Once the nausea disappeared, I worked my way through the Safeway cookie and candy aisle. Since I can't have caffeine or wine, I settled for chocolate."

Evidently, a boatload of chocolate, based on her appearance. Or maybe she was toting a fifteen-pound baby in her belly.

I opened the door to the timeshare office and ushered her inside. The crime scene tape had been removed, which made sense since the murder had occurred five days earlier. I crossed my fingers hoping the crabby manager would be out on her lunch break.

The man we'd seen earlier at the Riva Grille sat behind a desk in the same cubicle he'd been in on my previous visit. He held a cell phone to his ear, but he waved at us, so I gathered he wanted us to wait for him to finish his call. The second it ended, he hustled out of his office to greet us.

"Hello, hello," he said, shaking each of our hands. His gray eyes bugged out when they landed on Liz's belly. "My name is Marty Fenton. How can I help you today?"

Liz assumed her role without missing a beat. "As you can see, my family will be increasing any day now." She looked down at her belly in case he didn't get the picture. "It's so lovely in the mountains, and I thought a timeshare would be perfect for future vacations. I live in El Dorado Hills so it's just a ninety-minute drive up here. My friend and I noticed your sign and decided to drop in."

"You've certainly come to the right place. Our company offers a huge variety of timeshare weeks for sale. You'll be pleased when you see what kinds of deals are out there. Follow me to my office."

Liz waddled down the corridor and I followed in her wake. We sat in the chairs across from Marty's tidy desk. The only adornment was a photo of Marty and three strawberry-haired girls lovingly surrounding him. I leaned closer and confirmed he'd dined with his daughter. That made me feel better. Not that I presumed he was chasing after young girls, but still. Considering his line of work, I much preferred dealing with a family man.

He handed us each a trifold flyer covered with scenic photos of various projects and a three-page list of available timeshare weeks for sale.

"My goodness," said Liz in her most posh accent, "such a wealth of options to choose from." She batted her eyelashes at him. Even at eight months pregnant, Liz could still flirt with the best of them. "Are there any deals you consider better than others? You are the expert here."

Marty blushed and leaned forward, an instant addition to Liz's long list of male conquests. "There are so many different types of units to choose from. Why don't you tell me more about you and"—a disappointed look crossed his face as he noticed the large rock on Liz's left hand—"and your husband's interests."

"Well, we love skiing and boating. I suppose a week in Lake Tahoe would be the most practical purchase. Although it would be nice to travel elsewhere, Hawaii, Florida, Mexico," she elaborated. "Do you have timeshares for sale there as well?"

Marty's face lit up at the thought of selling multiple destinations to a new client. He spent the next half hour describing the "best" deals in various projects. The prices for the resales ranged as high as $25,000 and as low as one dollar.

"Why would someone sell their timeshare for only a dollar?" Liz asked him. "Talk about a deal!"

"Sometimes people run into financial difficulties and find it difficult to pay their annual maintenance fees. Or if they're suffering from a medical issue and can't make use of the unit, it's just not practical to own the timeshare any longer."

I scanned the list he'd presented to us earlier, stopping at a listing at a high-end fifteen-year-old project on the south shore of Lake Tahoe that had been marketed quite heavily at its inception. "I remember when these weeks first went on sale," I said. "My husband and I went to a presentation. Back then one week in peak season was going for around $35,000. There are several on your list that are asking only $5,000. How come?"

"It could be a number of reasons," Marty replied. "People purchase the timeshare weeks, then discover they aren't able to use them as much as they originally anticipated. That's why I enjoy my job so much. I can present you with the deal of the century with these resale options."

Deal of the century? Now why did I doubt that?

"Oh, dear, I'm not sure this would be such a wise decision after all," Liz said. "So many of these sellers have lost a small fortune since they first purchased their units."

"It's only because they purchased directly from the timeshare developer," Marty assured her. "By buying a timeshare through our company, you can save tens of thousands of dollars."

"Some of those buyers must be so frustrated," I mused. "Have you ever encountered an irate customer, Marty?"

He shook his head so vehemently, I worried he'd get whiplash. "Oh, no, our customers couldn't be more pleased with our services." He reached into a desk drawer and pulled out two sheets of paper. "Check out these glowing testimonials. We've even received a service award from the local chamber of commerce."

Marty's face clouded over. I wondered if he'd just remembered that award had turned into a bloody murder weapon.

His comment provided the perfect opening. "I read that one of your sales associates was killed here in this office last week," I said. "By a client?"

"Heavens, no." Marty's thick sandy eyebrows rose a full inch. "Actually, the police don't know who the culprit was. Probably a homeless person," he said. "Or a druggie."

"In the middle of the day?" I asked. "So you're saying the south shore isn't a safe place to vacation? That drug addicts walk in and just attack people?"

Liz swung her head to the left and right. "Perhaps we should leave if there are unsavory elements hanging around this office."

Marty's chair squeaked as he leapt out of it.

"Oh, no, not at all. In fact, it might have been an act"—Marty lowered his voice as he lowered himself back into his chair—"of passion."

"The man was having problems with a girlfriend, or an ex?" I asked.

Marty smiled, or maybe it was a smirk. "Exes. Plural. Gregg was quite a player. In all respects."

"Do tell," Liz cooed.

"Well, you didn't hear it from me, but the guy liked his guilty pleasures. Women, drugs, gambling. Tahoe's quite the party scene. For a few," he amended, realizing his comment wasn't aiding his sales pitch at all.

"Could one of his exes have killed him?" I asked.

"He broke up with one gal, Cherie, a dealer at Harrah's, a few months ago. He claimed she kept calling him, wanting to get back together."

"Was she a stalker type?" Liz asked.

Marty shrugged. "What female isn't?" When he noticed our matching glares, he explained, "I mean, given that scenario. From what I recall, Gregg just up and dumped her after he hooked up with someone else."

"Was he still dating the new girl?"

Marty peered over his shoulder, although I wasn't sure why since we were the only people in the office.

"Gregg and the office manager were, um, cooking for a while, then he broke up with her a couple of weeks ago."

"The guy certainly had commitment issues," I said.

"I'll say. The atmosphere in here was darn hostile until—"

I finished his sentence for him. "Until he was killed."

Marty's face reddened to match his polo shirt. "Yeah."

"No one else was in the office when the attack occurred?"

"Kimberly, the manager, and I were at an offsite meeting. Gregg was supposed to join us but, he was, um, obviously delayed." Marty was interrupted by the cacophony of a horn clamoring insistently.

"What is that?" I asked him.

"Just someone's car alarm. I wouldn't worry about it."

Liz awkwardly eased out of her chair and grabbed her purse.

"Where are you going?" I asked her. "You don't need to worry about that racket."

She turned and motioned for me to follow. "Yes, I do. That's *my* car alarm."

CHAPTER TWENTY-FOUR

It was amazing how quickly Liz could move when motivated. And Marty and I were right behind her. Through the plate-glass front office windows, I noticed a few people congregating, although for some reason they all remained at a distance from where we'd parked the Jag.

Liz flung the timeshare office door open, then stopped in her tracks. Marty wobbled and threw his arms out, but he managed to avoid crashing into her. Since I was only inches behind him, my nose bumped into his fleshy neck.

I stepped to the side, gently assessing my nose for injuries. The blaring of the car horn was injurious enough to my poor ears. What was going on?

Uh oh. Liz and I had forgotten a cardinal rule when visiting Lake Tahoe or any mountainous area in California.

Do not leave food unattended in your car. Even a candy wrapper has been known to grab the attention of the active black bear community in Tahoe. As for the remains of Liz's pasta lunch, they were long gone, as evidenced by the pleased look on the bear's face.

The bear sprawled in the front of Liz's powder blue convertible, oblivious to the noise surrounding him as he rested one huge hairy arm on her steering wheel, his other paw dripping marinara sauce all over my friend's car.

Liz was not going to be happy about red sauce dribbled all over her ivory carpet.

"Bloody hell," she shrieked as she moved toward her car. I grabbed her arm and pulled her back.

"Where do you think you're going?" I asked her. "Don't you see the large furry critter occupying your car?"

"Yes, and I am royally ticked off. Now how are we going to get him out of there?"

We? I hoped she was using the royal "we" because I didn't have a clue how to chase a bear out of a vehicle. I didn't think yelling "shoo" would have the same effect it did on my cat. I reached into my purse and dialed 911.

"What can I help you with?" the operator asked me.

"We have a situation," I said. "There's a bear in our car."

"Excuse me, I don't think I heard you clearly. Did you say there's a bear in your vicinity?"

"Yep. In our car. And he doesn't seem in a hurry to leave."

"Oh, dear. Give me your location and I'll get someone over there immediately."

The minute I hung up, my cell rang. The bear turned his enormous head in our direction. I squeaked out a hello to the caller, trying to decide whether locking eyes with the bear was a wise move or not. Liz didn't want him in her car, but I wasn't certain we wanted him out of the car either.

"Where's that report you promised me?" Adriana said in an annoyed tone of voice.

"Sorry," I said. "I needed to make an unexpected trip to Tahoe and I'm in a bit of a pickle here."

"I knew I should have found another agency. This is inexcusable."

I heaved a sigh, still keeping my eye on our furry intruder. "A bear got into my car," I informed her, hoping my comment would elicit some sympathy.

"Honestly, Laurel, couldn't you come up with something more plausible?"

Click. The call ended.

I shoved the phone into my purse, then heard it beep. I yanked it out again.

"Where are you?" asked Gran. "Aren't you coming to get me?"

Shoot. I'd forgotten about my grandmother cooling her heels at the local police department. "Shortly. We're waiting for the police to come here."

"Why? What's going on now?"

"A bear decided to grab a snack in Liz's car."

"What? Have you been drinking?"

Unfortunately, no. I explained the situation and told Gran we'd come get her as soon as the bear, and anything he left behind, were removed from the convertible. I hoped the bear didn't have plans to nosh on Liz's steering wheel for dessert.

Or any of the bystanders for that matter.

"Okay, I'll wait here for you," Gran said. "Good luck getting Yogi Bear out of the car."

Liz and I stared at the bear that was now leafing through her glove compartment, possibly in search of dessert. An explosion of colorful dots rained down on the car. Yogi had discovered Liz's emergency M&M stash.

Suddenly the alarm stopped clamoring. The silence seemed to startle the bear. He stood, all six-plus feet of him, then climbed out of the convertible, his shaggy head turning left and right as if assessing the best getaway. Then he loped toward the back of the shopping center in the direction of an open area I remembered was filled with tall pines backing onto a small nature preserve.

Tires squealed as a squad car spun a hard right into the shopping center entrance. The officer in the passenger seat jumped out and yelled at us.

"Where's the bear?" he asked.

I pointed in the direction the bear had fled. "He went thataway." The animal was barely visible now as he disappeared into the thick forest.

The officer smacked his hand on the roof of the car and yelled to the driver, "Follow that bear."

Liz circled her Jag assessing the damage. I joined her, wincing when I noted several deep scratches on the leather seats. One of the bear's claws left an indelible mark across the entire width of the leather dashboard. Smears of marinara sauce dotted the seats and the carpet.

Liz leaned against the trunk, her Ray-Ban sunglasses teetering on top of her golden curls. Marty approached us, his face pale.

"Never seen anything quite like that," he said. "You know you shouldn't leave—"

We interrupted him with a chorus of "we know."

He peered into the car. "Coulda been a lot worse."

True. He could've eaten one of us.

A black Mercedes SUV pulled into the vacant space next to the convertible. A shapely bare leg displayed itself, followed by a tall blonde. I recognized Kimberly, the manager of Timeshare Help, from our previous meeting. "What's going on?" she asked Marty. Then she noticed Liz and me.

"You," she exclaimed, removing her dark glasses and pointing in my direction. "You came in last week with that crazy old lady who threatened Gregg. What are you doing back here? Annoying the rest of my staff?"

Marty beamed at his boss. "These two women are considering purchasing some timeshare weeks from us."

She narrowed her eyes at us. "Yeah, sure they are." Her attention shifted to Liz's convertible. "What happened to your car?"

"A bear found our doggie bag," Liz said sadly as she used a tissue to wipe some pasta remnants from the doorframe. "And I have a feeling my trade-in value just plummeted."

"There, there," said Marty. "Why don't we go back inside? I'm sure purchasing a timeshare unit will take your mind off the damage to your car."

The three women standing next to Marty, including his boss, all glared at him. Marty was either one awesome salesman or a complete dunce. I couldn't decide which.

"I think these women have enough to deal with right now." Kimberly placed a hand on Marty's back and shoved him forward. As soon as they entered the office she slammed the door shut and posted a "closed" sign on the door.

Liz placed her hands on her hips and gave the timeshare office a very unladylike one-finger wave.

"Now what do we do?" she asked.

My phone pinged and I read the message from my grandmother. *Still waiting!!!*

"Let's go pick up our favorite murder suspect."

CHAPTER TWENTY-FIVE

We departed South Lake Tahoe with one very unhappy granny tucked into the convertible's tiny rear seat. For the next sixty minutes, Gran grumbled about the stale coffee at the police station, our tardiness picking her up and the cramped open-air seating. I still say it wasn't my fault her wig flew off after I negotiated a ninety-degree curve over the summit. We watched it soar over the guardrail, tumbling down into the Tahoe Valley one thousand feet below.

I sure hoped we didn't get ticketed for littering.

Liz remained silent through much of the trip, most likely mulling over her future automotive repairs. The odds of me ever owning a Jaguar convertible were zero, so I enjoyed our airy and scenic ride back to Placerville.

Since we arrived after five, I easily found a parking spot a half block from the agency. I handed the keys over to Liz, who set off for the District Attorney's Office to find her husband and show him the damage. Gran and I entered the agency and found it filled to capacity with almost every member of my family.

Jenna sat at my desk, reading something on her laptop, while the two eight-year-olds hovered over her shoulders, their rapt attention to the screen making me curious. And suspicious.

Gran muttered something about working the kinks out of her cramped legs. She hobbled across the carpet toward the restroom. I walked over to the kids, wondering what the three of them were looking at.

CINDY SAMPLE

"What are you doing?" I asked Jenna. Her injured ankle rested on a small box she was using as a footstool.

"I'm investigating." She pointed to her laptop screen. "Tom recommended I look up some recent robberies or related crimes. He thought it might help me find the guy who destroyed my car."

"And what are you two up to?" I asked the eight-year-olds.

"We're helping Jenna," replied Kristy. "She said Ben and me can be her interns."

Great. The agency now had more interns than detectives.

I noticed Gran exit the restroom and enter Tom's office to chat with my husband and stepfather. Tom's head shot up and he looked in my direction.

What now?

The trio walked out of the office with Tom in the lead. My six-foot-three husband wrapped his arms around me and asked, "What's this about a close and personal encounter with a bear?"

"No big deal," I said. "We weren't in any danger. Liz's car is the only thing that suffered any damage."

"How did it happen?" asked my stepfather.

I looked down at the floor and muttered, "Liz put her lunch leftovers in the backseat. And we left the top down."

"Mom," Ben informed me with a solemn look on his face, "you never leave food in the car when you're up in the mountains. Not even a breath mint. Don't you know that?"

"I certainly do." I plopped a kiss on his forehead. "Now why don't you and Kristy go play a game while the adults talk?"

The kids pulled out their iPads and were soon settled in chairs, engaged in one of their favorite video games while the adults moved back into Tom's office.

Once seated, Gran gave us an update on her situation. "They didn't book me so I guess everything is copacetic."

"Not necessarily," Bradford chimed in. "Did they give you an idea why they hauled you into their office? There must be some additional evidence pointing in your direction. Although obviously not enough to arrest you."

"Ali told me they didn't have any suspects other than Gran," I said.

Gran grinned. "Yeah, then your wife here asked Detective Reynolds why they've been sitting on their butts for the last five days when they should be out looking for the real murderer."

88

"I said no such thing." Although for some reason Detective Ali Reynolds always brought out the worst in me. Nothing I needed to share with my husband, her former partner. And former lover as well? Something I'd always wondered about but never dared to ask.

"Agitating an investigating detective serves no purpose." Tom pointed his pen at me and then at Gran. "Both of you. Please keep your cool."

Gran nodded. "Otherwise I may end up in the cooler for good. And I'm just too old and weak to survive being locked up."

Bradford snorted at his mother-in-law's description of herself.

"There must be some new evidence that pointed in your direction," Tom said to Gran.

She shifted in her seat. "Guess we had a bit of a miscommunication when we initially chatted."

"Clarify," Bradford barked at her.

"That Reynolds woman called both Iris and Herb yesterday. They might have mentioned the two of them stopped at the art gallery in that shopping center to look at some photos while I went on ahead to the timeshare office the day of the murder."

"Gran, why didn't you tell me that?" I squawked.

She shrugged. "Didn't think it was important. I waited in the reception area for a bit. No one came out. Then Iris and Herb walked in, and we decided to cruise through the office and see if someone was there. That's it. No biggie."

Tom, Bradford and I shook our heads. That was indeed a biggie. Especially since Gran failed to disclose it.

"Anything else you'd like to share?" Tom asked Gran.

"Nope. Nada. I'm good," she said.

"So did you and Liz learn anything at the timeshare office that was of any help?" Tom asked.

"Vacation ownership, as they prefer to call it now, is a complete rip-off," I said. "And I now know more about the timeshare resale market than I needed or wanted to know. We did find out from one salesman that the victim had broken up with two different women in the past four months. One of the women is the manager."

"That mean gal who shooed us out of the office the first day?" asked Gran. "I pick her for the killer. She's a cold-hearted b—"

"We saw her today," I said. "Kimberly drove up right after the bear made his getaway. She wasn't at all happy about Marty talking to us, even though he informed her we were potential purchasers. She practically dragged him into the office, then hung out the closed sign. That seems suspicious to me."

"I would think Ali would have questioned those women already," Tom said, "but I'll give her another call. See what I can find out."

"Yeah, tell her to get her head out of her…" Gran muttered.

"I might phrase it slightly different," Tom replied, "but I'm on it." He glanced out his office window to the main office, where the noise level of our progeny had increased by several decibels.

"Are you taking the kids home?" he asked hopefully.

"Soon. I just need to—" My phone beeped and I glanced at it. Adriana calling again. "Finish my report for my other client. The paying one," I informed my grandmother.

She chuckled. "How about a few dozen cookies to cover your fee?"

Her offer wouldn't help our bottom line nor my waistline, but her payment would certainly put a smile on my face.

I told the kids to pack up their things. Then I returned Adriana's call. With luck, she might be too busy to answer.

"Where's my report?" she yelled in my ear.

"I'll have it to you by the end of the day. Sorry about the delay. There were circumstances that were out of my control."

"Fine. Just tell me this. Did you catch Gino with another woman?"

I hesitated for a moment, but decided not to count Gino chatting me up at the bar. "No," I answered. "We tailed him to a bar down in Sacramento. The only people he met with were some scary-looking biker guys."

"Are you sure you followed my fiancé? Why would he meet with biker types?"

"Now that is a very good question," I said. "Especially since they handed him a parcel. Do you want me to continue to follow him?"

"I guess. It seems so odd, although I suppose it's better than him fooling around with another woman. We're getting together tonight. Let me find out his schedule for this week and I'll get back to you."

As long as she didn't also pay me in cookies, it was fine with me. Tom should be happy about a client who paid me by the hour to follow her fiancé.

Shouldn't he?

CHAPTER TWENTY-SIX

I walked into Tom's office to share the good news about my additional client work. He frowned when I told him I'd be tailing Gino a few more nights.

"Laurel, I think any surveillance requested by our clients should be done by Bradford or me."

I folded my arms and frowned. "And why is that?"

"You don't know anything about the subject of this investigation. As I said last night, it could be dangerous for you."

"Is that because I'm a woman? Did you tell Ali Reynolds the same thing when you were partners?"

He splayed his hands out. "That's different. Ali is a trained professional. You're still learning the business. You don't have any way to protect yourself if you're assaulted."

"Then I guess it's time I learned some new skills." I stood and left the office, too annoyed at my husband to continue the conversation. Just because I'd been bopped on the head a time or two, by a killer or two, didn't mean I couldn't handle tailing someone.

Yet I couldn't completely disagree with him. It wouldn't hurt to carry some protection with me. A gun was out of the question. I was more likely to maim myself than an antagonist. And my peppermint Binaca spray probably wouldn't stop an attacker, although they'd have pleasant breath while they bopped me.

Then I remembered that Robin, one of my former bank co-workers, sold Damsel in Defense products. She'd asked me several times if I would host a party for her at my house, but establishing the new agency had taken precedence over any social events.

I called Robin and she offered to bring her products to my house that evening. I instantly agreed. If I could demonstrate this damsel was prepared to defend herself, my husband might not worry so much about my nighttime detecting.

Two hours later, I hosted a mini-soiree comprised of my mother, my daughter and me. The little kids begged to be included, stating they didn't want to be victims either, so I let them listen to Robin's spiel. It turned out that her company not only sold defensive items, but they did presentations at local schools to keep students informed about their personal safety.

After Robin spoke with Ben and Kristy, I sent them off to play while the adults checked out her array of stun guns, pepper spray, portable alarms, fake hairspray containers that stored valuables, as well as purses to hold all of the assorted equipment.

"I certainly could have used some of these items in the past." I flipped through her catalog wondering if my new official detective status warranted purchasing every single product the company offered.

"Keep in mind when you travel that many states don't allow stun guns or pepper spray," Robin informed us. "But they're legal in California."

"You could get me some pepper spray for a graduation present," Jenna said to me. "It would probably be a good thing to have when I'm walking through the UCD campus at night."

"I've worried through my entire thirty-year career about holding open houses in the middle of nowhere and the potential for assault," Mother added. "You definitely found a new client with me."

"Should we get something for Gran?" Jenna asked. "For protection when she's out by herself."

Mother and I exchanged glances. My grandmother would likely stun herself or a friend. And even though the stun guns didn't have the power of a Taser, the shock wouldn't be too heart healthy for her elderly cronies.

Tom joined our group and smiled approvingly at our purchases, although he insisted on warning us, "Just because you're 'armed' doesn't mean you should do anything crazy. Or try to be a hero.

These items are to be used strictly for defensive purposes and only when absolutely needed."

We held up our hands and promised.

Then I kidded Tom, "I promise I'll never use my stun gun on you, no matter how much you annoy me."

He whispered in my ear. "You manage to stun me every day of the week, sweetheart."

Aww.

The next morning I was back in the office reviewing Iris's documents, not the most inspiring of investigative duties, but it needed to be done. Especially the fine print, which meant basically all of the five-inch stack of documents. Even with my mortgage underwriting background, the verbiage made my head spin.

If someone with my expertise struggled to wade through everything, I could imagine how overwhelmed Iris was. She merely signed the agreements, innocently believing what her telephone contact had promised her.

After Googling numerous timeshare resale companies online, all of whose names sounded similar, and all of which offered the same reassurances, I discovered scams were the real name of the timeshare game.

I found it interesting that within seconds of me beginning my Google search, my inbox filled up with timeshare solicitation emails. Timeshare resale ads popped up with every query I made, even the online searches not related to my timeshare research.

I began listing all the different companies. Halfway through, I realized Iris had made a big mistake, although an understandable one, since I might not have noticed it without compiling my lengthy list. The name of the company Iris dealt with was Timeshare-Helper located in Florida, where a majority of these firms were located. Her sales contact there was Greg Martin.

Not Timeshare Help and not Gregg Morton.

I sat back in my chair, aghast at the complexity of the timeshare market. Most timeshare owners were contacted by telemarketers, or if the timeshare owner used the internet, via the annoying pop-ups that continued to assault my own screen. All a person needed to do was complete a few simple questions, hit the send button, and a "customer service" representative would give you a phone call.

Easy peasy, right?

How many other people, many of them seniors, were in the same position as Iris? People who now found it difficult to travel? Or whose financial situation had deteriorated, making the annual fees and/or finance charges no longer affordable.

A situation that proved ripe for scam artists who focused on the uninformed.

My cell rang, indicating my paying client was on the line.

"Morning, Adriana," I chirped. Now that I was armed with my defensive equipment, I was ready for another round of "tail your suspect."

"I hope you're ready to earn your retainer. I don't want to hear any more lame excuses like a bear in your car. Honestly, Laurel."

I began to protest but decided it would be a waste of time. I grabbed a pad and pen and waited for her instructions.

"What do you want me to do?" I asked.

"Gino told me he'll be meeting a client Friday night in Tahoe. A big client with mega bucks to invest."

"And you don't believe him?"

She sighed. "I feel awful about not trusting him. And landing a wealthy new client would be wonderful for his business. I told Gino I'd love to join him on Saturday when his meetings ended. We could spend the weekend together. A mini-vacation for both of us."

"Sounds lovely."

"It does, doesn't it? But he declined. Said he had far too much work to do and couldn't take the time."

"Do you know where he's staying?"

"He always stays at Harveys. I guess they comp him a room when he needs one."

"Okay, it should be easy enough for me to get a room there since it's still early in the season. I assume you want me to watch his every move."

"Yes. You'll make sure he doesn't catch you, right? If Gino ever discovered what I'm doing…"

"He won't notice me. And I'll bring along an additional team member to help out with surveillance."

We hung up and I debated whose assistance I could procure. Tom and Bradford were scheduled to be in San Francisco on Friday for their insurance case. Stan would, of course, love to join me, but Gino would be able to recognize him from the other night.

I needed someone who could blend into the casino surroundings with ease. Someone Gino would never suspect was keeping an eye on him.

That left just one person perfect for the job.

CHAPTER TWENTY-SEVEN

I phoned my grandmother and she picked up at once.

"How would you like to help me with a new case and get some gambling in at the same time?" I asked her.

"Wait a sec. I better put in my hearing aid. It sounded like you wanted my assistance investigating."

"Yep. Up in Tahoe. Most likely at Harveys, but we might have to move around a bit. We'll be working as a team tailing someone."

"Well, I'll be gosh-darned. You won't regret it, Laurel."

On second thought, I probably would regret this decision, but I'd run out of assistants, so Hangtown's version of Miss Marple was officially on the case.

Around ten that evening, Tom and I cuddled on the sofa, watching the late-night news. I confirmed he would be home late Friday evening. Leaving me free to spend an overnight in Tahoe with my gumshoe granny.

Tom seemed less than enthusiastic about my pending casework.

"Laurel, this case sounds like it may require someone with more experience than you have. I do not like the idea of getting your grandmother involved."

"I'm not crazy about it either, but are you or Bradford available to help out?"

He shook his head.

"There's no way I can follow Gino by myself. I need some help. He won't even notice Gran in the sea of white-haired gamblers up there."

"Your grandmother isn't exactly the epitome of discretion, you know."

"I think she might surprise you." I snuggled closer to him.

"Hah. Your grandmother never ceases to surprise me. But that's rarely a good thing."

"We'll be careful. We can hardly get into trouble surrounded by hundreds of tourists and gamblers on the casino floor. Their security force keeps tabs on everyone. We only need to discover if Gino is engaged in a fling with someone other than Adriana or truly meeting a business client like he told her."

"You promise not to follow him into any more dive bars?" Tom demanded.

I nodded. One dive bar visit was sufficient for this detective. Hopefully on this trip, Gino would stick to more high-end haunts.

Tom sighed. "Maybe it's time to teach you some defensive maneuvers."

I sat up. "I'd love that. Do you want to try it here?"

He reached over and placed a silky kiss on my neck, followed by another, sending my tingle meter into high alert. "How about we work on those moves upstairs? On a softer surface."

Who knew detective work could be so much fun?

Friday morning I informed the kids I would be gone overnight working on a case. I had worried the kids might be upset, but Jenna surprised me by saying, "Of course I don't mind. You're doing a job you love." She threw me a broad grin. "And as soon as my ankle has healed, I'll be able to help you. Now go get 'em, Mom."

With my daughter's endorsement under my belt, I went upstairs to pack for my short Tahoe stay. I rifled through my closet and ended up choosing a variety of outfits. They ranged from casual tourist to business woman to sexpot, although my preferred plan was to remain as inconspicuous as possible this time around. I could select some of Gran's wigs to assist my disguise when I picked her up.

We couldn't check into the hotel any earlier than three, but Adriana assured me Gino would arrive long after us since she'd arranged a late lunch date with him. She promised to text me when he left Placerville. She would also attempt to keep tabs on his whereabouts to help us out. "Although," Adriana whined, "I don't want to come across as needy."

Adriana's situation seemed kind of ridiculous to me. Why not just confront Gino? Then I reminded myself that I'd been caught completely off guard when I discovered Hank cheating on me with one of his clients. Maybe Adriana had the right idea after all. Get the true story before her relationship with Gino evolved any further.

I certainly couldn't complain about today's workload, since following Gino around Tahoe would help the agency's bottom line.

And maybe I'd win a few bucks at the casino and help out my personal bottom line while I tailed him.

CHAPTER TWENTY-EIGHT

Adriana had texted me as soon as Gino left Placerville, so by five o'clock, our detective duo was in place. I sat in one of the lobby chairs, thumbing through glossy brochures on the multitude of fun activities Tahoe offered visitors. Gran had positioned herself on a stool in front of a slot machine next to the casino entrance leading into the hotel lobby.

Gran was disappointed her role did not involve a disguise other than being herself—a white-haired, bifocal-wearing senior playing the slots. I wore a taupe top and slacks, guaranteed to blend into any crowd. I borrowed one of Gran's neutral ash-blond pixie-cut wigs to complete my camouflage.

I kept my eyes peeled for Gino's navy Mercedes. Our quarry finally arrived a little after six. Gino, dressed in business casual, looked as handsome and self-assured as ever. He handed his keys to the valet and strolled in, pulling a small navy suitcase behind him, a hefty black computer bag slung over his shoulder. Without a glance in my direction, he headed straight for the registration desk, checking in at a line reserved for Harveys' priority guests.

With one of the brochures hiding my face, I peeked out to ensure that once Gino registered, he got on an elevator designated for hotel rooms only. When Gino eventually came back down, he would have to walk past me to get to wherever he was going. This time of day, a throng of hotel guests crowded the lobby, so I doubt if he even noticed me.

I texted Gran to see how she was faring. She sent me a thumbs-up emoji in reply. The slots must be paying off. I hope they stayed on the plus side or else Gran's expense report for her gambling losses might exceed our surveillance fees. We didn't have long to wait. Gino entered the lobby thirty minutes later. His curly dark hair looked damp so he must have showered. He'd also donned a new cornflower blue shirt, an excellent color in my opinion, since it made him easier to follow. Did his shower activity indicate an upcoming romantic meeting, or merely a necessity after a long, hot drive up the hill?

I felt comfortable Gran and I could easily keep tabs on Gino's whereabouts as long as he stayed in the area around the casinos. The one obstacle would be if he drove to his final destination. I'd parked my Subaru in the free self-park garage close to the exit. I figured by the time a valet brought Gino's car around, I could have my SUV in position to follow him if necessary.

Gino glanced at his watch, an expensive one, I gathered, since it gleamed in the light emanating from the lobby's chandeliers. Then he walked toward the revolving doors leading to the valet station. I groaned in anticipation of a mad run to the parking garage, but he stopped a few feet in front of the doors and remained inside. He rolled his shoulders, one of which must be tired from continually lugging his hefty computer case around.

This was definitely looking more and more like a business meeting. Adriana would be relieved if that proved to be the case. I continued to monitor Gino's movements from behind my travel brochure. A young family with two toddlers in tow struggled to get all of their gear through the door closest to my location. I smiled, remembering the days when we traveled with the kids, lugging strollers, suitcases, and far more crap than we needed. I wanted to help them but didn't want to draw attention to my location.

On the opposite side of the lobby, two men entered via the revolving doors. The bald, shorter and more squat of the two, the end of a cigar hanging from fleshy lips, scooted in Gino's direction. His companion, who was almost a foot taller and quite a few years younger, followed behind.

Shorty (I had to distinguish them somehow) vigorously pumped Gino's hand. The big guy maintained a respectful distance between the two men. He wore a beige linen sport coat, not your normal casual Tahoe attire, which made me wonder if he was some kind of bodyguard. His jacket could easily hide a shoulder holster.

Or had I watched too many crime shows?

They chatted briefly, then the man with the cigar thrust out his left arm toward the casino entrance. Good. They weren't heading toward the valet.

I texted Gran to look out for the trio. She already knew what Gino looked like and his attire. I just prayed she wouldn't do anything foolish.

Gran sent a quick text that she was right behind them. I followed a discreet twenty feet behind her, but after walking out of Harveys main entrance on Lake Tahoe Boulevard, I caught a DO NOT WALK sign at the intersection. My right foot tapped an anxious beat while the red light intoned the number of seconds before I could walk across the busy four-lane street without getting run over and enter Harrah's casino on the opposite side.

As soon as the WALK button came on, I zipped across the street so fast my wig almost flew off. As I entered the lobby, I straightened my hairdo while I frantically searched for my grandmother. Harrah's was even more crowded than Harveys, so I finally texted her for her whereabouts. I breathed a sigh of relief when she responded.

They're eating in that fancy steak place. You can find me in front of the slots trying to earn back my losses.

Uh oh. I better hustle before Gran lost her retirement savings. It was a good thing she usually stuck to the penny or nickel slots.

It only took me a few minutes to locate the steak restaurant. It took me a few minutes longer to find my grandmother.

She noticed me first. "Laurel," she said in a stage whisper, "over here."

I spun around and finally spotted her. She sat so short she remained hidden behind the large machines. I could barely see her, which made her an excellent choice for a tailing detail.

"Great place to hide, Gran. But can you see the guys over the slots?" I asked.

"Yep. I got a straight shot through these two." She beckoned me over, and I checked out the space between a couple of machines.

"Looks good." I plopped down on the empty stool next to her. "I think we can safely say Gino isn't indulging in any romantic activity tonight."

She shrugged her bony shoulders under a thin cardigan. "The night's still young and so is Gino. Once he's done with these bozos who knows who he might take up with."

"True. I hope we don't have to pull an all-nighter."

Gran scowled at the slot machine in front of her. "Me, too. These machines aren't paying squat tonight."

"Do you want to go back to the room, order room service and go to bed? I should be able to handle everything myself from now on."

Gran slid off her stool. "Okay, maybe you'll have a better run than I did. But if you need me, just call or text. I'll set the volume on extra loud."

Gran promised to text me when she reached our hotel room. I still felt uncomfortable having an eighty-nine-year-old partner, but she seemed to enjoy it. Except for her losses in the penny slots. I had a feeling after she had something to eat my grandmother might get her second wind and hit the machines once again.

I walked past the half-empty steakhouse and scanned the room. The trio was seated at a table not too far from the entrance. I went back to the slots and managed to lose ten dollars in ten minutes. Time to find a safer place to hide.

Or a less expensive one.

I finally found a large pillar about fifteen feet from the restaurant entrance. It provided an excellent view of the entry while I remained hidden. As I peeped around the pillar someone bumped into me.

"Hey, sweetheart," said a paunchy middle-aged guy dressed in a Ralph Lauren polo and khakis. "Waiting for someone?" He leaned closer, sharing his onion-and-garlic-scented breath with me.

I shook my head and moved away from him, but he didn't get the hint.

He looked around. "You all by your lonesome tonight? Like some company?" He veered closer and leered at me, his stance indicating a few beers probably accompanied his earlier meal.

"Nope. I'm good." I pushed him away, but the physical contact seemed to encourage him even more.

"A cute gal like you doesn't want to be alone. Tahoe is a place for romance." His bleary eyes started to brighten with anticipation. "My name is Bruce. What's yours?"

I tried to sidestep him, but he blocked my way. I attempted to push his arm away but he still wasn't getting the hint.

A flash of blue twenty feet behind him got my attention as it quickly faded from view.

Shoot. Gino was on the move and moving fast.

I glanced at the slot machine next to me. Someone had left half of their watery cocktail off to the side. I picked it up.

Oops.

It landed all over Bruce.

"Sorry. Let me get a napkin." I brushed past him, then zipped down the narrow aisle in search of Gino. I'd expected my quarry to saunter back to Harveys with his pals, but they must have remained behind in the restaurant.

Did that mean Gino had another meetup in mind? Or perhaps he wanted to get some gambling in while he was in the casino. The very large and expansive casino that stretched a football field in length.

Now where the heck did he go?

Fridays are big nights at Harrah's. People from the Central Valley and the Bay Area frequently drove to the Sierras for a weekend in the mountains. Plus, Harrah's offered an all-you-can eat seafood buffet on Friday nights.

As I looked to the right and left for Gino, I almost knocked over an elderly couple who were debating which slots to sit in front of.

Just pick one, people. You'll be able to lose your money in any of them.

After threading my way past the numerous slot machines, I found myself standing in front of a decent-looking bar that offered musical entertainment. Light rock with an emphasis on the light.

My face lit up when I spied Gino perched on a stool at the U-shaped bar. Although bar patrons could play a poker machine while they drank, Gino seemed far more interested in chatting up the long-legged blonde sitting next to him than gambling. Given my previous encounter with Gino at The Gray Goose, the man did have an eye for the ladies.

While I debated whether I should find an inconspicuous spot at the bar to keep tabs on him, the blonde reached for her purse and I got a clear look at her profile.

Well, well, well. This certainly put an interesting spin on things.

CHAPTER TWENTY-NINE

I hadn't known what to expect while I was following Gino, but I certainly didn't anticipate him sitting at a bar next to Kimberly, the timeshare manager.

Was this a chance meeting or were they longtime acquaintances? Or lovers?

By this point, I could have used a drink myself. But I wasn't certain my disguise was good enough to fool another woman, especially the sharp-eyed Kimberly, so I chose a table in a dark corner. It provided me with a full view of the couple and they would have to turn completely around to spot me. And from this distance I shouldn't be recognizable to either of them.

A server came by. I debated whether to buy a glass of wine while on duty but then realized I would look even odder sitting there without a drink in my hand. Besides, the house wine was only four dollars a glass.

I placed my order, then donned fake glasses just in case. My feet tapped along to the beat of the music—"Shut Up and Dance" by Walk the Moon. My bunions, trapped in too tight flats, thanked me for the break. Sitting at the table also provided me with some time for a little contemplation.

Detective work, so far, seemed far duller than I'd originally anticipated. My husband had warned me it wasn't anything like the TV shows I loved to watch. Stakeout duty definitely ranked near the top for ho-hum activity, although it paid the bills. The frosting on the cake was solving a case: finding missing persons, securing restitution for fraud victims, bringing long-lost relatives together. There were a multitude of ways a detective agency could help their clients. But it frequently took legwork and massive amounts of time doing online searches.

I sipped my wine. Maybe I wasn't cut out for this type of work after all. With Gino deep in conversation with Kimberly, I spent the next hour contemplating the pros and cons of my current profession.

The current negative, as I peered at my watch, were the hours. Almost eleven. I couldn't get a handle on the couple's relationship. While they seemed comfortable with one another, Gino kept his hands to himself. Was it possible they were business acquaintances? Maybe he was purchasing a portfolio of timeshares for his clients.

How are timeshare developments financed? Were timeshare loans sold in financial markets the same as home mortgages were? From what I knew, Wall Street moguls would sell their grandmothers if they could get a decent price for them.

My head swirled with images of dollar signs and my grandmother standing on an auction block.

I set my glass down. Alcohol on an empty stomach did not a good detective make.

Kimberly finally slid off her barstool, as did Gino. They walked out together heading toward the exit. I'd already paid my server so I waited a few seconds before following the pair. The big question was whether Kimberly would go up to Gino's room with him.

I grabbed my cell out of my purse and took a quick photo of the two of them together. In case I needed proof of some type of liaison. I wish I'd thought of it earlier when Gino was meeting with those two men, but the meeting had looked like your standard business dinner.

The couple reached the revolving door. Gino let Kimberly go first instead of crowding in with her. I held back, watching and waiting.

Then a strange thing happened. Kimberly kissed Gino on his cheek and headed toward the valet station. Gino waited for the light to change before crossing the street and re-entering Harveys.

Excellent. Hopefully the man was tired from a long day consisting of work, driving one hundred miles, and two meetings. I certainly was and my schedule had been light compared to his.

I remained a decent distance from my target. With less people cramming the casino this late at night, I'd be more obvious if Gino looked behind him. Halfway through the casino, he turned to the left and entered a room filled with a few men and even fewer women sitting around several tables. High-stakes poker. He joined one table and I continued to watch from a distance. Finally, since it looked like Gino had settled in for the evening, I decided to head for our hotel room.

Once in the elevator, I let out my breath. I'd successfully survived my second stakeout. Whether I'd learned anything important or not would be up to my client. I had only one thing on my mind.

A soft bed.

Hours later, after twisting and turning, punching my pillow numerous times, and attempting to find a pair of earplugs in my cosmetic case, I fell asleep as the sun began its ascent over the Sierras.

It seemed like only minutes later that my grandmother grabbed my shoulder and shook me so hard I thought we were experiencing one of the occasional California earthquakes.

"Rise and shine, Ms. Sleepyhead. Did you party hard last night?" Gran chortled at her comment.

"I didn't come back to the room until almost midnight." I sat up against the gold brocade headboard. "Your snores are loud enough to wake the dead. And keep the living awake." I blinked at the sun blasting through the plate-glass windows. "What time is it?"

"Nine. Don't we have more tailin' to do today?" she asked.

"I need to check with Adriana. After his dinner with those two guys, Gino met up with a woman. And you'll never guess who—Kimberly."

Gran's mouth opened wide, exposing her matching set of gold fillings along each side. "Well, I'll be. I told you the woman was up to no good. Stealing Gino from his fiancée."

"While they seemed friendly enough, it almost looked like more of a business meeting. He came back to the hotel alone."

"Are you certain?"

"I suppose Kimberly might have arrived later on. I couldn't stand guard in front of his room in order to find out."

107

"So are we off the clock?" Gran asked. "How about we do something fun this morning before we head back?"

My grandmother's definition of fun ran the gamut from zip-lining to an all-you-can-eat oatmeal buffet.

What was I in for now?

CHAPTER THIRTY

"What did you have in mind?" I asked her.

"The gondola ride to the top. I've never taken it," she said. "And this year they opened up earlier than usual. Plus, since it's Saturday, they'll have a big breakfast buffet. My treat."

I was half right. At least Gran would get her fiber this morning. Which would make her less grumpy this afternoon. I hadn't ridden the new gondola either, so it sounded like a fun expedition.

"Let me check in with Adriana. See if she knows Gino's schedule for today. If he accomplished everything he wanted to do last night, then he might already be cruising back down the hill."

I texted Adriana, who replied a few minutes later. Gino was still in Tahoe and supposedly meeting some clients for breakfast at the Tamarack Lodge at the top of Heavenly Valley Mountain followed by golf at the Edgewood Club. And, yes, she wanted us to continue our surveillance.

How fortuitous for us, since he needed to take the gondola to get there.

I showered quickly and Gran and I rolled out of the room by 9:45. I checked out and left our bags with the bell desk. We both kept our eyes peeled for Gino, but we didn't spot him in the casino. He was probably already at his breakfast meeting.

There is nothing I love better than multitasking. Riding the gondola, eating at a breakfast buffet, and completing our tailing detail were a perfect combination for today. The skies were brighter than the cerulean blue in Ben's crayon box with a few white puffy clouds drifting aimlessly above the snowcapped mountain peaks.

The gondola was situated in the middle of the Heavenly Valley Village, an attractive retail center comprised of natural stone and cedar-sided shops and restaurants. Even though early in the season, a line snaked from the ticket booth to the curb. We hotfooted it to the booth. No one moves as fast as my grandmother when she's on a mission and I barely kept up with her. Once we purchased our tickets, we moved from the ticket line to the gondola line. At this high altitude the sun felt hotter. I wiped droplets of perspiration from my forehead and wished I'd brought a ball cap with me.

Gran nudged my arm. "See that tall fella over there? He kinda looks like the big thug who was with Gino and the other guy wolfing down steaks last night."

I shifted a few feet to the left to get a better look. Gran was right. The very tall man with the platinum buzz cut, wearing a navy hoodie, did resemble the young fellow who dined with Gino and the cigar-chewing man. In fact, I was fairly certain he was the same guy. Was he a local or a tourist? Any chance Gino was here with him for his breakfast meeting?

I took off my sunglasses and squinted. The other man with Young and Tall, who was a few inches shorter, wore a white and royal blue ball cap and a blue polo shirt. A few dark curls stuck out from under the white ball cap. Could that be Gino?

As he entered the gondola car, the man looked over his shoulder and Gino's dark eyes met mine. Was there a flash of recognition or was my imagination overreacting? Either way, Gran and I would only be a couple of cars behind him. We could enjoy our breakfast and keep an eye on Gino while we were at the top.

Although so far, with the exception of the odd meeting with Kimberly last night, Gino's activities seemed to be on the up and up. But if tailing Gino brought some peace of mind to Adriana then my work was done.

The gondolas moved quickly, so quickly I had to shove Gran into a seat before the automatic doors slammed shut behind me.

"Ooph," she said.

I sent her an apologetic smile, then plunked down on the hard seat next to her. A vista view of stores, restaurants and hotels sprawled below. Tall pines loomed on both sides of the gondola car as we moved up the hill.

Suddenly, the panoramic expanse of Lake Tahoe spread out before us. The water, ranging from a pale sky blue to a deep royal blue, soothed me. I felt myself relaxing for the first time in a long time.

"This is great," Gran exclaimed.

I nodded in agreement because it was. According to the brochure, this gondola soared 2.4 miles as it rose almost three thousand feet to the resort's mountaintop summit. My stomach lurched as our car dipped from a gust of wind before settling back into a smooth ascent.

I switched to the seat on the opposite side from Gran so I could keep an eye on Gino's car. My view changed from the lake to rows and rows of tall pines.

As we neared the end of the line, I carefully watched to see which way Gino and his companion went, but they never got off. Did they change their minds?

I'd previously warned Gran we'd have to jump out since the cars didn't come to a complete stop at the top. They only slowed for a quick departure by the current riders before the car would swing around and load a new batch of passengers.

Gran leapt out before I could stop her. She sure was spry for an old gal.

I shot out of the opening, grabbed hold of my grandmother's arm and dragged her back into our same car.

"Hey," she said, her penciled-in eyebrows joined together in displeasure. "What's the deal? What about breakfast?"

"We'll get it the next go-around. I didn't see Gino and his companion get off the gondola."

Gran settled in her seat, a noticeable frown on her wizened features. I could tell she'd been looking forward to the oatmeal buffet, so I promised to make it up to her. Hopefully, they would let us go back up without paying twice, once I figured out a decent explanation of why we'd performed such a crazy maneuver.

Maybe I could blame it on a senior moment. I stared ahead, watching the expanse of blue growing larger as we descended. My feelings boomeranged from trepidation about following Gino to concern about my grandmother.

She could be darn crabby if she didn't get her morning fiber.

The gondola slowed as we began our approach to the base. I paid close attention to the cars directly in front of me trying to determine which one Gino was in. Before we even reached the staging area, a big man wearing a navy sweatshirt with the hood over his head leapt out of a car and raced off.

Someone sure was in a hurry. And that someone looked like Gino's companion. If so, was Gino going back up the mountain again?

Gran and I grabbed our purses, preparing to exit as quickly as possible.

I rose from my seat, then flopped back down as the gondola shuddered to a complete stop.

CHAPTER THIRTY-ONE

Multiple screams assaulted our ears. Since our car was stopped only a foot above the ground, I hopped out, Gran following on my rubber-soled heels. A teen continued to shriek, her high-pitched cries reverberating around the square. Her mother wrapped an arm around her in an attempt to console her. An employee, his face whiter than fresh snow, attempted to push back the oncoming passengers anxious to board the gondola.

Angry shouts and glares mixed with confused expressions as additional employees came to assist the young man. They extended a long gold braid between two poles, blocking anyone from entering the gondola area.

"What's going on?" Gran asked a staff member who insisted on guiding us away from the ride.

Freckles dotted his pale face as he pushed a thatch of bangs from his forehead. "Someone's had an accident."

"Is the someone dead?" asked Gran.

That's my grandmother. Subtlety is not her middle name.

His face grew even paler. "I can't say, ma'am."

I stood on my tiptoes trying to look into the gondola car where I'd last seen Gino, but it was closed off for now. A solemn-faced employee stood guard in front of the car.

My stomach plummeted. "This doesn't look good. We need to find out exactly what's going on," I said. Sirens in the distance indicated an ambulance and other rescue vehicles were on the way.

"Maybe that big dude bumped off Gino," Gran suggested.

I shivered. "I certainly hope not. But we may be the only witnesses to see that guy with Gino."

"Whoa. If we tell the cops what we saw, will we hafta go into witness protection?"

"Of course not," I said emphatically before stopping to consider her question. Wasn't witness protection just for eyewitnesses of mob or drug lord types of killings? Certainly Gino wasn't involved with the mob. Or drug kingpins.

Or was he? There was that odd meeting with the biker dudes. And his two companions last night seemed a tad on the seedy side. Especially the cigar-chewing fellow. What had we gotten ourselves into?

Navy blue uniforms arrived on the site and began milling around the square. One police officer was attempting to corral the gondola riders into a separate area cordoned off with crime scene tape. I walked up to him and tugged on his arm.

"I was riding on the gondola just three cars behind that one." I pointed toward the car that had carried Gino. "I'm a private detective working on a case. My grandmother and I may have witnessed something important."

"If there's been a murder, we know who done it," Gran said.

"Hey," he protested, looking around to make sure none of the bystanders overheard Gran's remark. "Nothing's been said about murder. This situation is being viewed as an accident."

I nodded. "Got it. My husband, Tom Hunter, used to be a homicide cop. You guys have to be careful what you say to the public."

The officer's face brightened. "You're married to Tom? He's a good guy. Tell him Frankie Vallejo said hi." He looked around the crowd. "One of our detectives is already here. Follow me."

Gran and I followed him through the crowd of onlookers that had gathered behind the huge swath of crime scene tape. Surprise, surprise. My favorite detective.

Frankie tapped Ali Reynolds on the shoulder. She whirled around, her arched eyebrows merging together in annoyance.

"Geez. What are you two doing here?" she asked. "Please tell me you're not involved in this mess."

114

"Just indirectly," I said. "Our agency was hired to follow a man named Gino Romano. This morning we spotted him getting on that particular gondola car with another man we saw him dining with last night."

Her jaw dropped. "You gotta be kidding."

Gran marched up to Ali and glared at her, her nose mere inches away from the detective's. "We don't kid about murder."

"We don't know if this is an accident or not," Ali said. "And I can't confirm the person's identity, but since you seem to be involved yet again," she said with a sigh, "why don't you go down to the station and complete a formal witness statement. Otherwise, you'll have to wait here to be interviewed." She waved her arm at the fifty-plus group of gondola passengers who'd been sequestered in one of the coffee shops.

I was pleased Ali considered our information helpful until I heard her mutter to Officer Vallejo something about, "those couple of crackpots again."

So much for bonding with our brethren in blue.

Two and a half hours later, Gran and I were still seated on uncomfortable metal chairs in the stuffy windowless room where Sergeant Vallejo had deposited us. Initially, we planned on leaving a formal statement, but we'd been ushered into this interview room instead. And left to twiddle our thumbs.

"This place is starting to get on my nerves," Gran said as her gaze roamed from the brown industrial carpet to the dirty beige walls. "Could use a decorator's touch, too. How long do ya think they can they keep us here?"

"I don't know. We came here voluntarily, or at least I thought so." I stared glumly at my cell phone. No service whatsoever inside the building. I wasn't certain if that was a Tahoe thing, since the area wasn't known for terrific cell phone service, or if they wanted to ensure suspects couldn't call their friends. Or partners in crime.

The door to the small room opened with a bang. Gran started, putting her palm above her heart. "Geez, Louise. You about scared me to death. Are you planning on leaving us here until I croak? I'm not as young as I look, you know."

Detective Reynolds ignored Gran as she lowered herself into one of the chairs across the table from us. The officer accompanying her carried a small device that I guessed would record our conversation.

"We've been busy interviewing other witnesses at the scene to see if they'd noticed anyone or anything out of the ordinary. Took longer than we expected."

"Did you have any luck?" I asked. "Did anyone confirm the man we mentioned earlier? The one who jumped off the car?"

She shook her head, her short glossy dark-brown hair remaining in place, as opposed to my coppery curls, which moved in multiple directions if someone merely sneezed.

"Tourists encompassed the majority of the people wandering around the square. We glanced through a few iPhone photos, but no one captured anything on their cameras other than scenery." She grimaced. "And way more selfies than I needed to wade through."

Ali nodded at the other officer and he clicked on the recorder. She asked for our names and other official information, plus our client's name and numbers, then proceeded to ask questions listed on a small notepad in front of her. Once we'd established the reason for our presence in South Lake Tahoe, the questions became more specific.

"So you claim to have inadvertently ended up on the gondola a few cars behind the man under surveillance. Why did you only follow him last night?" she asked. "Any competent detective would have continued to tail him this morning."

Now it was Gran whose hackles rose. "Listen, youngster, my granddaughter has more competence in her little toe than you have in your whole body."

I gave Gran a gentle kick under the table.

"To clarify," I replied, "I'd already discussed the man's schedule with his girlfriend. We knew he planned on dining at the Heavenly Valley buffet with a client. We didn't think we'd have any problem picking up his trail. All our client cared about was whether or not Gino was seeing another woman. Since we'd corroborated his dinner companions last night were men, we weren't as concerned about his plans."

Gran nudged me. "Don't forget about the gal. The crabby one."

"What gal?" asked Ali.

I explained Gino had met Kimberly in the bar for a brief time.

"It was an odd coincidence," I reflected, "that Gino and Kimberly were acquainted. But I don't know how relevant it is to his murder." Ali opened her mouth to protest. "If he was murdered. And I don't know how it's related to Gregg Morton's murder."

Ali narrowed her dark eyes at me. "It's also an odd coincidence your grandmother was at the scene both times. What should I make of that?"

I shrugged. "Bad timing?"

She snorted, but in a delicate manner.

"We appreciate your time, Detective Reynolds. We're anxious to assist you with this case."

She put her palm up. "Thanks for coming in but no further help, please. Stay far, far away from my investigations."

"But what if during our other casework, we discover something that would assist you in finding the killers? Certainly you won't refuse helpful evidence?"

"Helpful evidence from you?" Ali's voice crescendoed. "Talk about an oxymoron. Like I said, stay out of my way."

Sergeant Vallejo ushered us back to the lobby where Gran and I debated our next move. The police station was a few miles from Harveys. We could wait for a patrol car to drop us off, Uber or call for a cab.

"So what's next on our investigating schedule?" Gran asked.

"Didn't you hear what Ali said?" I reminded her as I clicked on my Uber app.

"She's not the boss of us."

True. And our agency had a client who had now lost her fiancée. Would Adriana be aware of his loss by now? My phone pinged nonstop as a multitude of texts popped up now that we were out of the police station.

Adriana – Did Gino meet with anyone?

Tom – Where are you? Why aren't you answering your texts?

Mother – Why aren't you and your grandmother home?

Stan – When's our next stakeout?

Liz – Is this baby ever going to come out?

Jenna – Why aren't you home? The senior dinner is tonight. I need your car.

Ben – Can we get a dog?

Sigh. You never realize how important you are to your family
and friends until you get stuck in an interrogation room for three
hours.

A black sedan arrived, indicating our Uber ride was here. Gran
and I piled into the back seat while I tried to call Adriana to share the
unfortunate news. Into voicemail once again. Hopefully, the police
had contacted her by now.

The driver slammed on the brakes as he slowed down for a light
behind a long line of cars. "What's with all the traffic?" I asked.

"Looky loos. Folks are saying some guy got his neck broke on
the gondola. Lots of police been talking to tourists. Makes me think
it wasn't no accident."

Gran and I kept our mouths shut during the two-mile drive that
ended up taking ten minutes. Ten very long minutes while the driver
practiced a standup routine he was working on for amateur night at
one of the local comedy clubs. I gave him two tips. One involved
cash. The other was to stick to his current profession.

"What's next?" asked Gran as we stood on the sidewalk in front
of Harveys.

"I'm going to try Adriana again although I hate leaving the news
on her voicemail."

"She's not going to be happy with you."

"Me?" I squawked. "She only hired me for surveillance, not to
be his bodyguard."

"Speaking of bodyguards, do ya think the big lug we saw with
Cigar Shorty last night was some kind of security? He had that look."

"Define look."

She pulled out her cell, scrolled through it and turned it toward
me. "I took a photo of them last night when they went through the
casino."

"You did?" I glanced at her phone, then grabbed it for a closer
look. "All I can see is the partial back of one man, a bunch of slot
machines and a lot of carpet."

"I'm still getting the hang of this thing. Scroll through some
more."

I scrolled to the left. A photo of Gran's shoes against the red-
flowered carpet. Nope. Then to the right.

"Hmm. It's not a bad photo of the back of that big guy although
his boss, or whoever he is, remains hidden. Nice work, Gran."

I quickly emailed the photo to myself before Gran could accidentally delete it. Then I'd forward it on to Detective Reynolds. Whether she wanted our help or not.

"I told you I could help out. I could be a consultant, specializing in old folks' cases. What do you think?"

I shuddered at how my husband and stepfather would respond to Gran's request to be a senior snooper for the agency.

"We'll see," I told her. "For now, let's just hope Tom and Robert don't fire me for letting the subject of a surveillance get killed right in front of us."

CHAPTER THIRTY-TWO

Throughout our relationship and subsequent marriage, my husband has managed remarkable restraint during some of my "adventures" or misadventures. But tonight, seated at the kitchen table, the steam figuratively coming out of my husband's ears easily matched the hissing steam from my teapot boiling on the stove.

I walked over to the refrigerator, grabbed a bottle of beer and handed it to him. He opened it, took a very long sip and then continued to harangue me. Albeit in a soft voice so the kids wouldn't overhear our conversation.

"Laurel, I told you that taking on a surveillance operation was a bad idea," Tom said. "What if the killers noticed you, either last night in the casino, or this morning? It sounds like your client's fiancé was up to his broken neck in trouble."

"It seemed like such a cut-and-dry case," I said as I poured boiling water into my flowered mug. "Find out if the guy is a philanderer. Isn't that the type of work detectives frequently take on?"

Tom sighed as he placed his beer on the table. "Spousal surveillance makes up the majority of most agencies' casework. I had hoped ours would handle higher-level cases. Financial fraud, insurance work, assisting the district attorney when needed."

"Not much we can do about it now." I looked at the rooster clock over my sink. The cocky fellow looked as bewildered as I felt. "It's almost nine thirty. I'm surprised Adriana hasn't returned my call."

The shrill sound of "Ding Dong the Witch is Dead" blasted from my cell phone where it rested on the counter.

Tom's head jerked up as I replied. "That's her ringtone now."

I grabbed the phone and greeted my client.

"Laurel, how could you do this to me?" she shrieked in my ear. Guess the cops notified her finally. I moved the phone a couple of inches away, hitting the hands-free button so Tom could listen in.

"I'm so sorry for your loss," I said to her. A somewhat meaningless condolence since, from my perspective, she was better off with Gino out of her life.

"If I hadn't hired you, this never would have happened." She sobbed quietly as I attempted to calm her down.

"Adriana, I feel for you. Truly I do. But it looks like Gino might have been hanging out with the wrong crowd. His death is still under investigation, but I think it's possible the police will consider it murder."

"It has to be a mistake. He went to Tahoe to see clients. Why would his clients want to kill him?"

Now that was the billion-dollar question. Why indeed?

Adriana's tone changed suddenly as she returned to her normal bossy self. "Well, you'll just have to figure out who did it. And bring justice to Gino. And me."

Although Tom remained silent, his head shook the answer to her request. A solid no.

But as I have reiterated on numerous occasions, I am my own woman. Free to make my choices. And I did feel a sense of obligation to Adriana. Obviously, it wasn't my fault Gino died while Gran and I tailed him. But if Tom suddenly died under suspicious circumstances, I would want answers as well. And as quickly as possible.

I walked to the refrigerator, grabbed another bottle of beer and set it in front of Tom.

"I'll do what I can," I assured her before ending the call.

I met Tom's angry gaze and wondered if helping Adriana would lead to the end of our marriage.

CHAPTER THIRTY-THREE

Before Tom could chew me out, my phone rang again. Jenna. What now?

"Honey, are you all right?"

"Yes, everything's fine. Nikki went to get the car so I wouldn't have to limp so far. She had to park at the back of the lot. But you'll never guess what I saw."

She was one hundred percent accurate about that.

"What?"

"I was hanging out front here, talking to some of the kids, when this white car whizzed by on Ponderosa Road. It barely stopped at the stop sign before taking off. And get this. The left headlight was out and the front bumper was dented. I think it could be the guy who rammed me."

"Whoa. You couldn't catch the license plate from that distance, could you?"

I could almost hear her shaking her head over the phone. "No, but I thought as soon as Nikki pulls up, we should try to catch up to him."

"Absolutely not. Way too dangerous."

"Mom, you put yourself in dangerous situations all the time."

True, but not intentionally.

"Look, I don't want any harm to come to you or Nikki. Her parents would kill me if you two ran into that car. And knowing how poor a driver he is, that's a possibility."

"Okay. You're probably right. Plus, he's long gone by now. I'll just have to find another way to track him down."

I breathed a sigh of relief. While I applauded my daughter's enthusiasm, I wished she'd take it down a notch. Her phone call had provided me with a brief respite, since Tom had disappeared from the kitchen.

I climbed the stairs and opened our bedroom door. The room was dark and Tom lay sprawled across our bed. No snoring emanated from the room, yet he didn't attempt to converse with me. I debated what to do, then silently closed the door.

After all, tomorrow was another day.

I woke early on Sunday, although Tom must have risen even earlier. His mug and a rinsed-out bowl had been added to the dishwasher racks. I didn't recall any early-morning meetings on his schedule. Especially on the weekend.

I poured the remains of the coffee into my own mug and pondered the relevance of his actions. It didn't take much of a detective to determine my husband was upset with me. Should I call him and touch base or wait for his irritation to subside?

Before I came up with a plan, two sleepy-eyed, tousle-headed kids slipped into the kitchen chairs on either side of me, brightening my morning immediately.

"What are you two doing up so early?" I asked, both curious and suspicious. I sensed they possessed an action plan of their own, and I wasn't certain I was prepared for their creative planning. Especially this early in the day.

"Guess what?" Ben asked, his hazel eyes earnest.

"What?"

"Dad found a rescue dog when he was working a couple of weeks ago. He didn't know where he came from so he took the dog to the pound hoping the owners would go there looking for him."

"Did the owner turn up?"

Ben shook his head. "Nope, so Dad took the dog home to Gran's house."

"How does Gran feel about that?" I asked. My grandmother has a kind heart, but I didn't recall her being overly fond of the canine population.

"She said"—Ben made air quotes—"'I'm too old to take on the caring and feeding of a dog.'"

"I'm not surprised. So what's your father going to do?" I asked before realization sunk in.

"Oh, no. We are not adding a dog to this family." I turned my gaze over to Kristy, who so far had let Ben handle their puppy petition. "And I'm sure your father would agree with me. We are all far too busy to take on another pet at this time. And Pumpkin would hate having a dog around."

"My pop said it was fine with him," Kristy replied.

Ben nodded. "Yep, he said it would teach us"—he pointed to his stepsister and then back to himself—"to be more responsible."

My husband, the traitor.

"When did you discuss this with Tom?" I asked the twosome.

"Yesterday. We waited and waited for you to come home so we could ask you. But you were late," Ben said accusingly.

"Your mother has different responsibilities now. And my hours will probably become even crazier. Which is why we won't be able to add a dog into our lives."

The doorbell rang. I glanced at the clock. Who could be calling at eight o'clock in the morning? The kids jumped out of their chairs and raced to answer it.

My stomach sank when I realized who was standing on our doorstep.

CHAPTER THIRTY-FOUR

"Are you freaking kidding me?" I tried not to shriek, but it was far too early to be greeted by my ex-husband and his furry companion.

His really huge black-and-white companion.

"Hey, I thought you were cool with adding him to your family," Hank said. "Tom didn't object."

My husband and I were headed for a lengthy discussion today. In the meantime, the ginormous dog managed to work his way into the foyer. He sat in the middle of my wood-plank entry, his head tilted to the left, deep brown eyes gazing soulfully at me.

I tilted my own head. "Why did he sit in that puddle?" I asked Hank before my caffeine-deprived brain did the math.

"Get a towel, Ben," I ordered my son before sending Hank and his oversized pet back to the porch stoop.

"He's not even trained," I complained.

"He's just stressed," Hank replied as the dog took care of the rest of his business by one of the evergreen bushes.

"That makes two of us." I took the towel Ben handed me, then gave it back to him. The kids might as well get their first lesson in dog care.

"So why are you here at this hour?" I asked Hank. "We need to have a family meeting before we add a dog to the mix."

"I've got an urgent job that came up. Do you remember Donald Lange, he owns a mammoth vacation home on the west shore of Lake Tahoe? He just drove up to the lake for the first time in four months and discovered his pipes froze. The place is a disaster."

"That's tough."

"Tough for him, but a great opportunity for me," Hank said with a sly grin. "The only hitch is I need to head up the hill immediately. Which is why I'm standing on your doorstep with man's best friend."

I sighed. "I suppose we could watch him on a trial basis. He would certainly help keep the kids occupied this summer."

Both kids threw their arms around me. "Thanks, Mom." Then Ben and Kristy raced up the stairs with their new pal galloping behind them.

My ex turned to go when I stopped him. "Hey, you never told me his name."

Hank grinned. "Scout. A perfect addition to your detective agency."

Two puddles and one broken vase later, this frazzled mother sat at the kitchen table relishing the quiet. A peaceful moment that wouldn't last long. And, based on our morning, would rarely make an appearance with the new addition to our family. I stared out the window and couldn't help grinning as I watched the kids playing with our new boarder, a one-hundred-fifty-pound Bernese mountain dog.

Just what we needed. Another family member with a big appetite and a small bladder. Although considering my recent record, Scout might prove more successful as a detective than me. He'd already dug up one of Ben's missing shoes from under the kids' trampoline.

I decided it was long past time for me to create a "to detect" list for my increasing caseload. No one loved lists better than me, except possibly my mother, the most organized person I knew. Although the best part of utilizing to-do lists was when you got to scratch an item off.

I grabbed a pen and lined pad from one of our junk drawers, refilled my coffee cup, then plunked back down in the kitchen chair and began writing.

1. Resolve Iris's timeshare issue. While it wasn't the most urgent topic on my agenda, it was my first real case and I was determined to see it through.

2. Determine who killed Gregg Morton. While his murder probably shouldn't command a spot on the list, with Gran still a primary suspect, it needed to be addressed.

3. Find out who killed Gino. And why.

I gnawed on my lower lip as I reviewed the list, a far cry from my normal weekly shopping lists. Especially since two of the three items involved a murder. Deep in thought, I almost didn't hear my cell vibrate. I'd forgotten to turn the ringer back on.

I stood and grabbed the phone, hoping it was Tom calling with an explanation for his early departure. I grimaced when I saw my caller's name.

"Adriana, are you doing okay?"

"Really? Do you seriously expect me to be okay when my beloved fiancé was just killed?"

"No, of course not. Just letting you know I care about how you're doing."

Her tone softened as she replied, "Thanks. I appreciate that. And I realize it probably wasn't your fault Gino was killed."

Thanks. I think.

"So what can I do for you?"

"I contacted the South Lake Tahoe police like you recommended, but they didn't say much, or even ask me too many questions. I told them how Gino and I met, how long we've been dating, and where I was yesterday when it"—her voice wobbled but she continued—"happened."

"I'm sure they'll have more questions for you later on. And for his co-workers. They'll have a ton of data to pore through."

"Right. That's why I'm calling you. I think we should go through Gino's house before the police drive down here."

"Gino's house? You mean together?"

"Yes, of course together. Between us, we might find something the police wouldn't realize was important."

"I didn't realize Gino had given you a key to his house."

The line went quiet for a few seconds before she responded. "Well, not exactly. I, um, sort of, removed a key from his keychain one night, made a copy, then returned it. He always used his garage clicker to enter the house, so he never noticed it had been missing."

Hmm. I wondered if Gino had realized how sneaky his fiancée was.

"When do you want to get together?" I asked, not sure when Tom would be home, although Jenna could watch the kids. She'd joined them in the backyard and all three of them laughed as Scout romped around the yard.

"I'll be at your house in five minutes or less."

Alrighty then.

CHAPTER THIRTY-FIVE

Adriana pulled her Lexus coupe into our driveway, right behind Tom's SUV, which had arrived seconds earlier. I stood on the front porch, attired in my oversized T-shirt and shorts, since Adriana hadn't left me any time to change.

Tom got out of his vehicle and greeted Adriana. They chatted and walked down the sidewalk together.

"I'm sorry you were too busy to handle my case," she said to Tom. "I'm sure my fiancé would still be alive if you'd been in charge."

My cheeks burned at her insinuation, and I was tempted to tell her to hit the road, but professional courtesy as well as a paycheck for the agency quelled my internal indignation.

"We're sorry for your loss," he said in a sincere tone before giving me the once-over. "What are you up to, Laurel?"

"Five-foot-four and a quarter," I said in jest, but neither of them laughed.

"Are you wearing that?" Adriana asked, eyeing my sloppy attire.

"You didn't give me much notice," I replied. "Come on in. You can update Tom on your situation while I change into something more suitable. All right with you, hon?" I said to my husband with a heavy emphasis on "hon."

Tom's heavy brown eyebrows drew together, but he merely nodded and ushered Adriana into the living room. I fled, taking the steps two at a time and wistfully hoping Tom would be more receptive to my investigating once Adriana shared her sad story.

I threw on a colorful Madras top and capri pants, and added some mascara, blush and lipstick to my otherwise pale face, managing to join them in less than seven minutes. Based on Adriana's nose twitching when she saw me, I should have spent more time rummaging through my closet.

The first question out of Tom's mouth had nothing to do with Gino's demise. Instead, he pointed to the backyard and asked, "Is that a horse in our backyard?"

"Nope. That's Hank's dog. The one he rescued. He said you agreed that we would keep him. It would have been nice to have been consulted on that matter," I said in a low voice as I plopped next to Tom on the sofa.

"What? I never agreed to any such thing. Hank completely misinterpreted what I said."

Not the first time Hank had done such a thing. He probably figured the kids would fall in love with the dog and our acceptance of Scout as a permanent house guest was a *fait accompli*.

"You better call Hank and tell him to come get his dog," Tom said.

"How about you tell the kids about your decision first." I stood, indicating to Adriana it was time to go. She rose from the sofa, checking the skirt of her sundress for any stray hairs our new pet might have left behind.

"Adriana and I have work to do."

Adriana and I drove off before Tom could respond. I was almost grateful for her company because it meant putting off some major marital discussions. Blending two families required patience, flexibility and the ability to compromise.

Plus, a whole lot of love.

Adriana remained quiet throughout most of the drive, as did I. As we drew nearer to Gino's house in Granite Bay, I broke the silence.

"What do you expect to find in Gino's house?" I asked.

She sent a quick glance my way, then focused back on her driving. "I don't know. You're the detective." She thumped the steering wheel with her right fist. "Don't you have some ideas?"

"Based on his recent behavior, and his murder, Gino must have been involved in some kind of illegal activity."

She shrugged as she hit the signal to turn into Gino's subdivision. As we drew near his house, I debated whether or not we should park in his driveway or farther down the street. Adriana made her own decision by pulling into the driveway and turning off her car.

"I'm not sure we should park here," I said. "We're so obvious."

"Why not? I'm Gino's girlfriend. I have a right to be here."

"I don't know if that's true. But let's just go in and get this over with." My eyes roamed around the neighborhood. No one outside their houses checking up on us so far. "I wonder if Gino's neighbors know what happened to him. As far as I can tell, his name still hasn't been released to the media yet."

Adriana's door slammed shut, indicating she was done talking for now. So much for my observation. She motioned for me to hurry up so I did.

Once inside Gino's house, I breathed a little easier.

"How did you know the code?" I asked as she disarmed his security system with speedy precision.

She blushed. "Oh, I pay attention to stuff."

The woman was devious enough to be a detective. I could take lessons from her. We decided to split up. Adriana would take Gino's bedroom, which was fine with me. I was not a fan of searching through men's underwear drawers. She pointed me toward his office on the opposite side of the sprawling ranch house, and I headed that way.

I passed Gino's immaculate kitchen, wishing mine were as tidy. My standards had lowered in recent months. I considered it a success when most of the dishes made it into the dishwasher the same day.

I would have loved to examine Gino's house inch by inch, not only for detecting reasons, but for a few decorating tips. But I worried the South Lake Tahoe police would not be far behind us, and I wanted to concentrate on any personal or professional records he'd stored at his house.

I pulled a pair of disposable gloves from my purse since I knew better than to leave any fingerprints. As Gino's fiancée, Adriana was free to lay her palm across every surface of his house.

Gino's office was a traditional masculine office with a modern cast. Dark cherrywood mixed with solid black surfaces. Floor-to-ceiling bookshelves filled with books and DVDs covered two walls.

I glanced at my watch. Going through Gino's office would be a monumental task. Should I look through the obvious? File cabinets, drawers, bookshelves? Or try to find more unusual hiding places like in the family Bible. Or hidden in one of the DVD boxes. Which could take forever.

Especially since I had no clue what I was looking for.

If I were Gino, what would I do? He certainly didn't expect anything to happen to him this weekend. So any relevant clues to some type of illicit activity might be hidden, or rather not hidden, as in plain sight.

Unless Gino realized what a nosy Nancy his fiancée was. Which meant he might not have anything tied to any nefarious activities stored in the house.

Still, if I were a crook, I would worry about keeping anything pointing to criminal activities in my place of employment.

Which brought me back to ground zero. Gino's home office.

I settled into Gino's well-padded desk chair. Comfy. The man didn't stint on his home décor. What would happen to all of his furnishings, his house? Who personally benefitted from his death? Family? Charities? Adriana? Another question I'd have to run by my client.

I looked around for any sign of a computer but could only find a printer and modem. Gino must have taken his laptop to the hotel, which meant the police most likely were in possession of it by now. The drawers of his contemporary-style desk opened easily enough. They were filled with ordinary business supplies, envelopes, etc.

A three-tier tray stood on the corner of his desk. The top shelf contained mail that had been opened and thrust into the tray. While I would hesitate to open his sealed mail, these previously opened envelopes seemed to be calling my name.

Ah ha. For a man with a supposedly lucrative profession, Gino appeared to be deep in credit card debt. Five-figure debt on three different cards. I didn't even know you could get credit card lines as high as $50,000.

Where was all that money going?

The next envelope proved even more mysterious. Not only did Gino have enormous credit card bills, but he owed a Reno finance company some serious dough. And I had a feeling said finance company probably charged even more exorbitant interest rates than the credit card companies.

I grabbed the bills and headed toward the other end of the house. As I neared Gino's bedroom, a scream echoed down the hallway, followed by heartbreaking sobs.

CHAPTER THIRTY-SIX

I burst into the master bedroom to find Adriana sprawled across the burgundy-and-navy bedspread, sobbing her heart out.

"What's the matter?" I dropped down next to her. A pile of cards, letters and envelopes lay strewn across the Ralph Lauren bedding. Had she discovered more traces of Gino's profligate spending? Or proof he was involved in another intimate relationship?

She sat up and pointed to the colorful cards dotting the bedspread. "He saved them."

"Saved what?" I asked.

"All of the cards and notes I sent him," she whimpered. "Every single one. I think Gino really did love me."

"Of course he did," I assured her, although I was also surprised at her discovery. Despite some of the things I'd recently learned about Gino, it seemed apparent he truly cared for Adriana.

"And if it hadn't been for me hiring you, Gino would still be alive today. It's all my fault." She burst into tears once again. I looked around but couldn't spot any tissues, so I went into the master bath and brought a few back for her.

"Adriana, I'm relieved we've confirmed Gino's feelings for you, but given some of the information I just found, Gino had a few financial issues. Which may or may not have had any bearing on his murder. Keep in mind Gino didn't accidentally die. Someone killed him. Murder happens for a reason."

"I suppose," she burbled, wiping her eyes with the tissue, which only served to turn her into a Rocky Raccoon lookalike.

I went into the bathroom again, grabbed a washcloth, wet it, then returned to the bedroom. Adriana stood in front of a four-drawer bureau, grimacing at her reflection in the overhead mirror. She peered over her shoulder at me.

"Did you find anything revealing?" she asked.

"Did you know Gino was in debt? Big-time."

I could see her scrunching her face in the mirror. "Don't be silly. Gino makes, I mean made, an excellent living. He treated me very well."

"Based on his credit card bills, he treated himself very well. He spent a ton of money at the big casinos. Did Gino have a gambling problem?"

She whirled around. "No. Why?"

"It looks like he owed money to the casinos and possibly a loan shark."

"A loan shark? Really?"

"Well, someone named Louie's Loans sent Gino a bill a few months ago with an astronomical sum of money due."

She plopped back on the bed, silent for a few seconds before she sat up again. "Gino did play poker with some friends occasionally. And one weekend when we went to Lake Tahoe, he made a small killing at the craps table." Her eyes started to water again. "That was the weekend he proposed and bought me my ring. He said I brought him good luck." She looked forlornly at her diamond. "I guess not so much."

"Rest assured whatever trouble Gino got himself into has nothing to do with you."

She grabbed my arm and squeezed tight. "Listen, you're still on my payroll. Figure out who did this to Gino. Please. Can you do that for me?"

I nodded, although I had a feeling my partners would not be too thrilled about it. I was about to reply when we heard voices yelling and pounding on the front door.

"Open up. We know you're in there."

CHAPTER THIRTY-SEVEN

Adriana rushed to the foyer with me right behind her. Given the racket, it was most likely the police, although it could also be Gino's killer.

She peered through one of the glass panes to the side of the solid oak door.

"Cops," she whispered. "What should I do?"

Sigh. It might be time to increase our hourly rate. I grasped the brass handle, opened the door and greeted my least favorite detective.

Ali Reynolds gawked at me. "What the blazes are you doing here? And who are you?" she said to Adriana, who was peeking over my shoulder.

"I'm here in my official capacity as investigative consultant," I replied to the detective. "This is Adriana Menzinger, Gino Romano's fiancée."

"You have no business being in this house," Ali said, her nostrils flaring in anger. I could tell they were flaring because her nose was barely an inch from mine.

"Adriana wanted to retrieve her personal items. She has a key so she has every right to be here. And I'm along to provide comfort to her." I wrapped my arm around Adriana to demonstrate just how comforting I could be.

Ali's dark eyes flashed as she noticed the arm I'd wrapped around Adriana ended in a hand ensconced in a fingerprint-prevention glove. "And I suppose you always wear gloves when you tag along to support a friend?" She shook her head in disgust, then turned to direct a team of crime scene investigators into the house.

"You need to get out of here. Both of you. Now."

"Can I finish getting my things?" Adriana asked her. "How would you feel if your boyfriend were suddenly killed and your world was turned upside down?"

Ali flinched and her face grew pale. With a softened tone, she told Adriana she had five minutes to finish up.

Adriana went back into the master bedroom, leaving me alone with Ali. The detective glanced at the papers I was still holding.

"What are those? You're not removing evidence, are you?" She snatched the credit card bills out of my hands and quickly scanned the statements.

"He had a lot of debt," I informed her.

"Brilliant deduction, Sherlock." She pulled an evidence bag out of the pocket of her windbreaker and stuffed them inside. "I thought this guy was some kind of wealth manager. Doesn't look like he knew how to manage his own wealth." She narrowed her eyes at me. "I hate to ask you this, but do you have any idea what was going on with him?"

"Gino might have had a gambling problem." I pointed to the evidence bag. "The bills included charges from multiple Tahoe casinos. Adriana said he also played poker with some other players on a weekly basis. But other than that, she was basically clueless as to his debts. Especially the one from Louie's Loans."

"Gambling debts frequently lead to even more serious consequences," Ali said. "Loss of home, family, a life of crime…"

"Murder," I added.

"Yep."

Adriana joined us. She clutched a small tote bag filled with what I presumed were cosmetic items.

Ali held up her palm, signaling she wanted a look in the tote. "I need to make sure you're not removing evidence," she said.

"Just my makeup and some love letters," Adriana sobbed.

The detective pawed through the assortment and handed it back.

"Will you keep me apprised of your findings?" Adriana asked as she reclaimed her love notes.

Ali nodded, although the odds of her keeping either of us informed were less than zero.

"And, of course, you'll share anything," Ali said, with her dark eyes fixed on mine, "absolutely anything you discover with me."

I nodded, then followed Adriana down the sidewalk to her car.

"She's kind of a bitch," Adriana whispered, "isn't she?"

I almost said, "It takes one to know one." But that comment would have landed me in the bitch category as well. Adriana had been remarkably nice today, especially given what she'd suffered in the past twenty-four hours.

The evidence techs hauled equipment from their van and up the sidewalk. I wasn't certain what they expected to find, but maybe Gino's walls, counters and doors would yield some fingerprints of well-known felons who'd visited his house.

"So what's next?" Adriana asked me as she reversed her car down the driveway. "Do we go undercover to find the killer?"

"We?"

"Sure. You want my help, don't you?"

Honestly. Everyone wants to be an amateur sleuth these days.

"Look, you have your own job to do at the bank. I have a team of skilled homicide detectives at the agency. I promise we'll put all of our manpower behind our investigation for you."

I just hoped those skilled homicide investigators agreed with me.

CHAPTER THIRTY-EIGHT

Adriana dropped me off at my house, where I was met by a scene resembling a sitcom on steroids. High-pitched shrieks, low-pitched barking and the smell of wet dog tempted me to run after Adriana and catch a ride with her.

To anywhere.

I threw back my shoulders and soldiered on, or in my case, mothered on, and marched into the family room, the scene of the chaos.

"Where have you been?" asked my husband in a strained voice. "I left you three messages."

"Mommy, Mommy, we gave Scout a bath, but he didn't like it," Ben shouted. It didn't take a detective to come to that realization. All it took was one look at the trail of doggy paw prints throughout the kitchen and family room.

"Where's Scout now?" I asked. A sharp bark outside the slider answered my question.

"We put him back outside." Kristy shook her head sorrowfully. "He's not a very cooperative dog."

I settled in an empty chair next to Tom and placed my hand on his. "And you thought chasing killers was tough duty."

His brown eyes crinkled and he gave me that half smile that never failed to make my heart beat faster.

"I hope you had a more constructive day than I did," he murmured.

139

"I think it's time we held an agency meeting." I was about to share some more details when Jenna hobbled into the room.

"Where were you?" my daughter accused. "Didn't you remember I needed your car for the senior banquet?"

"Yes, I remembered," I countered, clearly puzzled. "I rode with Adriana and left my car here for you."

"Doesn't do me any good when you have the keys," she said with a pout. "Next time you go tearing off with a client, leave your keys behind, not your cell phone." She picked up my phone from the charger and handed it to me.

I glanced at the screen. Eight texts from my daughter and husband.

I looked at Tom. "Couldn't she have driven..." He frowned and shook his head. His SUV was off limits to my teenager. And I couldn't blame him. Jenna was a good driver, but we'd already lost one car.

I sifted through my purse, pulled out the keys and handed them over. "Drive safe, sweetheart," I said, my heart racing again but not in a good way. How many days, months or years would it take for *me* to recover from Jenna's crash?

She grabbed the keys. Despite her injury, she practically sprinted out the door into the garage. The teen recovery rate was far superior to mine.

"I'm not sure we can handle the new addition," Tom said, tilting his head in the direction of our new pet, who added his two cents with a string of woofs. "When will Hank be back in town?"

"Not for a month or two. I'm sure Scout just needs to get adjusted to us." As if sensing he was the topic of our conversation, Scout sat quietly, pretending to be a well-trained dog.

"Let's give Scout more time," I said. "It's only been a few hours."

Tom looked at the kitchen clock. "Feels like a week to me. And what were you and Adriana doing all of that time? Given your mutual history, I'm surprised you're still speaking to one another."

"She's growing on me." I smiled at him. "Kind of like star thistle. Prickly, but you get used to it."

"She doesn't have any crazy ideas about you investigating her fiancé's murder, does she?"

My husband is such a good detective.

"Sort of. By the way, we ran into your old partner at Gino's house, shortly after we arrived."

Tom's face reddened, which seemed an odd reaction. "I suppose you mean Ali Reynolds?"

I nodded and waited for him to elaborate. When he didn't, I switched into interrogation mode. "You've never said anything about your relationship with Ali. Did the two of you ever date?"

Tom's face grew even redder. "Not really. She was very supportive during Carol's illness and afterward. That's all."

His comment about his wife's death made me feel like crawling under a rock so I switched investigative direction.

"You are correct that Adriana wants me or rather, our agency, to investigate Gino's murder. She's not real keen on Ali Reynolds."

"Ali will do a fine job. She's an excellent homicide detective."

Bully for her. With my hackles raised, I proceeded. "I'm sure she will. But Adriana is our client. I was there when Gino was killed. I feel an obligation to do what she's asked of us," I replied. "And she's paying our agency for the investigation. We can't simply ignore her request."

Tom rubbed his hand through his chestnut hair, mussing it up nicely.

"You're right. Let's go make a plan."

We spent the next two hours alone in our bedroom, making said plan. Someday we hoped to get a larger house with space for a home office, but for now, we sat propped against the pillows strategizing how to investigate Gino's murder.

Such a waste of a king-size bed.

"So you'll talk to Ali and see if you can get any leads out of her," I confirmed with Tom. "And I'll interview the loan shark."

Tom sighed. "I'm not crazy about you chatting with anyone in the 'shark' category, but you do possess more financial expertise than I do."

I shifted closer to Tom, and he pulled me into his arms.

"Have I told you lately how much I love you?" he whispered in my ear before leaving a trail of kisses down my neck.

My insides went mushy, and I turned to meet his soft lips.

Our brief rapturous moment was interrupted by pounding on our bedroom door.

"Mom, come quick," cried Ben. "Scout broke a lamp."

CHAPTER THIRTY-NINE

The following morning I woke up with murder on my mind. My number one victim—my ex-husband. The man who dumped the world's most rambunctious canine on our doorstep.

Although he did have the sweetest eyes. Scout, that is, not Hank. Scout's shaggy head rested on the console as I drove him to a local Doggy Daycare. Maybe they could teach him some manners this week while the kids were still in school. Otherwise, we were going to have to put bubble wrap around every breakable in the house.

At the daycare center, I bent over and gave our pet a goodbye hug. He returned the favor by licking off the makeup on one side of my face.

Once on the road, I headed east toward Reno. Lately I'd spent more time zipping up the mountainous highways than roaming the streets of Placerville. I hit the audio button and the strains of Carrie Underwood's "Before He Cheats" filled the car with music.

Just for fun, I'd Googled "Reno loan sharks" the previous evening and much to my surprise, the online yellow pages offered a category for them. Louie's Loans, the company whose name was on the bill I'd found on Gino's desk, held a prominent spot. Right across the street from Phil's Pawnshop. Both were conveniently located close to the major Reno casinos.

An hour into my drive, I realized I should have brought something with me that was pawn-worthy. I glanced at my diamond ring, which originally belonged to Tom's grandmother. There was no way I'd let this ring end up at any pawnshops, but it could be useful as a conversation starter.

Two and a half hours and one pit stop later, I pulled into pawnshop mecca. Skyscraper-sized casinos were interspersed with brick and stucco one-story buildings. Huge posters covered the pawnshop and finance company windows advertising their fantastic deals. The one thing both types of establishments bore in common were garish fluorescent lights advertising their business in one hundred-point font.

I slid out of the car and locked the door. Despite the sun shining in a cloudless sky, I still felt a chill as I walked down the slightly seedy strip. Maybe I should have dragged Gran or Stan along with me today. Tom was trying to finish his interviews for the district attorney so he could hopefully begin assisting me on this case in the near future.

I squared my shoulders and opened the door to Phil's Pawnshop. I could practice my spiel before I moved on to my real quarry—Louie's Loans.

The bell tinkled as I walked into the store. The two men behind one of the counters sized me up, down and sideways. While I'd expected to see glass cases filled with an array of jewelry, I didn't realize how many guns of all shapes, sizes and calibers would be for sale.

I shivered again as I cruised past more firearms than I'd ever seen displayed in one place. When I reached the two men, I smiled and stuck out my left hand for them to admire before I began my pitch.

They responded with a flat, "Five hundred dollars. Take it or leave it." The older man, who needed a year's supply of Crest white strips, threw his arm out and added, "We got more diamond rings than we know what to do with. Ya got anything else?"

My tongue nudged one of my molars as I contemplated the value of my two gold fillings.

"Not really," I replied. "Do you make loans here?"

He shook his head of thinning black hair. "Nah. But you can check with Louie over there. He does all kinds of financing deals." He pointed across the street. "Just watch yourself and read the fine print. Louie don't take no prisoners."

I had no idea what he meant by that elusive remark, but I merely thanked them and headed for the door. Once outside, I gazed at Louie's place. The building he was housed in was plain red brick, nothing outlandish. The garish "buy and sell signs" posted across the windows definitely got your attention.

I walked to the end of the street, caught the light before it changed and zipped across the pedestrian crosswalk. I ambled down the sidewalk, reading the catchy signs before entering the store. Louie's square footage doubled that of Phil's paltry shop. The store contained a staggering array of every possible item a person might pawn. Guitars galore, iPads, computers, tools and jewelry. Oodles of jewelry.

Despite bright lights shining down on the displays, a scent of sadness and despair permeated the atmosphere. I tried to shake off the depression that wrapped itself like a heavy cloak around my shoulders.

I had a job to do. And a mystery to solve.

An attractive twentyish woman with the elegance and appearance of a young Nicole Kidman stood behind one of the jewelry counters. She threw me a dazzling smile, and as I drew closer I grew more and more positive we'd met before.

"Can I help you?" she asked, smoothing her long auburn curls behind her ears.

"Yes, um, Phil"—I jerked my finger behind me toward Phil's store—"told me that your company makes loans to almost anyone."

She chuckled. "Not quite anyone. But if you have some type of collateral we can arrange short-term financing for you. What amount were you looking for?"

Uh oh. I wasn't prepared for that question. But Gino had borrowed a lot based on the bill I recovered at his house. I'd start high and work my way down.

"Forty thousand?" I asked.

"Whoa," she said, her bright blue eyes growing rounder. "That's not small. Do you have collateral or money due you soon?"

I chewed on my lip trying to come up with something feasible, wishing I did have forty thousand walking into my life in the near future.

"My husband and I split up and the house will be closing shortly. Would that work?"

She relaxed her shoulders. "Oh, sure. I'll go get you some forms for you to fill out." She went around the counter and headed toward the back. Her cell rang and she picked it up and greeted the caller with a "hello," followed by "this is Cherie."

Cherie! A unique name that fit her well. Now I remembered where I'd seen her before. It was when I won at the roulette wheel the first time Gran dragged me up to Tahoe with her. Cherie also worked at the casinos.

As my grandmother would say, now isn't that a coincidink.

Cherie returned with an armful of documents for me to peruse. As I skimmed through the extra-teeny font, I asked, "You look so familiar. Do you work in one of the casinos?"

"I'm a dealer at Harrah's. I only help out here when they're short-staffed."

"Do you enjoy it?"

"It's okay." Cherie shoved another errant curl behind her ear. "I prefer working at the casino. It's fast-paced and I meet interesting people. There are always a few losers, of course."

"In more ways than one," I replied.

She laughed. "True. But I've met some great guys while I was dealing." Her smile fell away as if she remembered something. "Mostly. Sometimes they're not the good guys you think they are."

Little bits of conversation were coming back to me as Cherie and I chatted. Marty at Timeshare Help had been a wealth of information, not only regarding timeshare resales, but also providing details about the personal life of Gregg Morton. Including an ex-girlfriend by the name of Cherie.

Was there a subtle way of asking Cherie if she once stalked the murder victim?

Nope.

"Sounds like you might have had a bad breakup," I said, trying to sound more like a sympathetic mom than an investigating detective.

Her eyes flashed. "Gregg was a..." She continued on using a descriptive vocabulary a sailor would have been proud of.

My, my, such a potty mouth on this beautiful young woman. But at least I confirmed her ex-boyfriend's name was Greg. Or was it Gregg?

"Well, it sounds like you might be better off without this Gregg person," I reassured her. "He's not bothering you, is he?"

She shook her head so vehemently one of her long curls almost smacked me in the face. As I stepped back, I barely heard Cherie mutter to herself.

"That SOB will never bother me again."

CHAPTER FORTY

Cherie flushed when she saw my face and realized I overheard her remark.

"Sorry. I shouldn't have said anything about my ex. It was inappropriate."

She was correct, but the more inappropriate the better, from my point of view. Would she next reveal she'd offed her ex? Instead, Cherie morphed into the perfect professional, reviewing some of the basic loan requirements with me.

My eyebrows lifted when I scrolled down to the last line of the agreement and noticed the percentage rate listed in a pale blue font.

"Whoa. Twenty-five percent interest and a five percent loan fee?"

Cherie shrugged. "If you want a lower rate then go to your local bank. We are basically a lender of last resort." She looked at her watch. "I need to head to the casino soon. Do you want to take the paperwork with you and come back when you're ready?"

I said yes and thanked her for her time. I crammed the documents in my overstuffed purse and was about to leave when I thought of an important question.

"Cherie, what happens if someone can't repay their loan on time?"

A voice behind me boomed, "Then we break their kneecaps."

I shrieked and dropped my purse, the contents bouncing off the glass display cases and onto the floor. When I bent over to retrieve the items, I ended up nose to nose with a cigar-chewing, bald-headed man.

"Sorry, miss. A little pawnshop humor." The man stood and handed over my lipstick and business card holder. He gazed down at my skirt, which in the kerfuffle had inched its way up my thighs.

"And we would definitely not break those lovely kneecaps," he said with an expansive smile that made his cigar bobble up and down before it settled against his thick lips. Then he held out his hand. "I'm Louie."

"I appreciate your, um, restraint, Louie. Thanks for the help, Cherie." I dumped the assorted items into my purse and scurried out of the pawnshop/lending operation.

Once outside, I shook myself like a dog, hoping any slimy remnants of my visit would shake off. I hustled to my car and scrubbed my hands with antibacterial soap while I sat in the driver's seat, attempting to assimilate everything I'd learned in the past hour.

Cherie, presumably Gregg Morton's ex-girlfriend, was ticked off big-time with the man. But could or would the young woman have killed him?

Cherie worked at the pawnshop that lent a ton of money to Gino. Did the loan have anything to do with his death? Louie had definitely been acquainted with Gino. Could he have been involved in Gino's demise? Although offing a borrower isn't the best way to receive payment on a loan.

I glanced at my watch. Having driven this far, I probably should go home via the south shore of Lake Tahoe. I could stop in at Timeshare Help and see if that very helpful Marty had anything more to share about Cherie. I could also stop at the Tahoe P.D. and see if Detective Ali Reynolds wanted to share anything more with me on either murder case.

The likelihood of that happening was even less than of me winning the Powerball lottery.

I arrived at the timeshare office at two thirty. I breathed a sigh of relief when I didn't spot Kimberly's SUV in the parking lot. I slipped out of the car, locked the door, then unlocked it again. I leaned over and removed the remains of my lunch—a few stray fries and a diet cola. I didn't want to meet up with any more bears this time.

I walked into the timeshare office and deposited my garbage in their wastebasket. Both Marty and another man seated in the cubicle behind him were on the phone. Marty looked up and smiled at me.

He either remembered me from our previous meeting or he was just plain friendly.

I lowered myself into a chair and riffled through the pages of a Tahoe magazine, my eyes landing on the summertime activities offered at Heavenly Valley. We'd have to bring the kids up here this summer for at least one weekend.

I leaned my head back in the chair and closed my eyes. So many activities. So little time. So many killers...So little...

I jumped when a hand landed on my shoulder, disturbing my murderous reverie.

"Hello there. You're back," said Marty. He looked around. "You didn't bring your friend?"

"Not this time. But she's still interested in buying some timeshares from you." Marty's smile grew even broader, the tiny piece of spinach wedged between his front teeth giving him a gap-toothed grin.

"So what brings you to Tahoe?" he asked.

"You were so persuasive the last time Liz and I were here, I've been thinking of purchasing a week or two myself. But I don't really have the money to do it, even at some of the reduced prices. I wondered what type of financing someone could get on a resale timeshare."

"Of course we can procure a loan for you. Timeshare Help is a full-service company." Marty ushered me to his cubicle. I relaxed into a chair while he gathered some handouts for me.

"This finance company is a subsidiary of Timeshare Help," he said. "Their rates are far better than using a credit card."

"Is it difficult to qualify?" I asked.

He shook his head. "Piece of cake. Do you work? You seem to be up here a lot."

"Yes, my husband and I own a detective agency."

He sat back and stared at me. "Wow. A real live P.I. Cool." He leaned closer and lowered his voice. "Are you working on any cases up here?"

"We have a few high-profile cases we're involved in. For instance, we're trying to collect information on your former associate, Gregg Morton. You mentioned previously his ex, a woman named Cherie, was stalking him. Do you know if she actually threatened to hurt him?"

Marty pursed his lips and pondered for a few seconds. "Cherie's a cute gal, very sharp. But one day Gregg was listening to his voicemails with his phone on hands free while he replied to some emails, and a message from Cherie came on loud and clear. She certainly didn't mince words. In fact, as I recall, she threatened to turn Gregg's"—Marty blushed, then continued—"uh, member into mincemeat."

"Ouch. What about Kimberly, your manager?" I asked. "I think you said she also dated Gregg."

Marty shrugged. "Kimberly comes on kind of strong, but I can't see her harming Gregg just 'cause he didn't want to go out with her anymore. Despite his flaws, Gregg was a great salesman. Made a ton of money for the firm. Kimberly wouldn't do anything to screw up her bottom line."

I was about to ask a question regarding Gregg's sales activities when the door to the timeshare office banged open.

Darn. Just the person I wanted to avoid.

CHAPTER FORTY-ONE

Kimberly strode into the office, fingers furiously texting away, completely ignoring Marty and me.

Whew. I had way more questions for Marty and I knew the minute Kimberly saw us together, she'd throw me out the door. Unfortunately, Marty didn't understand the complexities of investigating a murder because he called out to her.

"Hey, Kimberly. This woman's investigating Gregg's murder. You got any ideas who bumped him off?"

Kimberly whirled around, sending me her customary glare. "Are you here again?"

"She's here officially," Marty explained. "Trying to figure out who killed Gregg."

"Seriously?" she asked. I could see her eyebrows attempting to create a frown, but her botoxed brow refused to cooperate. "Oh, you're trying to get your granny off the hook. Good luck with that."

"Please join us," I said, patting the chair next to me. "I'm sure you have some ideas who did it. Besides my grandmother."

A wave of Chanel perfume filled the cubicle as Kimberly plopped her annoyingly tight butt onto the other visitor chair. "Why should we help you?" she snapped at me.

"Why shouldn't you?"

"Fine. Whatever. Gregg was an excellent salesperson. Quite the charmer," she said drily. "He could flirt with the best of them. As for little old ladies, and even men, he was persuasive enough to talk them into buying shares of the Brooklyn Bridge if we had any to sell." She slumped against the back of the chair. "We will miss him," she said softly.

"Is there anyone who disliked him besides Cherie, his ex?"

"That psycho bitch?" Kimberly's high-pitched voice rose even higher. "I wouldn't put it past her. Hers was the first name I gave to the detectives."

"Anyone else?"

"Gregg liked the party scene, the white stuff, you know." I shook my head in confusion, so she pointed to her nostrils. "Cocaine."

"So maybe he had a beef with a supplier?" I ventured.

"Possibly." She cocked her head to the left in the direction of Palomino's restaurant. "You can check out our local pizza king. Rumor has it he dabbles in drugs."

"How about that couple who came into the office a few times," Marty suggested. "The husband got real angry with Gregg. Said he sold him a bill of goods. Do you know what that was about, Kimberly?"

"Oh, yeah, I forgot about them. Every now and then we get a few dissatisfied customers who don't read the fine print and don't feel like they got a good deal. It seems to me this couple purchased a week from us at one of the Tahoe resorts, then a month later they found a similar unit for sale for five thousand less. The husband was royally ticked off."

"Can your company do anything to make it up to them?" I asked. "Give them a partial refund?"

"It's just plain luck. Some sellers are more desperate than others. You never know what will come on the market next. Kind of like the regular housing market. Constantly in flux."

"Any chance I could get their names so I could talk to them?"

Kimberly sighed. "I suppose I can track down their names. If I get the information for you, will you leave us alone?"

Silly woman. She had no idea what a pain in the butt I could be. But I merely nodded. She got up and walked down the hall to her office.

"You're a really good detective," Marty said admiringly. He pointed to a family photo of him and four women, three of whom I assumed were his daughters. "My middle daughter loves reading those Nancy Drew books."

"You have a lovely family. My oldest is going off to college this fall. I'm going to miss her."

"It's tough sending them off to college. My daughter just finished her first year at UNLV." He picked up the picture again. "They grow up way, way too fast."

I nodded in agreement, then stood to leave. While I was anxious to find out the name of their disgruntled customers, I also wanted to get Kimberly alone. I walked down the hall to her office and sat in one of the visitor chairs.

"I'm still looking," she said, pointing toward the door. "Wait in the lobby, please."

I ignored her. "As Marty mentioned, I'm a detective. We're working on another murder that occurred up here recently. A man by the name of Gino Romano. Were you acquainted with him?"

"Of course not. I don't hang out with murder victims." When I raised my brows, she replied. "Okay, one exception was Gregg. But I don't know this Gino guy."

"Are you sure?" I asked before I showed her a photo on my phone.

CHAPTER FORTY-TWO

Kimberly blanched. "Where, I mean, when did you take that photo? Have you been following me?"

"No. Should I?"

She recovered quickly. "Of course not. The only reason I didn't admit I knew Gino was that I...I met him through an online dating site." She glared at me. "Are you happy now?"

I couldn't understand why these women were so reluctant to admit they'd used an online site. First, Adriana was hesitant to own up to it. And now Kimberly.

"Lots of women meet their future husbands through dating sites," I commented.

"Yes, but look at me." Kimberly stood, displaying all of her wares for my inspection. Like she was auditioning for *The Bachelor*.

"So what's the deal with Gino?" I asked. "Did you two date for a while?"

"Barely. Our first meetup was at Harrah's. We arranged a day when he'd be up here on business. We had a couple more dates before he told me he'd met the woman of his dreams."

"Really?"

She rolled her eyes. "Really. So cliché, although I think Gino meant it."

"Why did you meet with him the night before he was killed?"

"Well, even though I wasn't"—she made air quotes—"his 'dream woman,' I admired his financial acumen. So I invested some of my savings with him. It was merely a brief client meeting."

I stared at her. How consummate of a liar was this woman? She worked at a timeshare resale company so she must have excellent fibbing skills when it came to potential customers. But her words rang true. I also sensed an underlying sadness when she admitted Gino met someone he preferred over her.

"Didn't Marty say you also dated Gregg?" I asked.

"Yes. Briefly. He charmed me into a fling a few months back, then broke it off suddenly. I was hurt for about two seconds, then relieved. It was time to find someone who was interested in a commitment, not just casual sex."

She mumbled under her breath. "Really great sex."

"You realize you've dated both Tahoe murder victims."

"Merely a coincidence. I was at a meeting with Marty the morning of Gregg's death. In fact, Gregg was supposed to join us but he never showed up. Then we found out why." She picked up a pencil and fiddled with it.

"What about your relationship with Gino. Is the Tahoe P.D. aware you dated him?"

"How would I know?"

"You didn't bother to inform them?"

"Look, Nancy Drew, no one asked me about Gino and I saw no reason to call them up and inform them I was a client of his. Along with hundreds of other clients. If they bother to search his client database, they'll run across my name eventually. Besides, the news said he was killed by some guy who jumped off the gondola before anyone could catch him. So why are you wasting my time?" She frowned and her knuckles grew white as she transferred her irritation to the pencil she was holding. The soft-leaded Number 2 favorite couldn't take the strain. It broke in half, and the sharp point flew across her desk, bounced off my sternum and disappeared into my cleavage.

Kimberly snickered while I shifted in my seat, hoping the piece of lead would eventually drop to the floor.

No such luck. I asked for the location of their restroom and Kimberly pointed to the rear of the office.

Inside the restroom, I fiddled around with my bra and the tiny intruder finally bounced onto the floor. I washed my hands while wondering if I could get any more out of Kimberly today. My phone rang as I dried them.

"Mommy, are you ever coming home?" whined Ben. "Grandmother won't let us watch cartoons. She's making us watch the Discovery Channel." Ben made a gagging sound. Heaven forbid the television be used as an educational tool.

"I'm almost finished up here. Behave for your grandmother. Now let me speak to her, please."

"Are you on your way here?" Mother asked. "I'm supposed to meet clients in an hour to list their house."

I peeked at my watch. Ouch. Interrogating potential suspects took more time than I'd anticipated.

"I'm on my way but I won't make it back in time. Have you checked in with Tom or your husband? Maybe they've wrapped up their interviews for the day."

She sighed. "Are you sure you want to continue this new career? The hours are so erratic. And you don't seem to be accomplishing anything."

"That's not true." My voice rose as I attempted to justify today's efforts. "These things take time. Aren't you worried they might lock up Gran for good?"

"Don't be silly. Obviously your grandmother didn't kill anyone..." A loud crash interrupted our conversation. "That dog. Hurry home."

Poor Scout. I almost felt sorry for him. For a change, I wasn't the klutziest member of our family.

I walked out of the restroom and knocked on Kimberly's closed door.

She looked up in annoyance. "You're *still* here? We are trying to run a business, you know."

"Of course. I'll get out of your hair as soon as you get me the names of those angry clients. I *so* appreciate your help."

Five minutes later, with the name and address of a couple named Lankershim, I trotted down the hallway and headed for my car. I would have loved to stick around just to annoy Kimberly some more. But Mother's call made me think another crime had been committed at the house.

By a klutzy and shaggy felon.

CHAPTER FORTY-THREE

Once in my car, I debated whether I really wanted to drive home to the chaos represented by my domestic life. I glanced at Palomino's Pizza. It was still early, not quite the dinner rush hour, but there was a steady amount of traffic in and out of the restaurant. I would regret having to make a separate trip up to Tahoe just to interview the "pizza king" Kimberly thought sold drugs to Gregg.

Plus, I could use a soda for the long drive home. I slipped out of my car and walked over to the pizza parlor. Once inside, my eyes adjusted to the cool darkness. The tables were half full so maybe the Tahoe crowd preferred early bird dining. Or maybe they offered a happy hour pizza special.

Two men in their twenties walked out of a back room, chuckling with one another. A few seconds later, Bruno Palomino emerged, a satisfied smile on his face. He walked around the counter, headed to the cash register and asked me what I wanted to order.

Shoot. I was so unprepared. Should I order a veggie pizza or something more exotic?

Like cocaine or ecstasy.

I leaned in and whispered that I had a special request. He moved closer as I murmured in his ear.

"I want a dozen Maggies," I said and then winked at him. Surely he'd know what I meant.

"What are you talking about?" he asked, looking confused.

Hmmm. I needed to pay more attention to my TV crime shows. Maybe those pills weren't called Maggies after all.

"I mean Margies." This time I winked twice, which did nothing to wipe the confused expression off his face. Then it clicked.

"Are you saying you want to buy some Mollys?" he asked before looking me up and down.

"Mollys? Are you sure?" I asked.

He grabbed a dish towel and began cleaning the counter. "Look, lady, we sell pizza and beer. That's all we offer." He moved closer, his handsome face darkening. "Now please leave before…"

I didn't need the "pizza king" to elaborate any further. I fled out the door, jumped into my car and was headed home on Highway 50 before you could say "drug baron."

I put the pedal to whatever metal my four-cylinder Subaru could manage and reflected on the day's activities as I maneuvered the car around the curves. The SUV wasn't as agile as Liz's convertible, but the mileage of the vehicle more than made up for its lack of vroom vroom.

My cell rang and I was tempted to ignore it, but I knew Adriana would just keep calling so I might as well find out what she wanted.

"Where are you?" she asked. "Are you working on our case?"

"Of course. You're my top priority," I replied, muttering "mostly" under my breath.

"What did you say?"

"Nothing important. I interviewed some of the staff at the pawnshop where Gino borrowed money."

"And?"

And I learned pawnshops make a pile of money on the backs of their customers, the people who can least afford to pay their usurious rates and fees. But what did that have to do with Gino's untimely death?

"And it was helpful. Now why are you calling? Aren't you at work?"

"I left the office early today. I'm having a tough time getting anything done at work. I talked to that homicide detective who's handling his case, but she wouldn't share anything with me."

"Did she say she wouldn't or she couldn't?" I asked, speculating that Adriana must have spoken with Ali.

"What's the difference? I feel so"—she paused for a few seconds—"helpless. Like I should be doing something. I don't even know who they'll release his body to or when they'll do it."

"Didn't Gino have any family?"

"He said his parents were gone and he didn't have any siblings. But maybe he lied about that, too. So I don't know if I should be planning a memorial service or...." Her voice broke and I waited for her soft crying to let up before replying.

"What would you like me to do next?" I asked. She thought for a few seconds.

"I came up with a great idea," she replied, sounding perkier.

"Okay..." I said, sounding way less perky than my client. Having worked for Adriana for almost six months, I knew she and I didn't always agree on what she considered a "great idea."

"I think we should go back to that dive bar together. You know, the one where you saw Gino and those biker guys meet and exchange that parcel. Between you and me, I'm sure we can coax them into sharing information with us. What do you think?"

I opened my mouth to tell her exactly what I thought of her lame-brained idea but instead slammed on my brakes with all the force of my size nine shoes. My head whiplashed toward the steering wheel and back to the seat as the Subaru narrowly missed colliding with an RV that had stopped in front of me. As I caught a panic-stricken breath, I watched a young deer spring across the highway and leap down the slope toward the river.

"Laurel, are you there?" Adriana shouted. "Isn't that an awesome idea?"

With my heart pounding from my near miss with a vehicle three times my size, all I could reply was "sure."

CHAPTER FORTY-FOUR

After my near-collision, I shut off my phone. I didn't need any more distractions on the way home. Especially distractions like Adriana, who was quickly turning into the client from hell.

I breathed a sigh of relief as I pulled into the driveway. I'd survived an almost car crash, and whatever Scout had broken couldn't be too disastrous. It's not like we owned anything valuable.

Then I walked into the house and discovered Scout had chased after Pumpkin. While the cat had found a safe location on top of our buffet, Scout's tail had taken down an entire wine rack, which in and of itself was no big deal. It was the eight destroyed bottles that comprised this personal crisis.

It takes a lot to drive me to tears, but the loss of my favorite chardonnay almost did it. Amazingly enough, Scout had scooted away from the wreckage before the bottles shattered, so we didn't have to remove any pieces of glass from his oversized paws. Mother, the Queen of Clean, had disposed of the entire mess by the time I arrived home.

"Scout is kind of a klutz, huh, Mom," Ben said as we stared at the dozing dog sprawled on the carpet. Although I had a feeling he was just pretending to sleep. The cat maintained her perch, calmly licking one paw.

"Yeah, I guess he really does fit into our family," I said in agreement. Scout lifted his head and lowered one eye.

Did that dog just wink at me?

I went upstairs to change into something more comfortable. Like my bed. I flopped on the bedspread and tallied up everything I'd learned in my day of detecting.

Much as I personally disliked Kimberly, she had an alibi for both Gregg's and Gino's murder, so that ruled her out.

Cherie, however, proved she had a temper and she did not take Gregg's breakup with her lightly.

Then there was Bruno Palomino. I might need to spruce up my drug buying skills for future investigations. Surliness didn't point to him as a killer, but I wouldn't mind finding a way for someone to arrest him for selling narcotics, assuming he sold them to buyers far more savvy than me. And he worked only a few feet away from the timeshare office.

I now possessed the name and address of the couple unhappy with their timeshare purchase. Since they lived in Placerville I should probably chat with them. Even if they seemed unlikely candidates for murder.

But when you think about it, how many murderers, other than a psychopath or two, actually fit the profile of a killer?

On that happy note, I fell into a deep slumber and woke up the following morning...

Just kidding. Soccer mom/private investigators do not have the luxury of napping. I quickly changed into doggie-proof clothes in the form of a T-shirt and shorts and trotted down the stairs to prepare dinner.

Much to my surprise, dinner had been delivered by none other than my grandmother, whom I found heating up a baked chicken casserole in my oven. I looked out the window but didn't see her red Mustang in the driveway.

"I don't see your car," I said as I grabbed a stack of plates from a cabinet.

"My chauffeur brought me," she replied with a giggle before pointing to her friend Herb, who was comfortably ensconced in Tom's recliner watching the local news.

"Hiya, Herb," I shouted, hoping to make myself heard over the volume that threatened to burst my eardrums.

"He don't hear so well," Gran said. "And the old coot refuses to wear a hearing aid."

Great. The "old coot" didn't hear well or see well. Some chauffeur.

"What's with the surprise dinner?" I asked.

"Your mother was complaining that your detectin' has been interferin' with your domestic duties. And since I'm your number one client, I figured this was the least I could do for my favorite granddaughter." She winked at me. "And favorite detective."

There's nothing I love better than a home-cooked dinner, especially when I'm not the person cooking it. The door from the garage banged shut, and a few seconds later Tom walked into the kitchen.

He sniffed. "Something sure smells good." He turned to me with a questioning look. "Did you make it?"

Hmm. Did my husband just insinuate I'm not a culinary expert, or was he merely an excellent detective?

I chose to take the high road and merely replied. "Gran's treat since I've been working *all day* on my caseload."

Tom wrapped his arms around me. "I can't wait to hear your update. You'll be pleased to know I'll have more free time to help you in a day or two. Let me wash up. It looks like dinner is about to be served."

Fifteen minutes later, with our stomachs stuffed with Gran's excellent casserole, I updated everyone on my discoveries. Gran and Tom listened intently, but I had a feeling Herb was more anxious to get back to *Wheel of Fortune* than learn anything about the timeshare victim and my slate of suspects.

"So this woman Gregg dumped still harbored a lot of anger toward him?" Tom summed up after I shared my conversation with Cherie.

"Very much so."

"How about the witch who runs the timeshare office?" asked Gran. "I'd love to nail her."

I shook my head. "Nope. She's got an alibi. She was with Marty, one of the other salespeople in the office, at the time of the murder. I made a sad attempt to get something out of Bruno Palomino, but it was kind of a bust. I guess I didn't do a very good job of portraying myself as a soccer mom needing a fix."

Tom shook his head. "No surprise there. You let me handle that angle."

Last year Tom spent six months undercover for a narcotics task force. He could far easier assume the persona of an addict than this naïve mom.

"Didn't you say there was a couple of folks real annoyed with Gregg and the timeshare company?" asked Gran.

"Yep. And Kimberly, after much prodding, shared their names with me. Paul and Sally Lankershim live in Placerville. Since I'm local I hope I can cajole them into giving me some information."

"I don't know them personally, but I'm pretty sure Iris does. Their names sure sound familiar. Let me see if she can set up something so Herb and I can chat with them," Gran said before glancing in Herb's direction. "He needs an activity other than watching TV all the time. How 'bout we help you out with your questioning?"

"Sure. They might be more likely to talk to you two than to me," I said.

What could possibly go wrong?

CHAPTER FORTY-FIVE

The next day started out exactly as planned. Which should have been a surefire warning that it wouldn't end that way.

With some referral help from Iris, Gran made an appointment with the Lankershims for that evening to discuss their mutual timeshare woes. She mentioned she and Herb, who would play the part of her husband, had some issues with Timeshare Help. They'd love advice from the elderly couple. The Lankershims invited Gran and Herb over for early cocktails and she instantly agreed. Gran was not one to turn down a free gin and tonic.

My assignment was simple. Drop Gran and Herb at the Lankershims' house and park a discreet distance away should they need assistance. In case the pair turned out to be killers. None of us thought it was a high probability, but a good detective is always prepared. My purse included my hot pink stun gun, pepper spray and hair spray.

Enough defensive equipment to take out an entire retirement home.

As I sat in the car pondering my next move in this investigation, my cell rang. Adriana.

"What?" I said breathlessly after digging the phone out of my purse and wondering why it was always so difficult to find.

"What time do you want to meet?" she asked.

"Meet?" What was she talking about?

"Remember, we decided to hit that sleazy bar in Sacramento tonight?"

Uh oh. I remembered her suggesting we visit the bar. What I didn't recall was actually agreeing to the plan.

"I'm not sure that's a good idea. That one biker guy might recognize me."

"Do they know you're a detective?"

I snorted. "Hardly."

"Then what's the problem?"

"Well, for one, I'm staking out a house for another client right now. I might not be free for a while. You're not my only client, you know." I looked at my watch. Five thirty. Gran and Herb had entered the house thirty minutes earlier. Since no cries for help had come from the house I assumed they were enjoying happy hour with the timeshare owners.

"C'mon, Laurel. This is really important to me. Can't someone else from your office relieve you?"

I sighed. "Tell you what. I should be done here in a couple of hours. We don't want to hit the bar too early anyway. Why don't we meet at the El Dorado Hills CVS drugstore at nine? Does that work?"

She accepted, although before signing off she warned me, "Dress hot, if that's even possible."

It was definitely time to raise those hourly rates.

By seven o'clock, I was hot, but only because the early evening temperature had soared well past ninety degrees. Still no peep from the senior detectives. I'd tried Gran's cell twice but each time it went directly to voicemail. I hated to interrupt them, but I needed to drop them off before going home and changing into something "hotter."

I moved my car from my current parking space four houses down and across the street from the Lankershims' home and pulled into their driveway. I waited a couple of minutes, thinking someone should have heard me drive up.

No such luck. I climbed out of the car and walked up their sidewalk, noticing their manicured lawn and perfectly pruned hedges. I wondered if Paul Lankershim demanded perfection from his lawn service or if he did the work himself.

I knocked on the door, then waited. And waited. Next I pounded on the door, thinking the elderly couple might have hearing issues like Gran and Herb.

I reached for the doorknob, which easily turned, and stepped into a small tile foyer. No sign of anyone. Where the heck could the four seniors have disappeared to? My gaze turned to the flight of stairs to the right of the entry. Should I go upstairs and look for them?

Then a scream pierced the air like an arrow through my heart.

CHAPTER FORTY-SIX

Since the scream sounded like it had come from behind the house, I rushed down the hallway into the kitchen in the rear of the home. No signs of blood or dead bodies.

But there weren't any live bodies either. I slid open the screen door and stepped onto a large concrete patio, where I found the four seniors. Herb and Sally Lankershim looked like they were attempting to contain their laughter but not entirely succeeding. Gran, who for some odd reason was holding a small fire extinguisher in her right hand, wore an abashed look.

Paul Lankershim, covered from his head to his wet Nikes in white foamy liquid, did not look pleased. In fact, he looked ready to murder my grandmother.

I walked toward the foursome. "What's going on?" I asked Gran.

"Paul here got the BBQ going, but the flames were so high they singed his eyebrows." She pointed to the handheld extinguisher. "I grabbed this and probably saved his life."

"You didn't save my life," Paul growled at Gran before shouting at his wife. "Get me a towel. Now."

Geesh. He was a crabby old buzzard.

"Hey, I meant well," Gran said. "Sorry about the mess."

Paul snatched the extinguisher out of Gran's hands. "Get out of my house," he yelled.

Herb shuffled toward the screen door with Gran not far behind. Sally whispered to Gran before wiggling her fingers goodbye. I followed the seniors through the house and out to my car, leaving my questions until we departed.

Once they were loaded in, I backed out of the driveway and headed for home.

"So how was your evening before the, um, incident?" I asked.

"Swell, until Ginny got carried away," replied Herb. He patted his stomach. "We coulda got a free dinner with them folks."

"I thought the man was on fire. You should be grateful I'm so quick-witted. We might have all burned up." From my rearview mirror I could see Gran fold her arms and move a few inches away from Herb.

"Well, I'm certainly grateful nothing happened to either of you," I said. "Paul Lankershim seems to have quite a temper. Did you learn anything about his timeshare dealings before the BBQ incident?"

Gran leaned forward. "His situation was different from Iris. He bought a timeshare that was a resale from Timeshare Help. Was all excited about it until a friend of his said he purchased a week in the same place for half what they paid."

"From what I've learned, those resale prices are all over the board," I replied. "It depends how desperate the seller is."

Gran nodded. "Yep. That's what Gregg Morton told Paul. Over and over, I guess. Sally confided Paul just couldn't let it go. They've been up to the timeshare office several times, but couldn't get anything resolved. At least to Paul's satisfaction. Guess they offered him a two-for-one dinner coupon for his troubles."

I smiled. Not exactly the same value. Unless it was for dinner at the Eiffel Tower, airline tickets included.

"Can you picture Paul as a murderer, though?" I asked her.

"He looked ready to clobber Ginny with his fire extinguisher," Herb chipped in. "Course that wouldn't be the first time someone wanted to clobber her. Remember when you accused George of cheating at poker at the senior center?"

"Man can't tell a heart from a diamond," she grumbled. "I guess I can get a tad overwrought sometimes."

I cleared my throat. "Back to Paul Lankershim. Do you think he killed Gregg?"

Gran rubbed her chin. "What's that saying your husband keeps bringing up?"

"My husband is never at a loss for words. I'm not sure what you're referring to."

She snapped her fingers. "Anyone can turn into a killer at any time or place."

CHAPTER FORTY-SEVEN

Based on Gran's comments, it didn't seem like I could rule out Paul Lankershim as a suspect in Gregg's killing. I dropped off the seniors at Gran's house and left them to their own devices.

I shuddered, wondering what the duo would get up to next. Although it was difficult to visualize them cavorting in bed, it might be the safest place for them to stay out of trouble.

I popped into our house to change my outfit into something more enticing than shorts and a T-shirt. Kids' laughter drifted in from the open screen door in the family room. I smiled as Scout attempted to catch the Frisbee Ben threw in his direction. My son's throw was a few feet short and Scout almost landed the catch before tripping over his own four feet and crashing into Kristy.

Watching our blended family enjoy an evening together made my heart pulse with joy. I also realized I might be able to change clothes and sneak out of the house before anyone even knew I'd come and gone.

I couldn't remember if I'd told Tom about Adriana's idea, and I wasn't certain he would approve of another sortie to The Gray Goose. I could be in and out of my closet in no time.

Not really.

After shoving inappropriate clothes right and left, it appeared my wardrobe needed some serious updating. Our honeymoon cruise a few months earlier had provided me with an excuse to purchase a cocktail dress and a few sundresses, but none of them qualified as "hot" enough to achieve our mission tonight.

Although, as I recalled, they were definitely hot enough to whet Tom's appetite on the cruise. Far more important in the grand scheme of things.

The odds were the biker dudes, if they even appeared tonight, would be far more interested in Adriana than me. I could be her sidekick. Her wing woman, so to speak. Whatever the heck that meant.

I threw on a pair of black capris and a tight-fitting raspberry top, dangling earrings and my one and only pair of stilettos. I evaluated my wig collection, courtesy of Gran, trying to determine the best choice for tonight.

The platinum pixie cut won this time. By the time I had my outfit on and my wig arranged, I almost didn't recognize myself in the mirror.

Boy, was I rocking the platinum do.

Approaching footsteps on our creaky stairs caused me to pause. Jenna? Tom?

"Who the...?" Tom entered our bedroom and stopped, his dark eyes confused and wary. Then he walked closer to me. "If I hadn't met you in our bedroom, I would never have recognized you. Nice disguise."

Then he frowned. "That begs the question. Why *are you* in a disguise? At least I hope there's a reason behind your new look."

"Night out with the girls?" I quipped.

He folded his arms, the firm biceps under his polo shirt causing me to drool and question my sanity. Why was I going out again?

Oh, yeah. "One girl. Adriana." When he frowned again, I explained, "It's a billable night out on the town. It doesn't get any better than that."

He moved forward, his large palms pressing lightly on my shoulders. "It better not, I mean—"

"All in a day's"—I looked at my watch—"or rather, night's work."

"Why would you ask our client to assist you?" he asked.

"Have you met our client?" I replied.

He grimaced. "Yeah, I get it. I won't bother wasting my time or yours by telling you to stay out of trouble. Just make sure your cell phone is charged and your pepper spray is in your purse. Got it?"

I saluted him. "Aye, aye, sir."

Then I grinned and left him with the kind of kiss that makes my man go wild.

CHAPTER FORTY-EIGHT

I texted Adriana I was on my way, then slid into my SUV. Although I'd wanted to say goodbye to my kids, I didn't think they needed to see me in my current disguise. Welcome to the seedier side of sleuthing.

I pulled out of the garage and ten minutes later turned onto the freeway. The empty gas light pinged, reminding me to fill up. Investigating these cases was taking a toll on my fuel consumption as well. Stopping for gas made me a few minutes late for my assignation with Adriana.

She took it well. Not.

"Laurel, need I remind you I am paying for your somewhat inept services by the hour," she chastised me as she slid into the passenger seat of my car. "Make sure you don't bill me for any time prior to your official arrival time of"—she looked at her elegant watch—"nine fourteen."

"I wouldn't think of it. I'll even give you the first hour free," I replied, shifting into reverse. "Deal?"

She sniffed an assent before flipping down the visor. She frowned at her image, reached inside a small clutch, then proceeded to apply more mascara to her overly full lashes. As she leaned forward, her mini slid up her thighs and her V-neck top slipped down, revealing a red lace bra underneath the plunging neckline.

I had to hand it to my client. She definitely knew how to look hot.

174

She flicked the visor back up and shifted her gaze over to me. I waited for an onslaught of criticism on my disguise.

"Not bad," she said. "I doubt you'll attract any men tonight, but it will be good to have you as backup. Especially since this is my first investigation."

I felt like stomping my foot at her comment, but that would entail removing my shoe off the gas pedal and since we were hemmed in by cars racing seventy-plus miles per hour on the freeway, I chose to take the high road and ignore her.

Once I pulled off the highway and onto Folsom Boulevard, Adriana began fidgeting with her purse, opening and shutting it.

"Something wrong?" I asked, although I kept my eyes on the road, not wanting to miss the turn into the strip mall.

"I guess I'm a little nervous," she admitted in a low voice. "This seemed like such a lark when I first suggested it, but in reality..." Her voice tapered off but I sensed her dark eyes boring into me.

"We'll be fine," I reassured her, although I kind of wished I had someone along to reassure me. Now why didn't I ask my hubby to join us?

Oh yeah. Despite Tom's early years doing undercover work, these biker dudes could most likely suss out he was a cop in seconds. And I really wanted to find out what kind of deal they had going on with Gino.

Although half of the strip mall stores remained dark, the flashing multicolored lights of The Gray Goose beckoned me into the small shopping center. I parked the SUV under a bright streetlight for safety reasons. Several expensive-looking motorcycles lined up with perfect precision in the parking slots near the front of the bar.

Adriana took her time climbing out of the car. Although her body looked hot, the expression on her face exhibited sheer terror.

I walked over to her and gave her a quick squeeze.

"There won't be a woman in the place who can compete with you," I said. "You got this."

"True," Adriana said, sliding her hands down her skirt, smoothing it down. She threw her shoulders back, thrust out her chest and said, "I'm ready."

"Trust me. You'll have the bikers eating out of your hand," I added. As I followed her across the bumpy pavement, wobbling on my four-inch stilettos, I just prayed this outing didn't come back and bite us on our butts.

CHAPTER FORTY-NINE

Adriana entered The Gray Goose first, as befitted the queen bee of our dynamic duo. Raucous chatter died down to muted whispers as she sashayed toward the bar. She plunked her posterior on an empty stool next to a burly guy dressed in leather, the silver studs in his leather jacket glittering under the bar's lights.

Jake! The biker who'd handed over the mysterious package to Gino last time. Just the man we wanted to discreetly question.

I slunk over to the empty seat next to Adriana and nudged her. When she turned, I cocked my head toward Jake and mouthed his name. She nodded and began chatting with him. Or flirting with him. She was a woman of many skills. I plopped onto the stool next to hers, but lost one stiletto in the process. When I bent over to retrieve it I bumped heads with the man sitting next to me.

I shot back up, which did nothing for the pain in my forehead. "Ouch. Why did you do that?"

"Sorry," he said with a guilty look as he handed my shoe to me. "I was only trying to help." He looked out of place in the bar, more like an absentminded professor than the usual Gray Goose patron.

"Thanks," I mumbled while attempting to shoe the narrow stiletto back on my noncompliant foot.

"Can I buy you a drink?" the man asked. "You know, to help ease the pain."

I couldn't think of a reason why not, so I accepted his offer. Then I remembered the hideous house wine from my last visit to the bar. I ordered a margarita, figuring there was no way the bartender could ruin tequila combined with lime juice.

I underestimated the bartender's skillset. Perhaps he was out of lime juice. And tequila, since my drink tasted more like Draino than a margarita.

I tried to pay for my "drink" but the man next to me insisted. He introduced himself as Derek. "I haven't seen you here before," he said to the back of my head since I was intent on eavesdropping on Adriana's conversation.

I swiveled in his direction. "Nope, not a regular," I said before whipping my head back in time to catch Adriana reaching into her purse. She pulled out her phone and handed it to the biker next to her.

What the heck?

"That's my boyfriend." Adriana pointed to Gino's smiling photo on the screen. "He passed away and I want to make sure his friends come to his memorial service." As a tear formed, she dabbed at her eyes with a cocktail napkin. "Did you know him? Gino said this was one of his favorite bars."

I almost choked on the sip of my drink, but I had to hand it to Adriana. She wasn't a half-bad actress. Or was she acting? Maybe she did want to include Jake and company on her guest list.

Perhaps her intent was to gather all of the suspects together at Gino's celebration of life. Kind of like a Hercule Poirot whodunit. Except we knew who did it. That big lug who ran away and remained unidentified. What we didn't know was why.

I shifted closer trying to hear Jake's response amid the loud chatter throughout the room. Derek moved closer to me, practically breathing down my neck. I would have whacked him with my purse except I didn't want to miss anything Jake and the pal who'd just joined him said to Adriana.

Jake grabbed the phone and showed it to his companion. Then he shook his head and said, "Never seen the dude."

Adriana blurted out, "That's not true. My friend saw you and him together." She turned to me. "Jake gave Gino a package out in the parking lot last week. Right?"

"Uh," I said, my brain working double time for an explanation that wasn't coming. I squinted at the two men. "Now that I think about it, I don't think you were the guys Gino was with that night."

"But, Laurel," Adriana insisted as I tried to quell her questions by signaling with my frantically blinking eyes. "You told me it was a guy named Jake." She placed her palm on Jake's arm and batted her eyelashes. "You referred to him as a stud of a guy."

"Must be another stud goes by the name of Jake," offered our suspect's friend. "I never met your boyfriend neither." The man stood and stretched, his grimy white T-shirt exposing a hairy belly. He gestured to Jake. "Time for us boys to hit the road."

Still trying to erase the image of the guy's matted gray chest while figuring out a way to silence my partner, I intervened with what would prove to be one of my less astute remarks. "Sorry to see you fellas leave. I barely got to chat with you all."

Ugh. Even my stomach groaned at my insipid line.

Insipid or not, it provoked a response.

Jake walked over to me and placed his paw on my shoulder. "You gals want to take a ride on our bikes? We promise you a good time."

Adriana slid off her stool. "That sounds like fun. What do you say, Laurel?"

I grabbed her hand. "I say we hit the ladies' room first. Be right back, fellas."

I practically dragged her to the restrooms in the rear of the bar. Once we were out of earshot, I asked her, "What is the matter with you? Are you deranged? Those men could be killers and you want to ride off into the sunset with them?"

"It's long past sunset," she corrected me. "Closer to midnight. I thought they would be more willing to discuss Gino if we bonded with them during a short ride."

"For all you know, a ride with them could be our last ride. Forever." I pushed on the heavy wood door marked "Gals" and ushered her inside the dimly lit restroom, the cracked vinyl floor littered with toilet paper and tissue.

"Yuck." Adriana flicked her eyes around the room. "This private eye stuff isn't so glamourous, is it?"

"Nope." I entered one of the two stalls and closed the door behind me.

"Ew, you're actually going to go in there?"

"I've been in worse," I replied. My kids often referred to me as Pit Stop Mama because I could describe in great detail the majority of the fast food restrooms stretching from the Bay Area to Tahoe.

Once I took care of business and washed my hands, I informed Adriana it should be safe to head back to the bar.

"But what if the guys are gone? We still don't have any answers," she whined.

"I'll get the rest of my team on it. I'm sure we'll figure out something. I am really ready to call it a night."

I opened the door to a pitch-black hallway. The forty-watt lightbulb must have burned out. As my eyes adjusted to the darkness, I sensed a hulking presence behind me. My neck prickled and I started to turn around.

The last thing I heard was Adriana screaming my name.

CHAPTER FIFTY

The pungent scent of days-old banana peels, rotten meat and a score of other disgusting smells woke me up from a brief and involuntary slumber. I shifted in the darkness trying to determine where I was. When I lifted my arm, a stream of jugs, heavy plastic bags, and a few glass bottles moved along with me.

A faint voice called out. "Laurel?" squeaked Adriana. "Are you in here?"

"Yes, I am. But where are we?"

A screeching sound assaulted my ears, but it was accompanied by the sudden vision of a moonlit sky up above us. I flailed around trying to stand up, but it seemed impossible among the detritus that surrounded both Adriana and me.

A slightly familiar face appeared above us.

"Thank goodness you're okay," said the man who'd been sitting next to me at The Gray Goose. The nerdy guy who bought me my drink. What was his name? Oh yeah, Derek.

"We're not okay," shrieked my client. "We're in a stinking dumpster."

I threw my elbow out to steady myself and ended up dislodging a bevy of bottles and cans.

"Stop that," Adriana yelled.

My eyes locked with our rescuer's, and I couldn't help giggling.

"Seriously, Laurel. How can you laugh at a time like this? And you," she said imperiously, pointing a finger covered in green gunk at our savior, "get us out of here."

"Be back in a sec," he said. "Don't go anywhere."

Everyone thinks they're a comedian.

"Hey," Adriana shouted but Derek had disappeared. I breathed easier when he returned a few minutes later, a short ladder in one arm, with the bartender close on his heels.

"What the hell are you gals doing in there?" he bawled. "Is this some kind of prank?"

Funny he should mention that. Who exactly was responsible for throwing Adriana and me in the dumpster? I presumed it was Jake and his pal. But why?

A prank? I thought not. A warning? Far more likely.

With the help of both men, Adriana and I climbed out of the dumpster. Once we were safely standing on the asphalt, I attempted to hug Derek, but he held back, evidently not a fan of our fragrant *l'eau de garbage*. The bartender remained a few feet from him and upwind from Adriana and me.

"Are Jake and his friend still in the bar?" I asked the bartender.

He shook his head, his bald pate glowing under the moonlight. "No, I saw them follow you gals but then got busy at the bar and didn't notice them after that. Not long after I heard their bikes roar out of the parking lot. Did you do something to upset them? That Jake has a bit of a temper on him."

I'd say. Although I doubted he'd thrown us in the dumpster due to a fit of anger.

"I'm sure you ladies would like to clean up," Derek said. "I found two purses on the floor by the rear door. They may be yours."

"Thank goodness," said Adriana. She attempted to run her fingers through her formerly glossy hair and shrieked when they connected with an eggshell.

"I am never going to recover from this," she said, spinning around on her stilettos, which had somehow managed to cling to her feet. Mine were buried deep in the dumpster, and as far as I was concerned, they could remain there.

"How could you let me do something so dangerous?" she asked as I struggled to keep up with her. My bare feet chafed from pounding the cracked pavement and I was worried I might step on something worse—like a nail or used needle.

"Don't you remember this was all your idea? I tried to talk you out of it."

"You should have tried harder." She mumbled something under her breath about getting tetanus and hepatitis shots, then flounced off, heading for the back door of The Gray Goose. The bartender followed behind her. Even as disgusting and angry as Adriana was, she still managed to put a little wiggle in her waggle.

I shook my head and started to follow her, but Derek stopped me. "I know you'd like to clean up," he said, "but I really need a word with you."

"Alone?" Was I about to be assaulted again? And why was my pepper spray never close at hand? From now on, I was only wearing clothes with pockets for these expeditions.

He pulled two business cards from his pressed jeans and handed them to me. Surprisingly, one of the cards was mine.

"Where did you get this?" I asked.

"I saw it lying on the hallway near your purse. Probably fell out. I noticed you're a private investigator."

I nodded and then nodded again to myself as I glanced at his business card. FBI agent. Well, well. That certainly put a different spin on things.

"Are you conducting an investigation?" I asked. "Or just slumming?"

He chuckled. "I can't go into details, obviously, but I picked up on some of the conversation you two had earlier with those two men. And I noticed the photo your friend showed them. Gino Romano, right?"

"Right."

"Can I ask what you're investigating? And does the other woman work for your agency, too?" The expression on his face was a mixture of confused and appalled.

"No, thank goodness. She's merely an extremely bossy and interfering client." I smiled, wondering if the time I'd spent stuffed in the dumpster could be considered billable hours. "This little incident might have taught her a valuable lesson. As you can see, subtlety isn't exactly her forte."

He nodded. "And your case?"

I tapped his card against my palm. "Tell you what, how about we save our chat until after I've cleaned up a little."

He reluctantly agreed and followed me back into the bar. I picked up my purse and joined Adriana in the ladies' room. After looking at myself in the mirror, I couldn't wait to wash up. But first things first.

There was someone I needed to call.

CHAPTER FIFTY-ONE

Tom arrived at The Gray Goose in under forty-five minutes, unshaven, hair mussed and eyes tired. My heart still leapt as he walked inside the bar. His eyes opened wide when he saw me.

He raced to my side before stopping and grimacing. Despite as thorough of a cleansing as I could manage in the bathroom sink, I basically reeked.

Then he grabbed me in his arms and showered me with kisses.

Did I have the best guy or what?

He stepped back. "I love you to death, but you stink, honey. We need to get you home ASAP."

"I agree, but we have to chat with the FBI guy first. He's hoping I can help him with his case and vice versa."

Tom looked over my shoulder. "So where's our friendly fed?"

"He went to walk Adriana to her Uber lift, which will take her back to her car. Derek wanted to talk to her more about Gino tonight, but she said she wasn't speaking to anyone until she shampooed and showered."

The door to the bar opened and the agent walked in. When he noticed Tom standing with me, he smiled and walked over. They shook hands and Derek said, "Well, I'll be. I didn't realize you were this woman's husband. How the heck have you been?"

Ah, the old boys in blue club strikes again. It seemed no matter what case we were on, Tom knew at least one of the officials involved. Which, from my perspective, was a good thing. Most of the time. Except when one of the officials was an ex-partner and possible ex-girlfriend.

Putting my feelings about Detective Ali Reynolds aside, I tuned into the guys' conversation and caught the tail end.

"… signs of money laundering," Derek stated.

"You mean Gino's been laundering money?" I asked.

"We think so, and the fact someone took him out of the picture made us even more certain."

"Is that why you were in the bar tonight?" I felt tired and confused, not to mention disgusting. But I wasn't going home until my questions had been answered.

Derek blew out a breath. "I guess it can't hurt to share at this point, particularly since the subject of our investigation is now deceased. One of the operations staff for Fidelity Wealth Management noticed discrepancies in some of Gino's accounts and reported it to their supervisor. Financial firms are constantly on the watch for money laundering."

"That's a high priority for your agency, isn't it?" Tom asked.

Derek nodded. "These thieves are becoming more and more sophisticated, but they still need to find a way to get their cash into the system."

"What kind of discrepancies did they find?" I asked, my financial background making me curious.

"Gino brought in several new clients in the past six months, and all of them purchased very large annuities. Worth hundreds of thousands of dollars. But then they cashed out the annuity fairly quickly, turning it into a liquid investment. And one we normally wouldn't catch."

"Clever stuff," I commented.

"Yep, and the only reason the firm caught it was because of a new staffer who had just seen a documentary on money laundering. She found it odd so many of Gino's client transactions were so similar in nature."

"Does this mean Gino was killed by some drug lord?" I asked.

Derek shrugged. "We haven't traced his activities that far. I've communicated with a Detective Reynolds at the SLTPD about our interest in his murder. She mentioned a couple of eyewitnesses saw the supposed killer jump off the gondola shortly before his body was discovered."

I raised my hand. "Yep, I'm one of the witnesses."

Derek blinked. "You get around, don't you?"

"Unfortunately, yes," replied my husband. "But I think it's time I took Laurel home. How about we follow up on this conversation tomorrow."

"You got it," Derek said. "Hopefully our next meeting won't involve any unintentional dumpster diving."

"With my wife," Tom replied as he ushered me toward the door, "always expect the unexpected."

CHAPTER FIFTY-TWO

After a long, hot shower the night before, I'd tumbled into bed and slept for nine solid hours. I woke to an empty bedroom and the smell of coffee wafting its way up the stairs. I threw on a clean T-shirt and shorts, ran a brush through my curls and entered the kitchen, anxious for my first cup of java to kick start my day.

My wonderful hubby had not only brought his disheveled wife home last night, but he'd brewed Kona coffee, walked the dog and made sure all three kids caught the bus to school. A Post-it note on the coffeemaker informed me he'd be at the D.A.'s office until noon.

The note also said: *Take a break this morning. Smell the roses for a change. XO, Tom.*

I sniffed the air, but my excellent sense of smell did not detect any flowery fragrances. I followed the scent to the family room, where a pile of fresh doggy doo doo awaited me. A grinning Scout sat on his haunches, the proud Prince of Poop.

I wondered if Costco sold pet stain remover by the case.

Once that unpleasant duty was taken care of, I could finally enjoy a cup of coffee. Or try to enjoy my coffee, since Scout was determined to climb on my lap, all one-hundred-fifty pounds of him. I finally seduced him with a doggie treat and eventually he lay under the table, his head resting next to my feet. I scanned the paper, happy to see our dumpster foray did not make the news.

Derek had told us he planned to interview Adriana in the morning. It would be interesting if she knew anything of importance about Gino's money-laundering clients. For her sake, I hoped not because that could be dangerous for her. So dangerous she might end up in witness protection.

Somehow I couldn't visualize Adriana agreeing to be dispatched to some tiny town hundreds of miles from the nearest city.

Did Gino's meeting with Louie mean the pawnshop owner hired Gino to launder money from his enterprise? Was the money laundering tied to Gino's death? Or was he killed for some other reason? Given the FBI was now probing Gino's murder, did that mean I was officially off the clock as far as Adriana was concerned?

While it would be nice to bring in more revenue for the agency, even I could tell when it was time for me to step back from an investigation. But I still wanted to find out what was up with Jake and his biker friend. Our questions must have hit some kind of nerve last night.

Or else the two bikers needed some dating tips.

I drummed my fingers on the table, which woke Scout from his slumber. He tickled my toes with his tongue before scooting out from under the table. It only took two woofs for me to realize he needed a potty break. I let him out into the yard figuring he could enjoy the fresh air while I got dressed.

As I was getting ready to drive to the agency, my cell played Adriana's theme song. I debated letting it go to voicemail, but I was concerned how she was holding up after last night's events and revelations by the FBI agent.

"How are you doing?" I asked her.

"Not great," she said in a low tear-drenched voice.

"Last night was tough," I commiserated. "But thank goodness that agent was there to rescue us."

A sound that was half sigh and half sob echoed over the phone. "I wish the agent had left me in the dumpster. I have nothing to live for. A dead fiancé who was also a criminal. How could I have been so stupid as to get involved with him?"

"Stop berating yourself. You are not alone when it comes to bad choices. Especially choices involving men. Aren't you grateful you didn't marry Gino before this all came out? You could have lost everything."

"I suppose," she muttered. "I guess we won't be solving his murder after all. Or will we?" Her voice almost sounded hopeful.

Maybe Adriana needed some kind of closure. Something more definitive than our dumpster rescue.

"Now that federal agents are involved, I'm sure they'll figure out what happened. But if I run across anything helpful, I'll be sure to let you know. Okay?"

"Fine," she said in a soft voice before clicking off.

Poor Adriana. I truly felt sorry for the woman. One blow after another. Maybe I should take her out for a drink sometime to cheer her up.

Although considering our previous night out, perhaps Starbucks would be a better choice.

The next day I holed up in the office phoning the timeshare resale companies that had guaranteed Iris the sale of her timeshare. I pretended to be a timeshare owner who was desperate to unload my timeshare points. The salespeople couldn't wait to help me out. They showered me with so many assurances and testimonials from grateful customers that I almost believed their sales pitch.

I still wasn't certain how to get Iris's money back without hiring a legitimate attorney, which meant even more money would need to be expended. I had pages and pages of notes but no practical course of action.

I nibbled on my pen before realizing my bottom desk drawer contained something far more nibble worthy. I yanked out the bag of M&M's and popped a few of the colorful candies into my mouth. Ah, just what I needed. Nothing like chocolate to rev up my little gray cells.

I could really use an expert to help me out on this. Would Kimberly be willing to give me some advice on how to get the money refunded from the Florida firms? I'd somewhat bonded with her at our last meeting. And she'd been kind enough to research Gregg's angry customers, the Lankershims, for me.

If I called Kimberly ahead of time, she'd probably come up with some excuse not to meet with me. It was only half past ten, so I could easily reach their office before lunchtime. I texted Tom and told him I was heading back to Tahoe for more research. I assured him I'd be back in time to cook dinner.

That text would probably have him quaking in his shoes. Not the fact that I was driving back to Tahoe. The threat that I would actually attempt to cook!

The trip to Tahoe took less than an hour. I was so wrapped up in my thoughts I barely noticed the scenery flying by me. I pulled into the Timeshare Help parking lot and looked around for Kimberly's black SUV, hoping I hadn't missed her. Although if Marty or another salesman were in, they might be able to give me a few tips.

My throat felt parched so I decided to stop at Palomino's. I could attempt another try at a drug buy or I could purchase a diet cola.

I went with the soda.

With my cup of diet cola in my left hand, I opened the door to the timeshare company. I heard voices coming from Marty's small office but neither Marty nor anyone else approached me. I hated to be rude, but I needed to get some questions answered and fairly quickly.

Just my luck — the one time I wanted to chat with Kimberly, she didn't appear to be around.

I headed toward Marty's office and as I drew closer he glanced away from his visitors. He beckoned to me, so I entered the office, where he introduced me to his wife, Veronica, and his eldest daughter, Meghan.

The two women stood. His wife, a graying blonde, shook my hand while his daughter merely nodded at me before walking out of the office without a farewell look or goodbye to her father. The older woman sent a fleeting smile to her husband, then scurried out after her daughter.

Marty motioned for me to sit while apologizing for his daughter's rudeness.

"Don't worry about it. You know how teens can be," I said. "My daughter's mood can change from one minute to the next."

"It's been a difficult year for Meghan," he said. "Boy trouble."

"Isn't it always," I said sympathetically. "I didn't mean to interrupt you while your family was here. I was actually looking for Kimberly."

"Kimberly's in Reno, but I'm more than happy to help. Were you ready to purchase one of the timeshares we looked at the other day?" His eyes lit up and I was halfway tempted to buy one of the timeshares just to put a smile on his face.

"Not yet. I'm working on my husband, though." I went on to explain Iris's situation. Marty was familiar with the types of scams some of the out-of-state resale firms engaged in.

"In California, timeshare salespeople are regulated by the Department of Real Estate," he said. "We're licensed the same as regular real estate agents and paid a commission on the sale of each timeshare. But in these other states, Florida in particular, these fly-by-night resale operations keep cropping up, taking advantage of timeshare owners. They set up boiler rooms with a hundred employees making telemarketing calls to people all over the country who have purchased timeshares. Occasionally there are enough complaints to shut them down, but then a few months later they pop up again using a different name." He sighed. "It gives the entire industry a bad reputation."

I couldn't agree more.

My cell pinged and I pulled the phone from my purse. A text from Liz stating she was with Adriana on her way to Reno.

"Excuse me a minute," I said to Marty. I went into the hallway and dialed Liz.

"Why are you and Adriana going to Reno? Shouldn't you be resting at home?"

"Adriana called and wanted company to drive to Reno and check out some pawnshop. I was bored and said I'd go with her. Maybe I can find a good deal on some china," said my British friend, who collected sets of china like some people collected stickers.

"Is she going to Louie's? Put your phone on hands free and let me talk to her," I ordered Liz.

"Hi, Laurel," said Adriana.

"What do you think you're doing driving up to Reno?" I asked, trying not to shriek at my client.

"Well, you said you were off the case after last night, and I kept thinking about Gino and that loan he had with the pawnshop. I thought I might learn something if I went up there and questioned them."

"That is the dumbest thing I've ever heard," I said hotly. "Actually, the second dumbest. The first is dragging a pregnant woman along with you to Louie's Loans."

"You're sure not doing anything to help me. It's my life and my fiancé who was killed." The phone clicked off before I could reply.

I stomped back into Marty's office and told him I needed to leave.

"I overheard part of your conversation. You mentioned Louie's Loans in Reno. That's where Kimberly is, in case you wanted to catch up with her. Maybe she'll have some ideas for you to help out your friend with the timeshare problem."

"Is Kimberly having financial difficulties?" I asked, thinking it might explain why she was always in such a bad mood. Maybe the timeshare business wasn't as lucrative as I suspected, and Kimberly was having to pawn some of her valuables.

He shook his head. "Naw, at least not that I know of. The woman owns more businesses than I can keep track of. Louie's Loans is one of them."

CHAPTER FIFTY-THREE

The drive up and then down the Kingsbury Grade contained more hairpin curves than this harried mother needed. And while I loved my Forester, the boxy SUV didn't appear to like the serpentine turns any more than I did.

Once I reached Highway 580 heading north to Reno, I relaxed my tight shoulders, although mentally I remained tense and annoyed with both Adriana and Liz. The thought of the two of them trying to pry information out of Louie was enough to make me nauseous. It was like Lucy and Ethel trying to interrogate the Godfather.

Yet if Kimberly was the actual owner of the pawnshop, I shouldn't have anything to worry about.

Should I?

My thoughts ping-ponged around my brain while I tried to concentrate on the highway and the speed limit. I hadn't tabbed Kimberly to be quite the entrepreneur Marty described. Although she had confided Gino handled her investments, so she obviously had money coming in from several sources.

As I reached the Reno city limits, I tried to remember the way to the pawnshop district and failed. I fiddled with my navigation system while I waited at a stoplight and the address popped onto the screen.

In less than ten minutes, I found a parking spot not too far from Louie's place. The street appeared deserted except for a couple of disheveled guys who looked like they'd spent the night in the casino and were trying to figure out where to lose their money next.

I grabbed my purse and keys and locked the car door. Neither Liz nor Adriana had attempted to call me in the hour-plus since I'd first conversed with Adriana and that concerned me. Perhaps they were ticked off with me. I had to admit I wasn't too cordial during our brief conversation.

Or maybe the two of them were buying out the store. As I recalled, Adriana loved to purchase jewelry, especially antique jewelry, and she had the financial wherewithal to do so. And with Liz's hormones running amuck, the veteran shopper could be doing significant damage to her credit card balances. They could be merely enjoying a fun shopping spree without party pooper me interfering and ruining their day.

But this party pooper also sleuthed for a living, and my intuition told me to prepare for anything. I returned to the car, unlocked the door, then reached into my glove compartment, stuffing my stun gun into one of the pockets of my practical beige twill cargo pants.

Then I called Tom, who for a change answered his cell.

"Everything okay?" he greeted me. Guess we were more of a "what's the trouble now?" kind of couple instead of a "how ya doin'?" husband and wife.

"Yeah, I think so. I'm in Reno. Ready to pop into Louie's again." I explained the call from Adriana and also my discovery that Kimberly owned the pawnshop along with Timeshare Help and numerous other ventures.

"Do you think they're in any danger?" he asked.

"Honestly, the only danger Liz and Adriana are likely to encounter is a drop in their credit rating from buying out the store. Still…"

"I could leave here in a few minutes," Tom replied, "but that's close to a three-hour drive." Then I heard him snap his fingers. "I know. I'll call Ali and see if she's available to meet you. What do you think?"

What did I think of me partnering with Tom's former partner/ former fake fiancé/possible former girlfriend?

Before I could respond, Tom put me on hold while he dialed her number. I sat in the car for five stuffy minutes, fuming and wishing I hadn't wasted the time calling him. What on earth was he doing while I waited and waited?

I glanced out the windshield and squinted, wondering if the heat was causing me to see a mirage. Was that Kimberly walking into Louie's? I slammed my finger on the end call button, shoved my phone into my purse and headed for the pawnshop.

I zipped up the sidewalk, my purse banging against my side, the stun gun whacking my right knee with every other step. If I hadn't been in such a hurry to catch up with Kimberly, I would have stopped to rearrange my hot pink protective device, but I didn't want to miss the opportunity to chat with her.

I pushed open the glass-paned door and scanned the room for Adriana and Liz.

Nothing. There was also no sign of Kimberly. Or Louie. Or the beautiful Cherie. Only one skinny young salesman wearing a short-sleeve shirt and belted slacks that were struggling to maintain themselves around his twenty-eight-inch waist.

So annoying when you see a man with a smaller waist than your own.

He pasted on a fake smile and greeted me as I approached the counter. "May I help you find something in particular?" he asked

I glanced inside the glass-enclosed cases. The colorful display of diamond rings, antique bracelets and brooches, Rolex watches and pinky rings spoke volumes to me. Each item must have a story behind it, a sorrowful tale most likely, because why else would you part with such an item unless forced to?

"Yes, you can help me," I replied. "Two friends of mine were in the store earlier. They asked me to meet them here, but I don't see them around."

"My shift started a half hour ago, and you're my first customer. Maybe they went to another pawnshop. There's quite a few in Reno."

"No, they were definitely headed here. One of them is a striking brunette and the other is blond and"—I mimed a pregnant woman—"about to pop. Not easy to miss."

He shrugged. "Sorry."

I blew out a breath and drummed my fingers on the glass top. I couldn't believe I made the trip for nothing. Well, if nothing else, maybe I could chat with Kimberly for a bit. If she was still in the store.

Before I looked for Kimberly, I decided to try calling Liz one more time. Her phone rang and rang. Loudly.

Far too loudly. As if it were close to where I was standing.

I shifted to the right toward the shrill sound of a ringing phone. It stopped ringing and I immediately redialed. Seconds later I heard the echo of the ringing phone coming from behind the glass counter. I stood on my tiptoes, leaned over the counter and spied a gray plastic wastebasket below. As the phone continued to ring, the salesman, who now stood on the opposite side of the counter, also glanced down. His face looked even more puzzled than mine.

As Alice in Wonderland would say, this day was getting curiouser and curiouser.

CHAPTER FIFTY-FOUR

"Grab that phone," I ordered him and he reached into the wastebasket and pulled it out.

I snatched the oversized iPhone with the baby blue cover out of his hand and stared at it. How had it landed in the garbage? Liz was admittedly a little ditzier these days, but I still couldn't imagine her agreeing to part with her phone under any circumstances.

My stomach contracted as the impact of my discovery sank in. Something was wrong. Very, very wrong.

"Do you know how this phone ended up in that wastebasket?" I asked in my most intimidating voice.

"I have no idea. Like I said, I just came on the floor"—he looked at his watch—"a half hour ago. It could of gotten pushed into the basket somehow and your friend not noticed it. Sometimes customers get excited about our displays and don't pay attention to their own stuff."

Yeah, right.

I dialed Adriana's number. No answer. At least it hadn't landed in the garbage as well.

I tapped my phone against the counter while I contemplated a course of action. The clerk's explanation seemed feasible. I'd once left my phone at Safeway when I was in a hurry. Liz could have lost her cell and not realized it yet.

"Is Kimberly here today?" I asked the clerk.

His eyes widened. "Yeah, she's the boss lady. Do you know her?"

"Old friends," I assured him. "Could you tell her Laurel McKay would like to see her."

"Sure, I'll go get her." He stepped from behind the counter, his long gangly legs striding toward the back of the store. He halted when a door opened up and two people emerged—Kimberly and a large man, who looked vaguely familiar.

I sorted through my mental database of contacts and as they drew closer, I realized where I'd last seen the man with the linebacker-sized shoulders and platinum buzz cut.

Jumping off the gondola the day Gino was killed.

CHAPTER FIFTY-FIVE

I did my best to present a poker face and not let the fear that assaulted every one of my frayed nerves show through my placid exterior. I'd spied on this guy twice—once when he'd dined with Louie and Gino, and again when he killed Gino. I sure hoped the Hulk-like villain didn't recognize me.

Kimberly's face bore her standard "not you again" expression. The lug accompanying her narrowed his eyes at me but remained silent, standing a few steps behind Kimberly in a surprisingly deferential pose.

"Now what?" Kimberly asked in a barely civil tone.

"Um, Marty sent me here," I said, promising to make it up to Marty the next time I saw him. The poor guy didn't need to get in trouble with his boss on my account. "I have a few more questions about timeshare resales."

"Honestly." She rolled her heavily mascaraed eyes. "Haven't you heard of Google?"

I bit back a smart retort and merely replied, "Yes, but you are much more knowledgeable than Google when it comes to the timeshare industry."

She gave me a small smile, while I attempted to keep from gagging at my own obsequious compliment.

"True," she said, "but my staff and I are busy doing inventory, so we'll have to chat another time. Ciao." She fluttered her pink shellac talons at me before pivoting and heading to the back of the store

200

once again. Big lug followed in her retreating footsteps, glancing once over his shoulder at me.

I cringed when I caught a glimmer of recognition in his icy blue eyes. But then he shook his head and continued in Kimberly's high-heeled wake.

"You forgot to ask Kimberly about your friends," the sales clerk reminded me.

I didn't forget. Not for one minute.

"I'm sure they're fine. Eventually Liz will notice her phone is missing," I assured him. "By the way, Kimberly mentioned she was in the middle of doing inventory. Do they keep a lot more merchandise in back? I might be interested in seeing what else is for sale. Can you take me back there for a peek?"

"Oh, I'm not allowed in the back." He leaned closer and whispered, "That's where the fine antiques and jewelry are kept. Only a small select group of clients are allowed in that area."

"You've never been in the back?" I asked. "Ever?"

"Nope." He shook his head so vigorously his glasses slid down his nose. He pushed them back up before explaining, "You gotta have a security code to get in there. I'm not high enough in the food chain for access."

"How do they acquire all of these high-end items?"

"Oh, they got a team of guys that goes all over and finds stuff. Kind of like them *Antiques Roadshow* guys on TV."

Seriously?

I glanced around the store, eyeballing the corners for any security cameras. Nothing jumped out at me, but knowing Kimberly, she'd hide any signs of surveillance activity from her customers. She probably stowed the camera in something unusual. Like the spooky owl clock in the corner. I could almost sense his beady eyes staring at me as I moved around the store.

I tucked Liz's phone inside my purse and said farewell to the young clerk. There wasn't much more I could do inside the store right now.

But that might not be the only option.

After I left the pawnshop, I returned to my parked car to catch up on my voicemails and texts. There was only one phone message from Ali Reynolds. *I have more important things to do than go traipsing to Reno to help you locate your pals.*

So rude.

With no help from the detective, that left just two options: I could call Tom and wait three or more hours for him to drive to Reno or complete a little investigative foray of my own. Even though I'd ostensibly agreed with the clerk's suggestion that Liz might have accidentally dropped her phone in the wastebasket, I considered it an unlikely scenario. And the clerk's comments about the super-secret valuable merchandise in the back piqued my curiosity.

I pulled out from my parking spot and drove a few blocks away. Out of sight of the pawnshop. Then I yanked my tote bag from the back seat. The bag currently contained four wigs, a cosmetic bag loaded with makeup essentials, a pair of clear glasses and a change of clothes. I covered my curls with the platinum pixie-cut wig and added the glasses, which I thought were a nice touch. Rather than change clothes in the car, I simply threw a long sleeve top over my current sleeveless blouse. Then I slipped off my wedge sandals and replaced them with a pair of navy Keds.

I moved my pepper spray from my purse to the back pocket of my cargo pants. I wouldn't win any fashion awards, but hopefully I'd disguised my identity well enough. I patted my pockets and decided I was ready.

It was long past time to find my pals.

CHAPTER FIFTY-SIX

My brief three-block excursion from my car to the rear of the pawnshop took close to ten minutes. Every time a vehicle passed by, I took cover by standing in doorways, behind parked cars and one time even crouched next to a mailbox. I undoubtedly looked more like a robber on the make than an undercover P.I.

Although masquerading as a thief might have gotten me better access to the back room of Louie's. After talking to the sales clerk I'd contemplated whether Louie's establishment dealt in illicit goods. They certainly wouldn't be the first pawnshop to do so. Too bad I'd already run into Kimberly today. She was far too smart for me to outsmart in my current disguise.

As I sidled near their loading dock in the back of the brick building, my eyes scanned all around me—from left to right and front to back. A revolving head would have been useful right now.

Or a partner. Even Gran. But, sadly, I was on my own.

A metal door screeched open and I jumped behind a dumpster. The combination of rotting fruit and days-old fish brought an unpleasant reminder of my brief dumpster dive a few days earlier. I shifted slightly to the right and peeked at the two men standing outside the back entrance. One of them was unfamiliar while the other, Big Lug, was too familiar.

They both lit cigarettes and walked away, in the opposite direction from where I currently hid from view. I calculated the distance from the dumpster to the doorway. No more than thirty feet. Could I race to the door and gain entry before they noticed me?

Assuming my foray into the back of Louie's was successful, what did I expect to achieve?

Insight into the pawnshop's operation? Discovery of my missing friends? Either or both reasons were sufficient for me to take a chance.

I inched my way out, then jerked back behind the dumpster as one of the men turned around. My heartbeat ratcheted up to ninety mph. The thumping of my heart sounded louder than a tympani solo. Could the men hear its frenetic refrain from so far away?

A sigh of relief escaped when the sound of both men laughing echoed back from a distance. This time when I snuck a look, they were disappearing around the block.

Time for me to break from my hiding place.

I scooted out from behind the dumpster and raced to the oversized metal door. I hadn't seen the men lock it, but that didn't mean it didn't lock automatically. I yanked. It barely moved two inches.

Whew. Someone needed to add bicep building to her to-do list. The door screeched as I struggled to push it open far enough for me to squeeze my curvy frame through the narrow opening. Once inside, it took a few seconds for my eyes to adjust to the dim lighting in the vast storeroom.

Small, medium, large, and gigantic boxes lined one wall of the storeroom. A multitude of televisions, computers and a host of other electronics were stacked on pallets reaching almost to the ceiling. I crept past a couple of large covered crates. Then I stopped and went back as my internal radar kicked in. I cautiously lifted the top of one of the crates, then recoiled, stunned to discover the type of artillery I'd previously only seen on my television screen.

Louie certainly didn't exaggerate. His motto of "We have something for everyone" rang true. His clients could load their automatic weapons while watching an eighty-inch TV screen, comfortably seated in an antique nineteenth-century brocade chair.

Ugh. Not a comforting visual.

I peeked at my watch. The men would soon return from their cigarette break. I peered around the room trying to detect hidden cameras but nothing jumped out at me. It would be foolhardy not to have some type of surveillance system considering their valuable and unorthodox inventory.

Which meant before long someone was bound to notice an intruder wandering around where she did not belong.

I noticed several doors on the far wall from where I stood. As I drew closer I heard murmurings from the other side of the wall. Did Kimberly and/or Louie have their offices back here? It wasn't the most elegant of surroundings, but the location was definitely out of the way. A discreet place to meet some of their less honest clientele.

I placed my ear against the wall, praying neither Kimberly nor Louie would come bounding out of the office.

The next words I heard were unmistakable. "Bloody Hell. Now what do we do?"

CHAPTER FIFTY-SEVEN

Liz! The other person's response was muted, but I determined it was definitely another female. I listened for a few more seconds but couldn't detect any deeper male voices. I softly tapped on the door.

"Liz, Adriana. Are you in there?"

"Laurel, is that you, luv?" Liz replied. "Have you brought the troops to rescue us?"

"Sure." No point discouraging them at this point. "Are you both okay?"

"Of course we're not okay," screeched Adriana. "And Liz is standing in a puddle."

"Is there a leak in there?"

"Only me," replied Liz in a subdued voice. "I think my water broke."

Talk about timing. My friends didn't need a detective to come to their rescue. They needed Wonder Woman.

Or an obstetrician.

I jiggled the door but, as anticipated, it didn't open. "Stay calm," I said. "I'm trying to find a way in."

Should I attempt to break the door down? Could I? The cops usually shot out locks when necessary, but I didn't carry a gun and didn't intend to. I patted my pockets. My stun gun and pepper spray were useless. Then I remembered a clever *MacGyver* episode where the star gained entry into a locked room using the filaments from a lightbulb.

I looked up. The few lights in the high ceiling were far out of reach. I rushed around the room, thinking there must be a ladder nearby to service the high shelving, currently holding electronics, appliances, even a few lamps.

Aha! I zeroed in on a Tiffany lamp sitting on top of a small mahogany table. I tilted the shade and let out a breath. Success at last. Two lightbulbs for me to have my way with.

I gently crushed the bulbs with the heel of my shoe and retrieved the filaments. Ten minutes later I was cursing MacGyver and the team of screenwriters who'd allowed him to utilize the same technique but in far less time. Only sixty seconds, as I recalled. My heart skipped a beat as I heard two sounds.

The first welcome sound was a soft click as my innovative implement finally succeeded in picking the lock.

The louder noise was the screech of the metal door in the back of the room signifying a person or persons had returned to the warehouse area.

Uh oh.

CHAPTER FIFTY-EIGHT

I kicked pieces of the broken lightbulb under a chest of drawers placed next to the door I'd unlocked. As the men's voices increased in volume, I grasped the doorknob and opened it. I put my finger to my lips as I entered the room.

In silence, I hugged both women. I didn't think Liz would let me go, but she suddenly bent over and clasped her stomach. She winced, then mouthed the word, "contraction."

"We need to get out of here," I said in a low voice.

"Obviously," Adriana grumbled. "What's your plan?"

Plan? Wouldn't it be great if I actually had one? My entire goal had been to find my missing friends. I'd never formulated an escape route.

My phone vibrated and I grabbed it from my pocket. Detective Ali Reynolds?

"Hello?" I whispered into the phone.

"Who is this?"

"Laurel McKay. You called me. Are you on your way?"

"I must have butt-dialed you. Remember, I have more important—"

"Yeah, yeah, I get it. But right now my friends and I are being held hostage in this pawnshop."

She snorted. "You'll say anything to get my attention."

"I can guarantee you delivery of at least one of your murderers. Send help, please."

"Fine, but it better be worth it."

"It will. Oh, we could use an ambulance as well. My friend is in labor."

That got her attention. "I'm on it. Stay safe."

Finally. troops were on their way. Hopefully from the Reno P.D. because South Lake Tahoe was still close to an hour away, even if the detective maintained top speed. Were we safe in this office? How likely was it the men would stop to check on the two women?

The click of someone shoving a key into the lock provided my answer.

I thought fast. The men wouldn't expect to find an additional woman tucked away, so I moved to the side of the door, hoping I'd remain hidden for a few seconds, giving me enough time to—

The door burst open, slamming against the wall where I'd planned on hiding.

Confused ice blue eyes met mine.

"What the—?"

Faster than you could say snickerdoodle, I whipped out my stun gun from the back pocket of my cargo pants and zapped his chest. He jerked back, rubbing his chest. One beefy arm smacked me across my right cheek and I fell to the floor.

The extremely dirty carpeted floor. My mother would have a fit at their shoddy housekeeping.

He roared and grabbed me by the collar of my T-shirt, lifting me close to the ceiling.

Then Adriana kicked him with the toe of one pointy heel, somehow managing to connect with one of his more tender organs. He dropped me like a boulder and I crashed onto the carpet again.

He whirled around and faced her. "So the hottie's got some life in her. How about I take you down a peg or two?"

As he reached for her, I rolled over, stuck my hand in my pocket and prayed.

CHAPTER FIFTY-NINE

Thank you, Damsel in Defense for making a pepper spray that can take down a giant. With his eyes closed shut and orange dye marking his face, the hulk roared in pain, stumbling around the room in search of relief. As he drew closer, I slammed the door into him and he toppled to the ground.

I hustled Adriana and Liz out of the office, then debated which direction to go. Out the rear door of the warehouse or try to find the retail section of the store? When a voice from the back of the store yelled "hey, you," I had my answer.

The three of us weaved between antique chairs, contemporary tables, stacks of boxes and crates, even a jukebox, stopping only once when Liz stooped over and clutched her belly. She maintained amazing control; not a single cry of pain was uttered, merely a mumbled British expletive or two.

By now, several men were chasing us. Their four-letter oaths grew louder and more emphatic, and they increased in volume as they drew closer to us. We zigged to the left and zagged to the right, throwing brass lamps, china plates, Waterford crystal, virtually anything we could lift, at the men. Whatever it took to slow them down.

I grabbed a small wooden box from a shelf and heaved it over my shoulder.

Score! The box must have contained ammunition because bullets rained down on the concrete. Curses interspersed with shouts of pain as one of our pursuers slipped and crashed onto the floor.

Our trio finally reached a double set of doors. I pushed on the safety bar and bright light welcomed us as we entered the safety of the pawnshop. The tall, gawky sales clerk I'd spoken with earlier stood off to the side of the doorway. He appeared to be rooted to the floor, his mouth open wide as he flicked his gaze back and forth between the three of us and a fourth determined woman.

Who was holding a gun. Pointed directly at me.

CHAPTER SIXTY

My canvas soles skidded to an abrupt stop on the slick floor. How to remain nonchalant when a gun is staring you in the face.

"Hey, Kimberly, nice Beretta," I said. "Your store has a great inventory of guns for sale."

She blinked before her face resumed its standard pissed-off glare.

"What the blazes do you think you're doing? You and your friends just destroyed thousands of dollars of merchandise in our warehouse."

"Sorry. My best friend"—I pointed at Liz—"is in labor." As if on cue, Liz bent over and let out a guttural shriek that made my insides crawl.

"Knock it off." Kimberly pointed the gun inches from Liz's head. My friend's normally porcelain complexion turned a pasty white. Then she sank to the floor, her billowing maternity dress wrapping around her like a shroud.

I dropped down next to Liz frantically fanning her face. One eyelid popped open and she winked at me.

What a trouper.

"I'm sorry about the damage," I said, looking up at Kimberly, "but why were my friends locked up in the office?"

"I can tell you why," said Adriana. "I accused her of killing my fiancé. Obviously, I was right."

"I told you I did not kill Gino." Kimberly bared her teeth at Adriana. "Although I can't believe he dumped me to marry you."

I interrupted her pity party. "Gino got on board the gondola with your employee. And a few minutes later, Gino was dead."

"I'm sure you're mistaken," Kimberly replied.

My voice rose as I tried to talk above the sound of approaching sirens. "I saw the man with my own two eyes."

Kimberly's attention drifted to the front of the store as the sirens grew louder.

I didn't want her to realize the police were nearing the pawnshop. At least I hoped they were getting close to our location, so I explained, "I called for an ambulance for Liz, so we'll be on our way and out of your hair in no time at all."

I helped Liz to her feet and we attempted to stroll away, Adriana following quietly behind us. We made it three steps.

"Stop right there," Kimberly cried. "No one is going anywhere." She turned to the lanky clerk, who cowered in the corner. "You. Go lock the doors and put the closed sign out." When he hesitated she pointed the gun at him. "Now, before I get angry. You don't want me to get angry, do you?"

He shook his head and scurried down the aisle. Within seconds, the doors were locked, the shades were drawn and the pawnshop turned into a barred-window fortress.

"Where's Hugo?" Kimberly asked one of the men who had chased us through the warehouse.

"He's out cold." The man pointed at me. "She must have a weapon on her." I shook my head, but Kimberly's eyes zeroed in on the bulge in my cargo pants pocket.

"Hand that over to Buddy," Kimberly demanded.

I folded my arms across my chest. "Make me."

She whispered in Buddy's ear and in less than a second, a knife appeared, barely an inch from my throat.

"Buddy can be most persuasive," Kimberly said. I didn't doubt it since Buddy's yellow-toothed smile seemed to widen as the knife inched closer to my carotid artery.

I slowly reached into my pocket, pulled out my hot pink weapon and turned it over to Buddy. He dropped his knife on a mahogany sideboard while he evaluated the stun gun.

Buddy smirked. "I can't believe this housewife knocked out Hugo."

Housewife?

Aaran

I shoved my hand into my back pocket, pulled out a tiny metal canister and aimed for Buddy's beady black eyes.

He screamed and raised his palms to his face, dropping the stun gun at my feet. With Kimberly's attention diverted by Buddy's howls, I picked it up and threw it to Liz, who was only inches from our captor. She zapped Kimberly with the might of a woman trying to save her child's life. Kimberly wilted and Adriana caught her Beretta as it dropped out of her hand.

I reached for a statuette of Elvis in his glory years. Much as I hated to destroy a collector's item of "the King," the sound of the ceramic smashing into Buddy's head was worth it.

I could almost hear old Elvis applauding from up above.

With all the racket the three of us had created, we almost didn't hear several people banging on the locked front door. They asked if anyone needed an ambulance.

Did we ever!

CHAPTER SIXTY-ONE

Hours later, actually twelve hours later, since Master Colin Daley decided to take his time joining the rest of us, I finally had the opportunity to update my family. Mother and Bradford had arrived several hours ago, long after Tom's speedy drive up Highway 50 with his best friend, Brian Daley—Liz's husband.

Brian and I had each held one of Liz's hands as she shrieked her way into motherhood. But one look at newborn Colin's bright blue eyes and she fell in love. Feeling that my part in the birth process was done, I left the new mother, father, and son alone, and walked down the hall into the waiting room, where my family waited for me.

I plopped into the empty chair next to Tom. The hard surface of the molded green chair didn't provide much comfort, but it was nice to get off my feet.

"Are you okay, dear?" asked Mother. "You've had a tough day."

I shrugged. "Faced a killer, helped deliver a baby. No biggie."

She shook her head. "I don't understand how you can joke about something like this. You could have been killed." She glared at me. "Yet again."

"But I wasn't. And I thought I handled it like a pro." I turned to my husband. "Didn't I?"

He threw his arm around my shoulders and drew me close. "Indeed you did. Even Ali was impressed at how you rounded them all up."

"She actually said that?"

215

Tom squirmed. "Not in quite those terms, but you handed her the leader of a huge burglary gang that has been operating in Tahoe and Reno."

"Not to mention a murderer," I added. "Did Hugo confess when he woke up?"

"He confessed that Kimberly ordered him to scare Gino. Hurt him a little. He said he didn't expect a jab from his elbow to Gino's neck would break it."

I punched the air with my fist. "I knew Kimberly had to be involved. Did she admit to killing Gregg in the timeshare office?"

Tom shook his head. "She hasn't admitted to anything. No murder. No robberies. The last I heard they were waiting for her attorney to arrive."

"Did Hugo explain why Kimberly wanted him to get tough with Gino?"

"Yeah, he did," Tom said. "After Ali offered him the possibility of a plea deal he's been spilling his guts. Evidently, Gino had been laundering money for the gang. Something to do with paying off big gambling debts he incurred and loans he got from Louie's. I don't have all the details yet."

"Hmm. Interesting. I wonder why Kimberly wanted to harm him if he was helping her?"

"Because he supposedly wanted out. Wanted to start over once he and Adriana got married."

"Aw, that's so sad. He really did love her." I looked around the waiting room. "Where is Adriana?"

"While you were busy coaching Liz, Adriana was informing Ali exactly what went on while she and Liz were at the pawnshop."

Once the cops rounded up all the suspects onsite, I'd only been given a few moments alone to chat with Adriana before they bundled Liz into an ambulance and allowed me to ride along with her to the closest hospital.

Although she was reluctant to admit it at first, it seems Adriana's interviewing technique lacked finesse.

"Guess I should have worked up to 'did you kill my fiancé?'" Adriana said to me. "She got real pissy after that question. Walked out of the office and locked us in."

"That's why you need to let the pros handle an investigation," I replied.

She reached out and gave me a hug. "You were kinda awesome, you know."

I smiled. I kinda was.

CHAPTER SIXTY-TWO

I woke with a start, the doorbell ringing nonstop like the chimes of St. Mary's during a hurricane. Since the racket refused to stop, I quickly slipped out of my nightgown and into a slightly more guest-worthy cotton shift. The clock read noon, a mere three hours since I'd fallen into a blissful sleep after our long drive home from Reno.

I peeked out the window, sighed and grudgingly opened the front door.

"What do you want?" I asked Hank.

"Nice greeting." He peered at me while I yawned back in reply. "Looks like you had a late night."

I covered a second yawn. "Yep. Knocked out a killer, busted a robbery ring and delivered a baby. All in a night's work."

"I'm impressed," he said. "Next thing you know they'll be making a Hallmark movie about you and your new career."

I smiled. Highly unlikely but it was nice to receive praise from my ex.

"Not to be rude, but I only got a couple hours sleep. What *do* you want?"

"I'm ready to take Scout off your hands."

"Scout?" I shouted.

Upon hearing his name, our rambunctious dog slid across the entry on all four paws, almost knocking Hank over in the process.

"Sit," I commanded and he did. Scout, that is. Hank never did anything I asked of him.

"You've even trained him. Thanks. He's going to be a great chick magnet." Hank beamed at the dog he planned to use as date bait.

"Wait a minute, buster. This dog isn't going anywhere," I said as I stroked Scout's head. "He's a part of our family now."

Hank gave me a quizzical look. "Are you sure? I was certain you'd be thrilled for me to take him back."

As if he could tell we were discussing him, Scout stared at me with soulful brown eyes.

"Quite sure."

Twenty-four hours later our household hummed with activity as Jenna prepared for her high school graduation, including practicing her class salutatorian speech. Her voice resounded with authority as she reflected on her high school years. I eavesdropped in the hallway, silently applauding her.

"Mom?" she cried out.

Jenna's bionic hearing would be useful in her crime-solving future.

I peeked my head around the doorway to her bedroom. "You sound great, honey."

Her face reddened. "Thanks. Is that last line okay?"

"Best commencement speech I've ever heard."

She laughed. "You're biased. How's your head feel?"

"I'll survive." I gently touched the bruise I'd received from Kimberly's henchman. "Sorry I missed your awards ceremony last night."

"It's no biggie. You caught a ring of thieves. That's so awesome."

"And at least one murderer." I brushed my hands together. "Anyway, my work is done. Now I'll have free time to spend with you kids."

"Don't forget we'll be working together," she said with a broad grin. "I can't wait to get started on some casework."

Which meant our firm better go out and round up some new clients.

The five of us made it to the Ponderosa High School campus seconds before the graduation ceremony was scheduled to begin.

Scout had decided to snack on Jenna's mortarboard while she practiced her speech one last time. He was chewing his way around the cap when Ben discovered him. Hopefully no one would notice her abbreviated gold tassel.

We pulled into the one remaining parking space in the crowded lot. As we rushed toward the football field where the ceremony would take place, Jenna stopped next to a beat-up white sedan with muddy plates and a crumpled front bumper.

"That's the car," she cried out. "The guy who rammed me."

Tom scrutinized the vehicle. "You're sure? Honda Civics are a popular model."

Jenna nodded, her tassel swinging in affirmation. "I doubt many Civics have a set of lime green foam dice hanging from the mirror."

"We can deal with this later," I said, grabbing her hand and running toward the ceremony. "You have a speech to give."

Mother, the Queen of Punctuality and Propriety, had managed to save a row of bleacher seats near the temporary stage for all four generations of our family. As one of the students who would address the audience, my daughter sat in the front row between Todd, the valedictorian, and Drew, the senior class president, who was also the school's star quarterback. Her long auburn curls glowed against the forest green gown like a beacon of light every time she moved her head. And for some reason she continually shifted in her seat, shooting glances in every direction while the valedictorian gave a lengthy and sleep-inducing speech.

What was she looking for? I hoped she didn't need a bathroom because the only options were a couple of portable toilets on the opposite side of the field. And her turn was next.

Jenna was finally introduced and as she climbed the stairs to the stage her head whipped to the left and right. If this had been a scene from a Stephen King movie, her head would have done a three hundred and sixty-degree rotation.

Not a good look for a salutatorian.

Jenna shuffled her papers, then reached for the microphone. Her words rang out loud and true, encouraging her peers to go out in the world, challenging them to be the best they could possibly be.

At the end of the speech, she added an impromptu one-liner stating "those who commit crimes against other persons will *always* receive their just reward."

Was that a warning to the driver of the Civic?

After a short presentation by the superintendent of schools, it was time for the students to receive their diplomas.

Just like every parent or relative there, our family screamed our lungs out when Jenna received hers. She settled into her seat and continued to chat with the boys on either side of her.

If I didn't know better, I'd suspect my budding criminologist was plotting something.

Seconds after Justin Zedesky received his diploma, cheers rang throughout the stadium, accompanied by five hundred mortarboards flying through the air. The graduates exultantly pummeled one another on the back.

With the exception of three students: Jenna, Todd and Drew.

All currently M.I.A.

After asking Mother to watch the kids, I grabbed Tom's hand and we maneuvered our way through the boisterous crowd. I already had a good idea where I would find Jenna.

We arrived at the parking lot to find Todd and Drew guarding the damaged Civic we'd noticed earlier. Jenna was bent over the broken headlight, snapping photos.

"I've got evidence," she shouted. She passed her cell to me and I looked at several close-up photos, all of which displayed periwinkle paint chips on the Civic's front bumper.

"Great job, honey," I said as four people approached the car. The two adults bore concerned expressions. The graduate wore a big smile, but the slightly older version of the graduate looked nervous, his eyes darting in all directions.

The father walked up to Tom. "What's going on?" he asked.

"I'll let this young lady explain the situation." Tom turned to Jenna. "It's your show."

And what a show it was. The kid's parents had no idea their son was responsible for a hit-and-run. They were upset about his reckless driving and had refused to pay the automotive damage, leaving it up to their son to save money for the repairs. Our brief meeting ended cordially with a full apology from the young man, and even more important, their insurance information.

Two cases closed in two days. Mother and daughter were on a roll!

CHAPTER SIXTY-THREE

After a tumultuous three weeks of crime-solving and celebrating Jenna's graduation, Tom and I decided the entire family could use a break. Since it was still early in the season, we lucked out and booked a three-bedroom lakefront condo in South Lake Tahoe for two nights. Hank said he would doggy sit Scout, and that was an offer we couldn't refuse.

The first day we spent on the beach building sand castles with the younger kids while Jenna relaxed on a chaise lounge. After four years striving for academic perfection, she was taking a well-earned break, a tattered mystery in one hand and a strawberry fruit smoothie in the other.

"This is nice," Tom said as we settled into our own chairs.

"Sure beats my last two trips up here," I replied. "From now on I'm sticking to white-collar crime. No more chasing after murderers."

"Good idea." Tom leaned over to kiss me. "Yum. You taste great."

"Passion fruit pink lip balm. Guaranteed to keep my lips luscious and lustrous."

"Honey, they don't come more luscious than you."

I fanned my face, wishing we could jump into the king-size bed and try it out. My cell rang, disturbing my fantasies. I reached into my beach bag and yanked out the phone. The clamor subsided but a resounding beep indicated I had a new message from an old nemesis.

"Why is Ali Reynolds calling me?" I asked Tom.

"Why don't you listen to your voicemail and find out?" said my practical husband.

I listened to her message twice before turning to Tom. "You're never going to believe this." I dropped the phone back in my bag, then pulled my paperback out.

"C'mon, you're not going to leave me in suspense, are you?"

"After that last remark I should." I waited a few seconds before blurting out, "Kimberly wants me to come to the jail."

"Whatever for?" Tom asked the question I'd wondered since I listened to Ali's message.

I shrugged. "To confess? To apologize? What do you think? Should I go?"

"Up to you. Don't forget we're taking the kids on the gondola ride tomorrow."

What a choice. Going back to the scene of the crime or meeting with the perpetrator of the crime. I had to admit Kimberly's request aroused my curiosity. If the kids gave me the okay I might skip the gondola expedition and find out what she wanted. Besides, given my propensity for disastrous encounters every time I visited Tahoe, the kids would be safer without me.

Tom dropped me off at the South Lake Tahoe Police Department the next morning. The second he drove away, I regretted my decision. The sky was a brilliant blue and the temperature a perfect seventy-five degrees, ideal for hiking on the mountain trails while enjoying spectacular scenery. Instead, I chose to meet with a killer.

Maybe it was time to make an appointment with a therapist.

Once inside the lobby, I gave my name to the clerk. After a brief call, she told me Detective Reynolds would be out shortly.

Thirty long minutes later Ali appeared. The dark circles under her eyes indicated the strain she was under to wrap up the murders in one tidy package.

Would my meeting with Kimberly unravel the strands of her investigation?

"Thanks for coming," Ali said.

"Anything I can do to keep Kimberly behind bars, just ask," I replied. "I still can't believe she held my pregnant friend hostage. Do you know why she wants to meet with me?"

"Clueless at this point, but the chief said it couldn't hurt. Just don't go and screw up my case."

Technically, Ali wouldn't have a case against the burglary ringleader without my assistance, but I kept that thought to myself. She did make that call to the Reno police, who ultimately rescued me and my friends from Kimberly's craven clutches, so I couldn't complain.

I followed Ali down a hallway covered with historical photos of police staff. We ended up in the same interview room Gran and I had previously visited. The décor had not improved since our last foray. Kimberly sat at the battered white table with her hands in cuffs. A uniformed officer stood in the corner. He straightened his stance when we entered.

Ali nodded at him. "Thanks, Gomez. I'll handle this." She started to sit but Kimberly protested.

"No cops. This is private. Between the P.I. and me."

"No can do," Ali said.

"What about my right to an attorney?"

"I'm sorry but I'm not a lawyer," I explained.

"Yeah, I realize that, but I don't need a lawyer right now. I need a competent detective."

CHAPTER SIXTY-FOUR

Kimberly complimented me? My initial smile morphed into a frown. What kind of con was she trying to pull now?

Kimberly lifted her manacled arms. "Look, Detective, I can't hurt her with my hands and feet shackled. And I need her help." She turned pleading cosmetic-free eyes on me. "Just hear me out for a few minutes. Please."

Darn. What would my husband do in this situation?

Ali turned to me. "It's your call. Gomez and I will wait outside." She winked at me, but I couldn't tell what she was trying to convey. I looked around but didn't see any signs of a secret mirror.

The two officers left the room. I was alone with a killer. My initial curiosity dissipated as reality set in.

"So what do you want from me?" I asked Kimberly.

She leaned closer and for the first time I saw how her time in jail had aged her. She looked every one of her forty-plus years.

"I want to hire you."

I sent her a scathing look. "To do what? You do recall threatening to shoot me and my friends."

"You practically destroyed my warehouse," she snarled.

I rose from my chair. "We're done here."

She lifted her manacled arms. "Stay, please. I'm sorry I threatened you and held your friends hostage. Things got out of control and I overreacted."

"You think?"

"How's your friend doing? You know there's no way I would have hurt her. I didn't realize she was so far along."

"No thanks to you, Liz delivered a healthy baby boy."

Kimberly looked relieved. "Tell her congratulations."

I rolled my eyes. Honestly, this woman.

"Here's the deal. Hugo's made a plea bargain with the District Attorney's Office and now they have me up on a double murder charge for both Gino and Gregg."

I nodded. No surprise there.

She continued, "I did not order a hit on Gino. Just a warning. It's not my fault that idiot Hugo doesn't know his own strength. And I absolutely did not kill Gregg."

"What made them finally charge you for Gregg's murder?"

"Marty went and changed his story. Initially, we alibied each other, since we were together at a breakfast meeting. But now he says he remembered I left for fifteen minutes to take a phone call." Her eyes blazed in anger. "I think he's still mad at me because during the meeting I threatened to sack him. Of course after Gregg died, I couldn't afford to lose Marty as well."

"Marty seems very nice. Why did you want to get rid of him?"

"He kept screwing up transactions. I had enough going on I didn't have time to cajole his irate clients. I tried to be patient after his daughter's suicide attempt, but that was almost three months ago. The guy needed to get a grip."

I put my hand up. "Wait a minute. One of Marty's daughters tried to kill herself?"

Kimberly nodded.

"How horrible. Which daughter? Is she okay now?"

Kimberly shrugged. "The eldest. She's alive. Not sure how okay she is. I don't know all the details but it had something to do with a guy."

We both sighed and in unison said, "Doesn't it always."

CHAPTER SIXTY-FIVE

My meeting with Kimberly ended a few minutes later. While she offered to pay double our normal rate to investigate her case, I wasn't certain Tom or Bradford would be too keen on the idea. On the other hand, everyone deserves a fair trial, or in Kimberly's situation, a thorough investigation.

Although getting paid could be a challenge.

I tried calling Tom but it went straight to voicemail. He and the kids were either engaged in a fun activity or else there wasn't any cell coverage up there.

What to do next? I could get a car service to take me to our condo and stretch out on a lounge. Or I could have them drive me to the timeshare office and find out why Marty's and Kimberly's stories differed. A more practical use of my time.

My ride pulled up and a few short minutes later I was banging on the locked door of the timeshare office. I peered through the glass but didn't see any sign of anyone moving around inside. Although, with one salesman dead and the manager locked up, that left a limited staff.

I tried Tom's cell again but still no answer.

My stomach growled, reminding me it was well past noon. Riva Grille was down the street. I could grab a bite and return later to chat with Marty. I walked the block to the lakefront restaurant and was seated on the deck after only a short wait.

The young server handed me a menu. I ordered an ice tea, reviewed the selections, and ended up with my usual—the BBQ

228

chicken quesadilla. Yummy. I glanced out at the lake. Boats of all shapes, sizes and prices dotted the area. The marina next to the restaurant did not lack for business.

I finished my meal, paid my bill and walked across the deck into the cool interior of the restaurant. Only a few guests dined inside. One family of five sat in the corner of the restaurant, the overhead light shining down on the patriarch's strawberry blond hair and Hawaiian flowered shirt.

Aha. I'd found Marty. Should have known he'd be at lunch. It was nice the way he squeezed in family time, even on workdays. I popped over to his table.

"Will you be back in the office later today?" I asked him.

"For you. Of course. Are you ready to buy a week or two?" he asked with a hopeful expression.

I hated to dash his hopes, but I had an investigation to complete. "Not quite yet." When his face fell almost into his salad, I added, "But as soon as I've finished with my investigation into Gregg's death."

The eldest of Marty's three daughters, the one I remembered was named Meghan, went pale. Her lip trembled as she asked, "Do you know who killed him?"

Her mother threw a comforting hug around her daughter's shoulders before glaring at me.

Hey, what did I do?

"I'm working on it," I said to Meghan. "Your father's boss, Kimberly, is in jail for Gregg's murder, but she claims she didn't do it."

The middle daughter pushed green-rimmed glasses up her freckled nose. "So you're a detective, huh. Like Nancy Drew?"

"Kind of," I replied. "Except I don't have a cool car."

She stared at me with the wisdom of an all-knowing middle school kid about to impart some valuable advice. "Gregg was a butthead. Ask my sister." She elbowed Meghan, who immediately burst into tears.

Wow. What was with that? The Fenton family dynamic was a little screwy.

Marty gulped the remaining half of his cocktail, flagged down the server and asked for the bill. The youngest protested she'd been promised dessert, but he shut her down saying he had work to do.

Mrs. Fenton gathered her daughters and with a quick goodbye to me and her husband set off with a trio of dejected girls trailing behind her.

"I'm so sorry. I didn't mean to break up your lunch," I said to Marty as he pulled some twenties out of his wallet.

"No problem." He stood and flicked his hand goodbye to me. I still wasn't finished with my questions, so I trotted along beside him as we walked out of the restaurant.

"Kimberly said you changed your story about meeting with her the morning Gregg was killed."

He shrugged. "So. I forgot she'd left the table to make her call. No big deal."

"She also mentioned you were away from the table when she returned."

"I visited the men's room." He stopped and put his arm on my elbow. "Are you always this annoying during an investigation? I thought you wanted to purchase a timeshare from me. You and your friend." His voice escalated as he drew me down the sidewalk away from the valet attendants. "You were just leading me on, weren't you?"

I squirmed in his grip. "Not intentionally. Liz really is interested in purchasing a timeshare. I'm sure she'll be in touch with you."

Marty mumbled and I leaned in. "Can't trust anyone these days. Co-workers, clients, kids." He dropped my elbow like it was a hot potato.

I rubbed my elbow but couldn't stop my inquisition. "Why was Meghan interested in finding Gregg's killer?"

He threw his hands up. "Girls. You raise them to do the right thing, send them off to college, then the next thing you know they let some jerk get them drunk and pregnant." He leaned into me and I could smell whiskey on his breath. "I tried, but I couldn't protect her from him."

A tiny alarm shrieked in my exceedingly slow brain as the wheels began turning. "From him. You mean Gregg?"

He stepped back, his eyes wild. "No, I mean—"

I moved closer but I kept my voice low and comforting. "Gregg got your daughter pregnant, didn't he? He really was a jerk."

Marty nodded, his breath shallow and fast. "When she told him she was pregnant, he gave her five hundred bucks and told her to take care of it and stop pestering him." His face grew redder and redder. "How could he do that to her? He'd known her since she was a kid."

I guided Marty to a bench close to the marina. I stroked his arm, hoping to calm him down. "What a terrible thing for a young girl," I said. "I bet it sent her into a huge depression."

He hung his head in his hands. I could almost feel the pain radiating throughout his body. I remembered the anger I felt when we caught Jenna's hit-and-run driver. What would it be like to discover your co-worker had gotten your daughter pregnant, encouraged an abortion, all of what led to...

"She tried to kill herself," he said, lifting his head, tears forming at the corner of his eyes. "If I hadn't come home early from work, she'd be gone. All because of that monster."

"I completely understand. And I'm sure the police will be sympathetic as well."

Marty's head snapped toward me. "What? You're going to turn me in to the police?"

Uh, well, yeah. Or better yet, have Marty turn himself in.

"It will be much easier if you go there of your own volition," I explained.

"I don't think so," he said before shoving me to the ground.

CHAPTER SIXTY-SIX

Ouch. Thank goodness for the excess padding on my butt. I winced as I untangled my legs and slowly rose while trying to keep an eye on Marty. He sped across the parking lot far faster than I would have expected a pudgy middle-aged man to move. Before I could blink twice, he'd raced down the narrow wooden walkway leading to the marina. A man clad in swim trunks and his bikini-clad companion had just pulled their turquoise speedboat into a vacant spot along the pier. The woman jumped onto the dock, a thick rope in her hand. Marty rushed past her, leapt into the boat and knocked the man into the water. Then he turned on the ignition and took off.

I hate when a killer makes a daring escape. So annoying!

The woman helped haul her companion out of the water. The former boat occupants hustled over to the marina office. I scanned the empty slips for some mode of transportation, but the only available watercraft was an unoccupied pedal boat. That would take me two days to get across the lake.

The roar of a returning Jet Ski carrying a single occupant resolved my dilemma. As he drew close to the pier, I showed him my business card, which was not nearly as effective as a badge, but it seemed to do the trick. Or maybe it was my cleavage when I bent over to display I was a card-carrying P.I.

Either way, before he could think twice, I'd stepped out of my shoes, strapped on his flotation jacket, attached the kill switch to my wrist, and hit the start button. I maintained the five m.p.h. speed limit until I exited the no-wake zone, then pushed the watercraft to the max.

While I'd been a passenger on several occasions, I'd never been in charge of the controls before. It felt very liberating. Very "I am woman, hear me (and my Jet Ski) roar."

Now all I had to do was stay upright and catch a killer.

All in a day's work for this detective.

CHAPTER SIXTY-SEVEN

Marty's boat had left the dock heading straight north. But this was a big lake with seventy-two miles of shoreline. And Marty's boat probably wasn't the only turquoise one out there. Was he trying to make a run for it on a permanent basis? Or only trying to get away from me?

Did he even have a plan at this point? Did I?

I vaguely remembered Marty saying he lived in Zephyr Cove, Nevada, a twenty-minute drive from his office. An even shorter ride across the lake. If he planned to escape, he might need a passport.

Or maybe he needed to head home to destroy some incriminating evidence in his house.

As I pondered various alternatives, a large ski boat filled with drunken sailors crossed in front of me. The turbulent wake they left behind caused my watercraft to rock and roll.

The Jet Ski leaned to the left and so did I. It took every rarely used muscle in my body to keep it from tipping over but I succeeded.

Definitely getting to the gym when this case was over.

I looked in both directions to ensure no other boats were close to my chosen path and veered the machine to the right heading east.

If my conclusion was correct, I could catch up to Marty at the Zephyr Cove Marina and hopefully talk him into turning himself in. If not, I'd call Ali Reynolds and tell her about Marty's admission of guilt to me.

That probably wouldn't be sufficient to keep him behind bars unless you combined it with Kimberly's confirmation of his absence from their breakfast meeting. Not to mention his boat theft. It might suffice until they reexamined the evidence from Gregg's murder.

With my hair flying in the wind and the Jet Ski skimming the lake, I managed to locate my quarry just outside the no-wake zone. A turquoise speed boat driven by a man with strawberry blond hair wearing a floral shirt.

Gotcha. Now all I had to do was sneak into the marina without Marty noticing me in pursuit. The roar of a racing boat coming up behind me got not only my attention, but Marty's as well. When he saw me closing in on the pier, he yanked his steering wheel to the right and maneuvered the boat around, now heading back out on the lake.

Directly at me!

Marty pushed his speedboat to the max, completely ignoring the five m.p.h. speed signs posted in the area around the marina.

I'd already slowed the Jet Ski for entry into the marina. With the prow of his boat set on a collision course with me, I froze momentarily.

Then I regained command of my senses. I accelerated and veered to the right.

Marty's boat missed me by mere inches. My heart dropped to the bottom of the lake while I caught my breath.

Boom.

The sound of two boats colliding echoed off the sides of the mountain. I turned my craft around to view the disaster.

The racing boat appeared to be damaged in the prow, but it remained afloat. The young couple looked stunned but physically okay. At least, from this distance. Marty, however, hadn't fared as well. He thrashed in the water, calling for help.

The occupants of the other boat threw him a life preserver, and as he swam in their direction, a Douglas County patrol boat drew up beside him. The deputy pulled a dripping Marty onboard and steered for the marina.

I headed in the same direction, anticipating enough charges against Marty to keep him locked up until an official murder charge could also be brought.

And when this was all over, I definitely needed a glass of chardonnay.

Better yet, a bottle.

CHAPTER SIXTY-EIGHT

A few weeks later, we celebrated Father's Day with new papa Brian Daley and doting mother, Liz. The guest list included all generations of my family, a few close friends, and Adriana, who made the cut by default since she'd shared prisoner status with Liz. The last few weeks had been hectic for the new parents and for me as I wrapped up my investigations.

This was my first chance to relax and share all with our friends and my former client.

I looked at Adriana, smiling down at little Colin, who snuggled on her chest while Liz played hostess serving drinks all around.

Who would have thought Adriana was the maternal type?

"I feel that I contributed considerably to Kimberly's eventual arrest," Liz said as she handed off a daiquiri to me. "Perhaps a killer consulting fee?"

"How about an official commendation letter from the agency?" I offered. When she scrunched her nose, I added, "And a bottle of your favorite champagne."

"What about me?" asked Adriana. "Don't forget my impressive karate kick to that goon. When do I get my champagne?"

Stan, a morose expression on his face, chimed in. "I can't believe you three had all the fun without me."

A trio of matching glares was his reply. "Aw, you know what I mean," he said. "I got boring stakeout duty, and you guys took down a huge burglary ring. How awesome is that?"

I grinned. It sure was.

"I still don't understand what was going on between Gino, Jake and the other biker dude," Adriana said. "What was their deal?"

"Another money-laundering arrangement," Tom replied. "Our FBI contact caught up with them, and they are currently behind bars for drug trafficking and money laundering."

Adriana's lip quivered as she handed Colin back to his mother. "I don't think I can ever trust a man again."

I patted her hand. "You feel that way now, but given time, you'll be back out there. I guarantee it."

She shook her head, her shiny dark locks flowing down the back of her sundress.

"Nope. Won't happen. I'm done with men forever."

Then she lifted her designer sunglasses over her forehead and squinted toward the sidewalk where a tall man approached our group, a six-pack in one hand and a broad smile on his face.

Adriana did a type of shimmy wiggle that somehow made her look even sexier. She fluffed her hair and smiled seductively as the guy stopped next to us.

"Well, hello there," she said in a throaty voice, putting out her palm. "I'm Adriana."

"Nice to meet you," he replied, shaking her hand with his free one. "I'm Hank."

CHAPTER SIXTY-NINE

Close to midnight that evening, Tom and I sat on the glider on the back patio, reflecting on the events of the past month. My kids were spending the night with their father, and Kristy was enjoying an overnight with Tom's parents.

Alone at last.

Unsurprisingly, our conversation focused on murder.

"I feel so sorry for Marty," I said. "Obviously, he went too far, but his daughter's attempted suicide ultimately pushed him over the edge."

"As a parent, we want to protect our kids every second of their life." Tom stared at his shoes. "I get it. But violence against another person serves no purpose."

I sighed. "I still hope his attorney can get him a reduced charge. I almost feel guilty about going after him. If it weren't for me, he might have escaped and destroyed his daughter's diary."

Tom leaned in and drew me closer. I snuggled next to him, his lime aftershave reminding me of the daiquiris Liz had served earlier.

Both equally yummy!

"You did what you had to do. And it looks like you managed to successfully wrap up your entire caseload," Tom said. "Nice work for a newbie."

"Hard to believe the murders were the easiest cases to solve. Getting money back from those lowlife timeshare resale companies proved to be the most difficult."

"That was nice of your mother to purchase Iris's timeshare points."

I laughed. "She's so funny. The woman is bound and determined to make Bradford take a vacation. Even if she's stuck paying timeshare dues forever."

Tom maneuvered so we were facing one another. "I wouldn't mind booking a vacation somewhere. Maybe your mother would let us use her points sometime."

I lifted an eyebrow. "What did you have in mind?"

"An isolated beach, turquoise blue waters, palm trees waving in the breeze. Just you and me together alone on the sand, where I can do this"—he placed a kiss on my neck—"and this"—another kiss—"and..."

Every nerve ending in my body screamed "woo hoo" but I made a valiant attempt to continue our conversation.

"According to Iris, those plum resorts are difficult to book."

Tom lifted his head, his brown eyes glimmering in the moonlight. "As long as I'm with you, sweetheart, it doesn't matter where we go. I have only two requirements."

I sat up, curious what Tom required before we took a vacation.

Tom ticked them off on his long supple fingers. "One—none of your family comes along."

"No problem," I said. "And two?"

"Isn't it obvious?" he replied. "No dead bodies."

I grabbed his hand and placed it over my heart. "It's a deal."

THE END

AUTHOR'S NOTE

I hope you enjoyed reading this book as much as I enjoyed writing it. If so, please consider leaving a review. Favorable reviews help an author more than you can imagine.

All the Laurel McKay Mysteries are listed below.

Dying for a Date (Vol. 1)
Dying for a Dance (Vol. 2)
Dying for a Daiquiri (Vol. 3)
Dying for a Dude (Vol. 4)
Dying for a Donut (Vol.5)
Dying for a Diamond (Vol. 6)
Dying for a Deal (Vol. 7)

To find out about new books, upcoming events and contests, please sign up for my newsletter:

http://cindysamplebooks.com/mailing-list/

ACKNOWLEDGEMENTS

Many thanks and hugs to the awesome friends who willingly read my early drafts: Jana Rossi and two of my favorite mystery authors, Heather Haven and Linda Lovely. As always, my critique group was there to answer my countless emails and plotting questions: Kathy Asay, Pat Foulk, Rae James, and Karen Phillips, my amazing cover artist.

A special thanks to Denise Haerr for helping with my South Lake Tahoe research.

Thanks to my editors, Baird Nuckolls and Lourdes Venard.

I'm so glad that Cheryl Redfearn-Escobar entered her Bernese mountain dog in my "Dying for a Dog" contest. Scout is the perfect addition to Laurel's family. Congratulations to Claudia Kennedy. Your entry was the winner in the "Help Me Write a Chase Scene" contest.

I am so grateful to my Facebook friends and readers whose prayers, positive thoughts and encouraging words lifted my spirits during my recent surgery and chemotherapy. Thanks to the friends who sent flowers and cards, chauffeured me to appointments and fed me. Special thanks to Cathy Allyn. You are an angel!

The support and encouragement I receive from my fellow Sisters in Crime (Sacramento and Northern California), Sacramento Valley Rose, and NCPA keeps my creativity flowing.

Thanks to the Assistance League of the Sierra Foothills for their ongoing support, as well as the wonderful work they do for our community.

And last, thanks to my family back in the Midwest for their loving concern and my children, Dawn and Jeff, who are always there for me.

ABOUT THE AUTHOR

Cindy Sample is a former mortgage banking CEO who decided plotting murder was more entertaining than plodding through paperwork. She retired to follow her lifelong dream of becoming a mystery author.

Her experiences with online dating sites fueled the concept for *Dying for a Date*, the first in her national bestselling Laurel McKay mysteries. The sequel, *Dying for a Dance*, winner of the 2011 NCPA Fiction Award, is based on her adventures in the glamorous world of ballroom dancing. Cindy thought her protagonist, Laurel McKay, needed a vacation in Hawaii, which resulted in *Dying for a Daiquiri*, a finalist for the 2014 Silver Falchion Award for Best Traditional Mystery.

Laurel returned to Placerville for her wildest ride yet in in *Dying for a Dude*. The West will never be the same. Then on to *Dying for a Donut*, a lip-smacking mystery set in the Apple Hill area.

It was time for Laurel (or maybe that was Cindy) to take another vacation. You can't beat a Caribbean cruise as the setting for *Dying for a Diamond*. Unless your setting is Lake Tahoe, the scene of the crime in *Dying for a Deal*.

Cindy is a five-time finalist for the LEFTY Award for best humorous mystery and a past president of the Sacramento chapter of Sisters in Crime. She has served on the boards of the Sacramento Opera and YWCA. She is a member of Mystery Writers of America and Romance Writers of America. Cindy has two wonderful adult children who live too far away. She loves chatting with readers so feel free to contact her on any forum.

Sign up for Cindy's newsletter to find out about upcoming events, contests and new releases. http://cindysamplebooks.com/mailing-list/

Check out www.cindysamplebooks.com for the latest news and blog posts.

Connect with Cindy on Facebook and Twitter
http://facebook.com/cindysampleauthor
http://twitter.com/cindysample1
Email Cindy at cindy@cindysamplebooks.com

Made in the USA
San Bernardino, CA
15 January 2020